The Rock & Roll Queen of Bedlam

Marilee Brothers

Medallion Press, Inc.
Printed in USA

DEDICATION:

For my husband, the First Reader,
thank you for believing.

Published 2009 by Medallion Press, Inc.

The MEDALLION PRESS LOGO
is a registered trademark of Medallion Press, Inc.

Typeset in Baskerville
Printed in the United States of America

ISBN 978-1-93-475546-4

10 9 8 7 6 5 4 3 2 1
First Edition

ACKNOWLEDGMENTS:

Without a career in public education where I experienced the best of the best, the worst of the worst and (thankfully) the vast majority between the two, this book would not be possible.

The Rock & Roll Queen of Bedlam

Marilee Brothers

Chapter 1

*P*anty hose are a tool of the devil.

On a tall woman, the crotch hangs at knee level, so she's forced to crouch and shuffle like Quasimodo. If a woman's vertically challenged, the things slither downward, pooling around her ankles like a reptilian second skin. My troubles began with panty hose.

For a Friday, it had been relatively tranquil. No fights, no blood spilled, no weapons displayed. All in all, a good day for a teacher in a classroom of behavior disordered teenagers with a few felons thrown in for good measure. The queen of Bedlam: that's me.

After school, I scoot across the parking lot as fast as my walking cast will allow. In forty minutes, I'll be cast-free and ready for my third date with Michael LeClaire. Seriously hot, comfortably rich Michael LeClaire. Rumor has it his parents have ordered him to go forth and multiply. Enter Allegra Thome, stage right.

I threw together a killer outfit. Short, clingy black

1

dress with a neckline that dips down—tastefully—to allow a glimpse of cleavage. Wispy lace panties and strappy heels. Successfully field-tested and ready for action, it's stashed in a shopping bag behind the seat of my red Ford Ranger.

Zipping across town to the clinic, I think about my leg and how it will look cast-free: pasty, shriveled and, in all likelihood, sprouting coarse dark hairs. Did I throw in a pair of panty hose? Of course not! I slap myself in the forehead.

Braking hard, I swing into Sid's Gas'n'Grub. Because Sid is the father of one of my students, Crystal (in for shoplifting), I like to give him my business. Sid sits on a stool engrossed in a tabloid, his big belly pressed up against the counter. He marks his place with a pudgy finger and looks up. "Hey teach! How's my kid doin'?"

"Not bad, Sid. Just a little language once in a while."

The corner of his mouth draws down. "Hey, Suze! Didja hear that? Goddam kid swears at school!"

Sid's wife Suzy stands up from behind the Plexiglas case, where shriveled hot dogs rotate over a heat lamp. She talks around the cigarette dangling from her lips. "What are ya gonna do?" She shakes her head. Ashes fly.

I assure them, compared to her classmates, Crystal is a veritable poster child of good conduct. I pick out my panty hose and rummage through my purse for $6.73 while Sid peruses the package. He beams his approval. "Good choice, Ms. Thome. Ya gotcher midnight smoke, lace highcut panty, nude toe and heel. New boyfriend, huh?"

"Sort of," I mumble, regretting it immediately. Oh, what grist for Crystal's mill. I'd pay. I wave goodbye as Sid assures me, "Let me tell ya, I'll have one serious fuckin' talk with Crystal about her language."

I step into the parking lot where a midnight blue Honda Accord with flipper wheels sits next to a beat-up Chevy, both of them nosed into the line of poplars marking the back of Sid's property. I know this car. It belongs to another of my students, Jose Delgado. Jose is relatively crime-free, assigned to my class due to spotty attendance, two weeks on, one week off, like clockwork. With his multiple gold chains, smooth olive skin, and dreamy eyes, Jose is the hands-down favorite of my behavior disordered girls.

I lift my hand to wave. But it isn't Jose behind the wheel. It's his guardian, the man he calls Tio Estefan, talking earnestly to a man in the passenger seat. I stuff my new panty hose behind the seat and look at my watch. I still have time to speak to Estefan about Jose's attendance. Dragging my cast, I skitchity-hop across the parking lot calling out in my pathetic Spanish, "Hola, Estefan."

He looks less than thrilled to see me and makes shooing motions with his hand, which I ignore. As I lean over to remind him of his responsibilities, a series of events explode like a string of firecrackers.

Doors slam. I gape in openmouthed astonishment as the man in the passenger seat points a gun at Estefan. I am grabbed from behind and pinned against the car. A rough male voice growls in my ear, "You're coming with me, lady!"

Heart leaping in my chest, I scream, "Sid! Suzie! Help me!"

With a howl of rage, I slam my cast into the man's shin. He mutters an oath, spins me around, rams a shoulder in my midsection, and hoists me into the air as I shriek and struggle. My captor, grunting with effort, tells one of his henchmen, "Get the goddamn door open. She weighs a ton!"

What?

"It's the cast!" I yell as he stuffs me into the back seat of the Chevy.

Frantically, I try to scramble out of the car and, in the process, bash my nose into his elbow. Blood gushes from both nostrils. The man recoils, and I finally get a look at the guy who not only assaulted my person but implied I'm overweight. Big, mean-looking guy. Cheeks dark with stubble. Bloodshot, pale eyes. Strings of greasy hair hanging below a baseball cap turned backwards.

"Wha— wha—?" I stammer as he digs a filthy-looking bandana from his jeans pocket and tosses it at me. I press it against my nose, gagging from the rancid odor of motor grease and sweat. He backs out of the car, slams the door, and tells the guy behind the wheel, "You know where to take her."

At his words, I feel the air leave my lungs. I scrabble for the door handle. There is none. I fight for breath while my brain books a one-way ticket on Air Terror. Who are these people? What do they plan to do to me? Shoot me up with heroin? Sell me into white slavery? Will I end up in some third world country dragging my cast behind me as I walk the streets, forced by a sadistic pimp to turn a trick in exchange for a crust of bread?

"Nooo!" I howl as the driver executes a perfect three-point turn and pulls out of the parking lot. Sid and Suzie stand in the doorway of the Gas 'n' Grub, eyes wide with surprise and mouths agape. I pound on the window and scream, "Call the cops!"

The driver pulls out into the street. "Take it easy, lady. We are the cops. What in the hell are you doing in the middle of a drug bust?"

I sink back in the seat, pinch the bridge of my nose to stop the bleeding, and moan, "I just wanted to invite him to parents' night."

Three hours later, I'm locked in a small room inexplicably painted pink. Periodically a man with chubby, dimpled cheeks steps in to check on me. He tries to look intimidating but fails miserably due to his squirrelly, chock-full-o-nuts demeanor. He tells me I have to wait for Sloan, the DEA agent in charge, the key to my freedom. Bereft of personal belongings, I pass the time tormenting Squirrel Cheeks.

"My aunt dates a lawyer who loves to sue people," I say. "In fact, he specializes in false arrest."

The last part's a lie, but I see a flicker of fear in Squirrel Cheeks' soft woodland eyes.

When Sloan finally slams through the door, I rise to a half-crouch with a feral growl. "You're in big trouble, pal! This is America. I know my rights!"

The corner of Sloan's mouth twitches. He winks at Squirrel Cheeks. "You okay? She's pretty scary."

"You'd better let me go, or . . ." I stutter to a stop when he yanks off his cap and his long, greasy hair comes along for the ride. He sails it across the room where it lands on the floor at the base of a mirrored wall in a crumpled heap, like a dead porcupine along the side of the road.

Lifting my astonished gaze to the mirror, I see Sloan studying my backside. I whirl to face him. "You're checking out my ass!"

He shrugs and swipes at his close-cropped dark hair.

I turn back to the mirror, assuming it's one way and Sloan's superiors are standing behind it. "First he bashes me in the nose, then he abducts me, and now . . ."

"There's nobody behind the mirror," Sloan says with a smirk.

I whirl around and put my hands on my hips. "Are we done?"

I desperately want out of this room and away from Sloan, whose scary, pale blue eyes and overbearing presence make me want to scream.

Sloan opens the door and leans against the frame. "You're free to go. Chuck will take you to your car."

I clomp to the door to squeeze by him. As I turn my head to blister Sloan with one last glare, my walking cast snags the doorjamb and I lurch sideways, falling against his body. His arms wrap around me as I teeter off balance. Pressed up against him, I feel a jolt of heat pass between us, the feeling so intense I inhale sharply, reach up, and touch my hair to see if it's standing on end à la Albert Einstein.

Sloan leans down, his breath warm on my face. "Good way to break your other leg."

Oh, yeah, the cast. I feel my anger return. He releases me, and I back away to put some space between us. "If not for you, my cast would be gone and I'd be on a date with my boyfriend." I pause so he can digest this information and apologize. He doesn't.

On the brief ride back to my car, I pump Squirrel Cheeks, AKA Chuck, for information about the drug bust and whether or not Jose is involved. But Chuck, hands locked on the steering wheel at ten till two, is afraid to look at me, much less speak. After collecting the Ranger, I head home with a sigh of relief.

Grandma Sybil's roomy two-story house seemed the perfect fit when I slunk back to Vista Valley after my short, disastrous marriage. When Grandpa Mort died, Grandma sold his string of auto supply stores but flatly refused to leave the family home. I have my own apartment upstairs. Grandma and my thrice-divorced Aunt Dodie share the main floor and finished basement. Basking in my family's support, I'm comfortably at home in apple-, peach-, pear-intensive Vista Valley, Washington, whose unofficial motto is "We never met a fruit we didn't like."

When I burst through the front door into the empty house, I find a trail of notes, in Dodie's handwriting, taped to the banister. I read each one as I mount the stairs.

5:15 p.m. "*Allegra! Where the hell are you? Dr. Myers said you didn't show up for your appointment, and he missed his massage.*"

Dodie's the office manager for Whole Health Clinic, where three generations of Myers doctors offer cradle-to-grave services. Dodie does not tolerate missed appointments.

7 p.m. "*Susan called. Sounds upset. Says call her about Nick.*"

8 p.m. "*Michael called. Thinks you stood him up. He called your cell but got voice mail, and is he ever pissed!*"

8:15 p.m. "*Word of warning: Your grandmother is with a client.*"

With a little hiss of dismay, I crumple the last note and shove it in my pocket, wishing I could turn off images dancing in my head, the ones featuring Grandma Sybil and her diligent efforts to help mankind.

I mentally sort the messages as I climb the stairs. Too late for Dr. Myers. I decide to let Michael cool off before I call. Nick, on the other hand, can't afford to be upset. His life depends on it. At sixteen, he functions fairly well considering he has cystic fibrosis. Nick and I became close during my short-lived marriage to his Uncle Harley. I adore his mother, Susan, having forgiven her for introducing me to Harley.

Susan answers on the first ring. Her voice is taut with anger, which I know springs from desperate worry. "It's that girl in your class. Sara. He won't talk to me. If he gets sick again . . ."

"Yeah, I know," I say, feeling guilty even though it's not my fault Nick is in the throes of a king-sized crush. A single parent, Susan struggles to hold down a job as an accountant for the Quail Hollow Winery and tend to her son.

I want to say more, but Susan slams down the phone and yells for Nick to pick up the extension. After a click and the alarming sound of Nick's fluid-filled struggle to breathe, I hear him say, "Sara's gone."

An alarm bell clangs in my overloaded brain. Sara's foster mother, Patsy, is no prize, but she keeps close tabs on her charge.

"Gone, as in—?"

"She told me to call her tonight. When I did, Patsy told me Sara left a note and took off."

His voice trails off into a deep, racking cough.

"Nobody saw her leave?"

"No, they were out shopping. Sara was gone when they got back. She wouldn't do that. I know she wouldn't!"

I hear panic in his voice and struggle to find the right

words. "You know, bud, Sara's had a rough life. Maybe she's fed up with Patsy. Maybe she has a new boyfriend."

"She doesn't have a boyfriend. I'd know!"

"What did the note say?"

"Just the usual crap. 'I'll be okay, don't worry,' stuff like that."

I finally convince him to let it ride over the weekend and promise if she's not in school Monday, we'll file a missing persons report. Before we hang up, Nick says, "You think you know Sara, but you don't."

His remark is so strange I'm not sure how to react. "I know her dad's wanted for dealing drugs, her mom's in prison, and she has a little brother somewhere. Is there more?"

"Oh yeah, Aunt Allegra. There's more. Lots more." Nick sounds old and tired, as if he's bearing a burden far too heavy for a kid of sixteen. He clicks off before I can question him further.

I decide to face the music and listen to Michael's messages on my cell phone. When I reach for my purse, I realize it's still in the truck and then trudge back outside, feeling each step reverberate in my throbbing nose. I grope around behind the seat, retrieve my purse, and start back toward the house. Then it hits me. The shopping bag containing my man-catching outfit and new panty hose? It's gone. That creep Sloan stole my underwear!

Chapter 2

Monday

So I'm lying in a hospital bed," I tell my friend Marcy as we dash down the hall to our respective classrooms. We dodge groups of slow-moving students while keeping a sharp lookout for R.D. Langley, our principal, who has huge issues with punctuality. Since we're both late, we're fair game for one of R.D.'s "corrective action requested" memos.

"Hospital bed, huh?" Marcy muses, an avid gleam in her eyes. "Then what happens?"

I lower my voice as we pass a drifting group of freshman boys. "I'm lying naked under a sheet. The room is dark, but the door is ajar and light is leaking in from the hall."

I pause for a minute, savoring the memory of a dream so sensual, so real, that when the alarm went off, I whapped the snooze button and slipped back into the action without missing a beat.

"Hurry up! We're almost to my room," Marcy urges.

"I see a hand—it's Michael's hand—he's holding a bath sponge. He tugs at the sheet and it slides off ever so slowly.

He holds the sponge over my naked body and squeezes. I see droplets of water suspended in air like tiny crystals. Then they splash down on my bare skin and slide across my body like warm honey, touching each and every sensitive nerve. My whole being feels bathed in fire . . . a good kind of fire."

Marcy pulls me toward a bank of lockers. "Come on! Get to the good part."

"He moves to my breasts with the sponge, softly stroking, round and round, back and forth until I'm moaning and gasping . . ."

"Hurry!" Marcy says. Her eyes are huge. She's breathing hard.

"He pulls the sponge away, and I hear the splash of water as he dips it into the basin. He takes my left foot in his hand and draws the sponge along the inside of my leg. Ever so slowly, starting with the ankle, then the calf, to the inside my knee. Onward and upward to the inner thigh. He leans down and follows the trail of the sponge with his mouth. His tongue is hot and wet, moving higher and higher. I'm going crazy. Oh, God, so close to heaven!"

"Yes!" Marcy shouts and gets a puzzled look from a sleepy-looking kid slumped against his locker.

"Here's where it gets weird," I say. "I lift my hand to stroke his hair to, you know, encourage him?"

Marcy nods eagerly.

"But he's wearing a baseball cap, and his hair feels greasy. I'm so shocked I pull my hand away and plop!"

Marcy blinks. "Plop?"

"Yeah. The cap, the greasy hair, the whole thing lands on my bare belly like a dead raccoon. Michael turns his face to the light and morphs into him. Sloan! The guy I told you about. He smirks and says, 'Surprise!' I wake up screaming, and that's why I'm late."

Marcy looks disappointed. "But he's hot, right?"

I shake my head in mock despair. "You're sick."

As I walk away, she says softly, "I may be sick, but I'm not the one having sex dreams about him."

I hold up one finger. "*Dream*, not *dreams*. Just one."

As I approach the cluster of students leaning against the wall outside my classroom, I'm greeted by Jimmy Felthouse (grand theft auto). "Hey, Ms. Thome, your cast is gone."

I dig through my tote bag for keys. "Yep, cast-free and ready to kick down the walls of ignorance."

My lame humor evokes a chorus of groans. I glance down at my newly freed ankle. Thank God for Dodie, who persuaded Dr. Myers, the elder, to meet us at the clinic on Saturday.

My students settle into their seats, and Nick checks attendance. Because his coughing is disruptive, he spends most of his day with me. I pitch him assignments; he bats them over the fence. In exchange, he acts as my teacher's aide and keeps my records in order.

He points silently at Sara's empty chair, a worry line creasing his pale forehead.

"We'll check it out after school," I say, distracted by an escalation of hostilities between Jimmy and Roger (breaking and entering).

Crystal makes her entrance ten minutes late, her eyes bright with secret knowledge. She tosses her pass on my desk and in a voice loud enough to be heard atop Mount Rainier, declares, "Jeez, I hope the cops let you go in time for your hot date, Ms. Thome. Hate to see them smokin' new panty hose go to waste."

"Those panty hose," I correct automatically.

All noise ceases, and twenty-four pairs of eyes sparkle with interest. I hadn't seen that look since I bent over to pick up the chalk, split my trousers, and mooned the class with my faux leopard skin panties. Finally, a teachable moment.

Later, Nick returns with the contents of my mailbox, including a note that reads, "See me at precisely 12:14," signed, R.D. Langley.

Momentary panic sets in. Had R.D. been silently stalking Marcy and me as we sprinted down the hall? Would he write me up for something as trivial as late arrival?

At the appointed hour, I present myself to R.D.'s watchdog and personal secretary, Sally. She checks me out with a disapproving sniff but waves me in.

R.D., looking GQ in a charcoal three-piece suit, cowers behind his desk taking care not to make eye contact with the other two people in the room, Sara's foster parents, Patsy and Dwight Hewitt. R.D. looks happy to see me. Something's definitely wrong.

"Ms. Thome," he says in a juicy baritone. "I presume you've met Mr. and Mrs. Hewitt."

I nod and perch on a chair under an enormous Boston fern. Lantern-jawed and greyhound thin, Dwight Hewitt sits across from me clutching the wooden arms of his chair with white-knuckled hands. His gaze darts around the room as if mapping out an escape route. By contrast, Patsy, plump and freckled, is as still as a statue, fat little fingers folded across her belly.

R.D. shifts in his chair and clears his throat. "Parents are always welcome at Vista Valley High School. How may

I be of assistance?"

"The girl run off," Dwight says.

"Oh, what a shame," R.D. gushes, clearly relieved.

I bat at a frond tickling the back of my neck and stifle a grin. At last, I know why I'm missing my lunch. R.D. thought the Hewitts were coming in for a bitch session and wanted reinforcements.

"We brought her stuff back." Patsy points to a stack of books on the floor next to her chair.

"Thank you so much for dropping by. We're truly sorry about Sara. I'm sure Miss Thome is happy to get her books back."

Dr. Langley stands. Dwight catapults to his feet, poised for flight. I forget about the fern and rise, bonking my head on the pot. R.D. inhales sharply and examines his fern for trauma. I rub my head and say, "I hear she left a note. Did you call the police?"

Dwight twitches and gazes imploringly at his wife.

Patsy rises. "We called her case worker."

"Did Sara say where she was going?"

"I'm sure the Hewitts didn't come here to be interrogated," R.D. says, herding us toward the door. A look of triumph flashes in Patsy's slightly bulging eyes.

I persist. "I'm surprised she'd run away now, so close to the end of school. What did the note say?"

R.D. shoots me a warning glance.

Patsy glares. "She said not to worry about her."

I wonder what I've done to deserve such hostility, but soldier on. "Handwritten?" I ignore R.D.'s little huff of disapproval.

"Yes, it was handwritten," Patsy snaps and glances

at Dwight, who yanks the door open and shoots through. Patsy waddles behind. I pick up Sara's books and sidle away quickly before R.D. can ream me out.

After school I jot down scathing messages I plan to hurl at Sloan and fire up my cell phone. He isn't in. "Would you like to leave a message," he growls, "on my voice mail?"

"Hey, Sloan. Remember the stuff you took when you abducted me and bashed me in the nose? I want it back!"

Not at all satisfying. I call back and listen for more options, press zero, and get a real live person. When I ask to speak to the top dog, the head honcho, the big cheese, I'm told Sloan is in the field. *Damn!* I'll have to improvise.

"Is this Chuck?"

"No, ma'am. It's Ernie."

"I want to leave a message for Sloan."

"Your name?"

"He'll know. Write this down. I want my underwear back."

Ernie makes a strangling sound.

Much better. I click off and tear into a pile of essays that need correcting. A few minutes later, my cell phone chirps.

Before I open my mouth to answer, Nick blurts, "I got a letter from Sara. Postmarked Friday. It says, 'Tell your aunt to come over and get her book.' What book is she talking about?"

"The Hewitts brought my books back today."

"No, no, not those books." He sounds peevish and impatient. "This is different. You must have lent her one of your own books."

Since this is so important to him—I know not why—I rack my brain trying to remember if I've lent Sara a book from my personal collection. "Read the rest of the letter," I order.

He mumbles through the first part. I barely catch "that thing we talked about."

"Hold it! What thing?"

"There's stuff you don't know."

"So tell me."

He pauses, and I hear him breathing. "I can't right now. Later. But I know one thing for sure. Sara didn't run away. Something's not right."

"You're watching too much TV. I'll stop by later."

As I tidy up my classroom, I pause by Sara's desk. I can see her in my mind's eye, sitting with one foot tucked beneath her, twisting a strand of long, dark hair around one finger as she labors over an assignment. Clutching her favorite purple pen, she begins to write. As her hand moves across the page, her silver charm bracelet tinkles softly.

Sara the bright and beautiful. Sara the damaged. With her luminous blue eyes and sweet smile, she slipped into my classroom and stole Nick's heart. Now he's convinced Sara's missing and is ready to saddle up and ride to her rescue. I have a couple of hours to figure out how to stop him.

Nick is still in my thoughts as I pull into my driveway. A black Lincoln Navigator is parked at the curb, probably one of Grandma or Aunt Dodie's admirers. I'll pop in, mumble a few pleasantries, and head upstairs. Unless . . . do I smell meatloaf?

Vlad the Impaler, Grandma's XXL tomcat is parked in front of the door. As I approach, his malevolent gaze zeros in on my ankles. Vlad's the reason my panty hose drawer is empty. I reach over him and open the screen door a crack. "Meatloaf, Vlad. Check it out!"

I follow him through the door to find Sloan in the middle of the living room, my Wonderbra dangling from his outstretched finger. Grandma sits, giggling, in her extrasmall, made-to-order recliner. Aunt Dodie is perched on the couch sipping a glass of red wine.

"Hi, sweetie," Grandma Sybil says. "This nice man brought back your things. He said you called and left him a message."

"I aim to please." Sloan has a nasty grin and a *don't mess with me* look in his pale blue eyes.

Oh, shit. Be careful what you ask for, Allegra.

"Grandma, you shouldn't let strange men into the house," I say.

Grandma's tiny hands flutter like rising birds. "He showed me his ID. You could at least thank the man."

"Thank him? He's the guy who broke my nose!"

"Not broken," Dodie offers. "Dr. Myers said so."

My feet feel stuck to the carpet as Sloan crosses the room. He grasps my chin with one big hand and tilts my head this way and that. "Definitely not broken."

He glances at my leg. "And the cast is gone. You'll live, Blondie."

Before I can regain my senses and pull away, he touches the tiny circular scar directly under my right cheekbone. "Looks like somebody with a ring knocked you around."

"Harley the Horrible, her late husband," Grandma says.

"West Point ring," Aunt Dodie adds.

"He's dead?" Sloan asks.

"He is to us," Dodie says.

"He's very much alive, and we're divorced," I say, reaching for my bra.

But Sloan isn't listening. He's gazing over my right shoulder. I turn to see Michael LeClaire standing on the porch, his lanky frame frozen in place, one hand lifted to knock. I mutter vile curses while Dodie drains her glass and leans forward in anticipation.

"Oh, hi, Michael!" I dash to the door and fling it open so violently it bangs against the wall. Michael says nothing but steps through, his eyes fixed on Sloan.

"Uh oh, here comes trouble,'" Grandma says.

I then attempt to explain to Michael why Sloan is standing in the living room fondling my underwear. By the time I finish, my face is hot with embarrassment and Michael and Sloan are staring at each other like two mongrels protecting their turf. I decide to throw in a little offense.

"Why didn't you return my calls, Michael?"

He ignores the question. "My parents were waiting to meet you. We had a special table reserved overlooking the eighteenth green."

"I didn't know your parents were having dinner with us."

"Would that have made a difference?" Michael glances at Sloan. "Is that your bra, Allegra?"

With a hiss of frustration, I say, "Haven't you been listening?"

The bemused expression on Sloan's face puts me over the edge, and I screech, "Tell him what happened!"

Snap! Snap! Grandma Sybil's recliner pops into full upright position, and she shoots out. "Time to eat, folks. Meatloaf and garlic mashed potatoes, Allegra's favorite.

Lemon pie for dessert. Come and get it!"

My jaw drops in amazement. Surely she doesn't think sharing a meatloaf will sort out this mess.

Michael mumbles an excuse, and I say, "I'm not hungry. You guys go ahead."

Sloan turns to trot happily after my grandmother, who, upon hearing my words, stops so suddenly Sloan almost runs her down. It's then I notice my black lace panties tucked in the back pocket of his jeans. I glance at Michael. Oh yeah, he sees them too.

Grandma glares at me. "Allegra, when you're done talking to Michael, join us in the dining room."

Michael, lips compressed into a pale, narrow line, makes for the door. I'm right on his heels. "Michael, wait. We need to talk."

"I don't need this crap."

Exit Michael LeClair, Vista Valley's most eligible bachelor. *Probably its only eligible bachelor,* I think bitterly, as his baby blue Mazda Miata peels away from the curb. I sidle toward the staircase leading to my private quarters. Moping and cursing require solitude.

"Allegra!" Grandma says sharply.

Sloan drops my panties and bra onto the couch and follows Grandma into the dining room. On leaden feet, I cross the room and tuck my undies behind a cushion. Dodie rolls her eyes and stands. "This should be fun."

She picks up the open bottle of wine and heads for the table. I trail behind, thinking, *Things can't possibly get worse.* Once again, I'm wrong.

Chapter 3

We're well into our third bottle of wine, and the tip of my nose is numb. Sloan eats heartily, sliding away from questions like a true Teflon man.

"Have you been a DEA agent long?" Dodie asks.

"Long enough. These mashed potatoes are great."

"Is Sloan your last name?" says Grandma.

"You can call me Sloan."

"Ha!" I cry. "I knew it. He has a hideous first name, like Chauncey or Aloysius, maybe even Harold."

Grandma perks up. "I have a client named Harold."

Sloan takes a sip of wine. "Client?"

I spring to my feet, knocking my chair over in the process. "Pie, anyone? I'll get it."

"We're in the middle of dinner, Allegra. Sit down," Grandma says. She turns to Sloan. "My granddaughter doesn't like hearing about my job."

"Ah." Sloan rakes me with a curious glance as he sets my chair upright. I sit down and hunch over my plate.

Grandma sets her fork down. "You've heard of the little blue pill? The one men take when . . ." She lets Sloan fill in the blanks.

"My daughter," her hand flutters toward Dodie, "works for a gerontologist. Long story short: old guy takes the pill and wants to see if the hydraulics still work. That's where I come in."

Sloan's eyebrows shoot up. I squirm. Grandma smiles. "I'm what they call a sexual surrogate. It's like therapy. Dr. Myers refers them to me. I give them a test run and get paid for it!"

"More like the Indy 500," I mutter.

"Well, I'll be damned." Sloan's teeth flash in a wolfish grin.

Grandma giggles. "Ain't life grand?"

"Win-win situation," Sloan agrees then turns his laser beam eyes on me. "So what's your problem with Grandma earning an honest living?"

I draw an outraged breath. He gives me a knowing grin. "Oh, I get it. Grandma's getting more action than you. And now, with your boyfriend seriously pissed off—"

"Exactly right!" Grandma says. "It's why she's so grumpy all the time. We had such high hopes for Michael."

"You mean she needs *therapy*?" Sloan says.

Dodie and Grandma burst into laughter.

"What a load of crap! I don't need a man to make me happy." My tongue feels too big for my mouth.

"She can't hold her liquor," Dodie says.

"Which is odd," Grandma adds. "Since Thome women can usually drink a man under the table."

Desperate to change the subject, I search my memory

banks and blurt, "A student of mine has disappeared. Sara Stepanek."

"Are you talking about Joe Stepanek's kid?"

Sloan's all business now. "Stepanek fell off the face of the earth. We wanted him bad. Still do. You check with the local PD?"

"She left a note, so they'll assume she's a runaway."

"Any reason to think she's not?"

"Sara's a good friend of my nephew, Nick. He claims she'd never run away so close to the end of school."

"I remember her when we hit the place. She in a foster home?"

"Yeah, and they don't seem worried." I push my plate away.

"Gut reaction?" Sloan leans forward to stare into my eyes.

"It's hard to say. She sent Nick a letter. He's convinced something's not right."

Aunt Dodie clears the table, and Grandma disappears into the kitchen to make coffee.

"The bust was a disaster," Sloan says. "Somebody— we never found out who—gave Stepanek a heads-up. He split and let his wife take the fall."

"Meth lab?"

He nods. "In the shed out back, along with a few kilos of marijuana. We'd been told Joe had a big operation and was supplying half of Vista Valley. We tore the place apart. If he kept records, he stashed them someplace else."

"Sara adores her dad. She talks about him all the time." I sigh. "Go figure. She hates her mom, but she's still daddy's little girl."

"Has she heard from him?"

"She's never said anything to me. Nick might know."

"Huh." He falls silent. I can almost see the wheels turning in his head. Finally, he says, "Maybe I'll do some poking around."

"Will you let me know what you find out? My nephew's not well, and I don't like to see him upset."

He ignores me and digs into his pie. "Probably not."

"What?" I can't believe this guy. "You wouldn't know about this if I hadn't told you."

"You're a civilian."

"Look, I just want to find out what happened to Sara." I'm dying to add "you arrogant ass," but it remains unspoken.

He doesn't answer.

"Okay, fine," I mutter. "I'll do some poking around on my own. I'm not without resources."

He frowns. "I wouldn't if I were you."

Sloan and I eat our pie in stony silence. Dodie skips dessert and pours another glass of wine. Grandma chatters about our upcoming gig. "The three of us entertain at retirement homes. We sing the oldies—not too old—tunes from the 60s, 70s and 80s. Yep, Serenity Bay Assisted Living is the place to be Saturday night."

I scrunch down in my chair.

Sloan points his fork at me. "Blondie here sings, too?"

"Don't call me Blondie."

Grandma's on a roll. "Allegra has a lovely voice, and she knows how to move her body. When we sang 'Old Time Rock and Roll,' Mr. Wamsley jumped up and started boogying with his walker. He tripped, and Allegra tried to catch him, but he fell on her. That's how she broke her ankle."

"Wow." Sloan gives me a half grin. "Have you been banned from Serenity Bay?"

Grandma says, "Oh, no, they love Allegra. Now that her cast is off, we'll be doing the Pointer Sisters next Saturday night."

Sloan chuckles.

Thankfully, he departs after the pie, kissing Grandma's hand and praising her culinary skills. On the way out, he pats me on the head. "See you soon, Al."

"Don't call me Al and, no, you won't see me soon."

"We'll see," he says and is gone.

"Hot-cha-CHA!!" Aunt Dodie fans her flushed face with a napkin. "Watching Sloan walk away is like crème brûlée for the eyes. He sure does fill out a pair of jeans."

"The front's not bad either," Grandma says.

"Settle down, you two." I gather up the pie plates.

Grandma sips her coffee and muses, "Things happen for a reason, Allegra. Michael may be out of the picture, but now you have Sloan."

"Yep," Dodie says. "When one door closes, another opens."

"I don't want Sloan. He's a jerk."

"Michael's not right for you," Dodie says. "He's a pouter. My second husband was a pouter."

I'm saved by my cell phone.

Labored breathing. A whispery voice. "Ms. Thome, it's me—Sara. I need . . ." She stops mid-sentence with a squeak of surprise. I hear a *clunk* like the phone's been knocked from her hand.

My heart does a double flip in my chest, and I shout, "Sara? Sara? Where are you?"

The line is dead.

"Hang up, and press star sixty-nine," Dodie orders.

I obey quickly and punch in the numbers of the last incoming call. A disembodied voice tells me my party is not available. "Damn!"

"Call Mr. Sloan, and have him trace the call," Grandma says.

"Forget Sloan. I'm calling the cops."

As I relate the one-sided conversation to the authorities, I begin to have doubts.

"Yes, ma'am, I'm writing this down," a bored-sounding detective says. "You say she sounded afraid?"

Was it fear I heard in her voice or excitement?

"You're sure someone knocked the phone out of her hand? Did she cry out?"

"It wasn't exactly a cry . . . more like a yelp."

"A yelp," he repeats, not bothering to hide his skepticism. "Surprise or pain?"

I admit I don't know. When I ask if Sara's disappearance has been reported, he says he'll check and then tells me to call back tomorrow.

Questions without answers make my head hurt. In an effort to clear my mind, I load the dishwasher and clean up the kitchen. Still no wiser, I kiss Grandma's soft cheek and wave nightie-night to Dodie. Before heading for Nick's, I scoop up the paper with the mystery phone number. I know Grandma's busy little fingers won't be able to resist, and Sloan will be back in the picture. I need time to think without his overbearing presence.

Nick squirms in embarrassment as I read Sara's letter aloud.

Hey, Woodstock,

    Something's come up, and I gotta go. Remember that thing we talked about? You're right.

    I've decided not to do it. Take care, and tell your aunt to come get her book.

    Give Clementine a hug for me.

                  Luv ya – Magpie

                  Daniel 3:17

I feel a headache coming on. Sara's letter is a mish-mash of noninformation. References to a mysterious thing. A Bible verse. Birds. And who the hell is Clementine? I need answers, and I know Nick has them.

"Okay, spill it," I say. "What's going on with Sara?"

He blushes and looks at his feet. "She calls me Woodstock, like the bird in Peanuts."

With his fair, spiky hair and big eyes, the name suits him. "And you call her Magpie?"

He ignores the question, picks up a retractable pen, and begins clicking the button with his thumb. When he looks at me, his eyes are wary. "Sara was sneaking out to see her dad. She made me promise not to tell 'cause there's a warrant out for his arrest."

"Was she planning on taking off with him?"

"I talked her out of it," he says. "What kind of a life would that be? Her dad's on the run. She'd have to drop out of school.

I point at the letter. "It says here she's decided not to."

"That's why I know she's in trouble," he says. "Don't you see? Sara promised she wouldn't take off with her dad, and she has no other reason to leave. I think somebody was watching her write this letter, somebody who . . ."

I throw my hands up. "She's just a kid, Nick. Kids change their minds. Things probably got hot for her dad, and he talked her into leaving. Makes sense, doesn't it?"

He won't look at me. His thumb goes faster. *Click. Click. Click.* I want to grab the pen and shake him until the truth rattles out. I know there's more.

"Well, doesn't it?" I ask, hoping to loosen his tongue.

When he doesn't answer, I know it's time to switch gears. "Okay, maybe the Clementine she mentions is Clemmy in our class."

"I called her. Clemmy said they weren't friends. She and Sara hate each other."

"Okay. What about the Bible verse? Did Sara go to church?"

"Yeah." Nick mumbles and looks away.

"Which one?"

"Church of the Holy Light," he snaps and folds his arms across his narrow chest signaling the end of the discussion.

I ignore his surly behavior. "Did you look up the verse?"

"Yeah, it's about three dudes who get thrown into a hot furnace."

"Oh, yes," I say, eager to share my biblical knowledge. "Shadrach, Meshach, and Abednego."

Before I was big enough to fight back, my mother dragged my sorry butt to Sunday school every week, praying I'd be scared straight. I still have a visual of Mrs. McPherson's felt board with Shadrack, Meshach, and Abednego standing in the fiery furnace, orange flames licking at their feet.

"Whatever," Nick says.

"To test their faith," I add. "God saved them."

He stands suddenly. "We need to go to the Hewitts'

and look for your book."

Back to the book. When Nick bows his neck, it's useless to argue. But I try. When I ask him how such an innocuous letter can possibly make him believe Sara is the victim of foul play, he looks away and says, "I just know."

We make plans to go to the Hewitts' tomorrow after school. Though I'd planned to tell him about Sara's call, I, too, decide to hold something back.

Later, alone in my apartment, I douse the light and tumble into bed, curling up on my side to gaze out the open window at the night sky. The wind rustles softly in the huge maples bordering the street in front of our house, a gentle lullaby that softens the edges of my worried mind.

My last thoughts before drifting into dreamland are of Sloan's magnificent denim-clad butt. Hey, I'm only human.

Hot-cha-CHA.

Chapter 4

*P*ull in here." Nick points to a long gravel driveway bordered by an overgrown hedge.

Two small boys pummel each other in the front yard of a shabby 50s bungalow set back from the street. A scrawny gray cat with a notch in his ear crouches nearby looking ready to jump into the fray.

"Davie and Dwight Junior," Nick tells me.

I grab my tote as we exit the truck. The screen door flies open, and Dwight senior appears. "You two, knock it off. Davie, get to mowin'."

"But it's his turn," Davie whines, giving his brother a shove.

"Is not!"

"Well, it better get mowed, or you'll both be sorry," Dwight snarls.

He retreats into the house yelling, "Patsy, that teacher woman's here."

Davie and Dwight junior stare at us with dull eyes.

Nick nudges me. "Look."

I follow his gaze further up the driveway, where a shiny new Dodge Caravan is parked.

"New wheels?"

"Uh huh."

Patsy appears at the front door. She smiles at Nick and grunts at me.

"Great car, Mrs. Hewitt!" Nick gushes as we step into the darkened living room. Dwight sucks on a cigarette and stares at a big-screen television.

Nick says, "Plasma screen? Wow!"

Patsy looks pleased. "Dwight's doing real good at the mill." She gives me a scathing look. "Some folks have to work for their money."

A prepubescent girl sits cross-legged on the couch with a bag of Cheetos. Her sandy hair and unfortunate overbite mark her as one of Patsy's brood.

Nick sits down beside her. "Hi, Doreen."

"Hey," Doreen replies, offering the bag to Nick. They munch in companionable silence. Patsy and I stand mute in the middle of the room.

Finally I say, "Could I have a look at Sara's books? I lent her one that was my grandmother's favorite." The lie slips easily off my tongue.

"Doreen!" Patsy screeches. I jump in alarm. "Take her to Sara's room and show her the books."

"Why do I have to do everything around here?" Doreen licks orange Cheetos dust from each finger and drops the bag onto Nick's lap. She slips into oversized wooden mules and clomps toward the back of the house. As I hurry after her, I hear Nick say, "Can I go look at your new car?"

I follow a pouty Doreen through the sticky-floored

kitchen to a small enclosed foyer with three steps leading to the back door. She makes an abrupt right turn and starts down a flight of slick concrete stairs leading to the basement. Guided by some feral instinct, Doreen disappears into the shadows, leaving me to fend for myself. I thrust a hand against the wall for balance but recoil quickly when I encounter a spider's sticky web. Visions of walking casts dance in my head.

"Hey, Doreen! How about turning on the light," I call.

Teeth flash white in the dim light, and I heard a disembodied voice. "I can see just fine."

"Don't make me call your mother." My voice has risen to a screech.

"Jeez, I was just kidding. Why are you teachers always so crabby?"

Deep sigh. Clomp. Clomp. Clomp. I hear her fumble with a chain, and suddenly an overhead bulb illuminates the dreary basement.

I stand at the end of a long L-shaped room strung end to end with an indoor clothesline. The far end of the room is lined with floor-to-ceiling cupboards. An ancient coal furnace lurks in the shadows against one wall. I count four rooms opening off the main room: three with closed doors and one open wide, revealing a washer, old-fashioned stationary tubs, and a shower head positioned over a drain in the floor.

"In here." Doreen opens one of the closed doors. A tiny window set high in the wall at ground level throws a small rectangle of daylight into the room revealing a neatly made single bed and little else. Glancing around for a light switch, I see none. However, on a wooden apple box by the bed sits a small gooseneck lamp. I picture Sara lying in bed reading in this dismal little room and feel a wave of pity so strong my eyes fill with tears.

I switch on the lamp as Doreen points to a bookcase formed by plywood boards and concrete blocks.

"That there's her stuff."

"Okay, thanks. I'll look through it."

I hope she'll take the hint and leave. Instead, she leans against the wall, folds her arms, and scowls at me. I sit on the bed and check out the items on the shelves. A grubby Cabbage Patch doll, four paperbacks, and a dried corsage. A fruit jar holds a colorful bouquet of feathers. I think about Sara using the plumage of birds to create something beautiful in this dreary room, and I try to swallow the lump in my throat.

I pick up the corsage and set it carefully on my palm.

"That's from when Sara and Nick went—" Doreen starts.

"I know." I dig a tissue out of my bag and blow my nose. "I helped pick it out."

I didn't need Doreen to tell me about the prom. How Sara's eyes sparkled when one of my many bridesmaid dresses fit her perfectly. How Nick, awestruck at taking the prettiest girl in school to the prom, hyperventilated and had to breathe into a paper sack.

"Are you going to sit here all day?" Doreen demands.

"As long as it takes to find my book."

Moving in exaggerated slow motion, I set the brittle corsage carefully on the shelf and pick up a paperback, feigning interest in the blurb on the back.

Doreen taps one giant shoe. "There's more under the bed."

When I tug at the cardboard box, I feel it bump something. I peek under the bed, pull out a one-liter bottle of cola, and then hand it to Doreen, who eyes it with interest. When I start to unpack the books, she heaves an impatient sigh and leaves. I hear her clatter up the concrete stairs.

Scanning the stack of books, I see nothing of mine. To lend credence to our story, I grab a few paperbacks. But when I bend over to turn off the lamp, I spot a slim, hardcover book caught between the bed and the apple box. I pick it up and find out I'm not a liar after all. The title of the book is *Best Loved Poems* and the name on the fly leaf is Sybil Thome. Somehow, Sara has one of Grandma's books. Did I give it to her? If so, I must have been in a stress-induced blackout.

With the books tucked under my arm, I switch off the light and leave the depressing little room. When I step through the door, I come face to face with the furnace. Each time Sara leaves her room, she sees the furnace. The fiery furnace. Now, at the beginning of June, the cold, dead furnace. The perfect place to stash something in a household short on privacy. I dig a penlight out of my bag and illuminate the furnace's gaping maw. Nothing.

A toilet plunger and push broom rest against the left side of the furnace. Feeling a little silly, I play the light over the other side, a narrow opening between the furnace and a freestanding metal cabinet. I see cobwebs, dust, and what looks like an old brown sweater pushed back against the wall.

Squatting down, I take one last look. At this angle, I pick up a flash of white peeking out from under the sweater. I reach in, trying not to think about venomous spiders licking their chops at the sight of my bare arm. With a shudder, I retreat and use the push broom to pull the sweater toward me. My pulse begins to race when I pick up the sweater and find it's wrapped around a Tyvek envelope embossed with the U.S. Postal Service logo. Inside, I find a Bible and a spiral notebook. "Property of Sara Stepanek" is written on the front in purple ink.

As I stuff it back into the envelope, a brown, hairy spider scampers across my hand. With a silent scream, I flick it off and do my spider stomping dance, dropping the envelope in the process. I bend over to pick it up and nearly levitate when Doreen bellows, "Ma! She's snooping around!"

Caught up in my mission, I failed to notice she'd sneaked back down the stairs barefoot.

I turn my back to block her view as she marches toward me. With my heart in my throat, I grab the sweater and cover the envelope. In a semi-crouch, I let the envelope slip into my tote.

I stand up, turn, and shove the sweater at Doreen. "Is this Sara's? I found it by the furnace. You should put it with her things."

She shrugs and tosses it over her shoulder.

Without waiting for Doreen, I hurry up the stairs to collect Nick and get the hell out of Dodge. I find him sitting behind the wheel of the new van while Patsy fiddles with the CD player. I wave the books at him and shout over the sound of the lawn mower, "Gotta go, bud."

With a few last words to Patsy, he scrambles out of the van. Patsy doesn't look up.

I set my bag on my lap and fire up the Ranger.

"You found it, huh?"

I hand over the loot. He opens Sara's notebook and

scans the pages.

"Oh, great," he says. "Poems. Every page has a stupid poem on it."

"Teenage girls like to write poetry."

"Not Sara. Remember the fit she threw when you made the class write poetry?"

Nick flips through the pages again and then checks out *Best Loved Poems*. "She didn't write these. She copied the poems from this book. Each one has a date. Weird. Why would she take the trouble to hide a bunch of poems? Doesn't make sense."

"Maybe there's something in the Bible."

I glance over at him and see disappointment in his eyes. He turns away and stares out the window. "I wonder where Patsy and Dwight got the money for a new car and plasma TV."

"Maybe they have good credit."

"Sara said they made her answer the phone 'cause collection agencies kept calling them." He turns his head toward me.

I feel the urgency in his gaze.

"They bought the car at Better Buy Auto Sales. We could go there and pretend we want the same car. Maybe we can find out if they financed it or paid cash," he says.

I roll my eyes. "Gimme a break! You wanted the book. I got the book. You think Patsy and Dwight are involved in some sort of conspiracy?"

He doesn't answer, but the stubborn set of his jaw tells me he won't let it go.

I drop him off with the pirated goods. He climbs out

and, before he shuts the door, says, "Tomorrow. After school. Better Buy Auto."

I murmur something noncommittal and head for the barn.

Chapter 5

Wednesday

Where's Allison?" I ask the next morning, counting noses after the break.

Her best friend, Janie, nibbles on bright green fingernails and mumbles, "She asked Coach Thorndyke if she could TA for him next fall. He said she had to try out."

"Try out?" I shriek while watching two girls give each other the stink eye. The stud muffin responsible for their bad blood slouches nearby, a proud smile on his narrow, pimply face.

"Jeez. Chill out, Ms. Thome. He makes all the girls try out," Crystal says.

Janie gives a sniff of disapproval. "I told her not to."

I count to ten and scan the approved list of sanitized curse words posted on my bulletin board. Totally unsatisfactory. "Listen up, class! You *do not* have to 'try out' to be a teacher's aide."

I smack my hand on the desk for emphasis.

"Oooo," Crystal mocks. "Thorndyke better be careful.

Ms. Thome's flippin' out."

Because Nick is now in his advanced math class, I send an SOS via Janie, offering to buy Marcy dinner Friday night if she'll cover my class for a few minutes. A deal is struck, and I go in search of sweet, dull Allison, who's in my room by default. She wasn't sneaky enough to run away when two other girls set fire to the trash in the bathroom. Allison is no more an arsonist than Stella and Stanley, the classroom goldfish.

Her problem is more complex than simple arson. Large of bosom and fair of face, her desperate need for attention makes her an easy target for teenage boys looking to score. Donny Thorndyke is a different story. Though he has the morals of a goat, he is presumably an adult male, albeit a recently divorced one. Damned if I'd let him manipulate her.

I find her in Coach Thorndyke's office. The door's ajar, and I see Crystal standing on a chair in her mini skirt and three-inch heels. She holds a bottle of glass cleaner in one hand, a wad of paper towels in the other. Donny Thorndyke leans back in his chair and enjoys the show as she sprays, rubs and wriggles, reaching for the top corner of the window.

In a towering rage, I throw the office door open. The front legs of Thorndyke's chair crash to the floor and Allison squeaks in alarm. The glass cleaner slips from her hand and she teeters precariously. I grab her hand and help her down.

I try to keep my voice calm. "It's class time, Allison. Wait for me in the hall and I'll walk you back."

I usher her out and shut the door.

"What the hell are you doing, Donny?"

He stands up and blusters, "Hey, hey, babe. Take it easy. She asked to be my TA. I figured if she's one of yours, she's short on credits. I'm trying to help her out."

Spittle gathers in the corner of his mouth. "I gave her an interview—you know, like a real job—and asked her what she was good at."

"Yeah, I'll bet you did." I take a deep breath. "Here's the deal, Donny. Allison will *not* TA for you. If you ever pull that stunt again with Allison or any other girl, I'll go to R.D."

His gaze slides away from mine and then comes back hot and angry. "You threatening me, babe? Go ahead. Do your best. R.D. and I are like this."

He crosses his middle finger over his index finger and jerks them skyward effectively flipping me off. He seems to grow larger in the small office. The air is thick with hostility. He takes a step toward me. I fold my arms and hold my ground but feel a flicker of fear when I realize Donny would like nothing better than to punch me in the face.

"Just stay away from Allison." I reach for the door.

He gives a snort of disgust and shuffles papers on his desk.

My classroom is in chaos when Allison and I return. Marcy, looking like a trapped animal, hisses, "Boy, do you owe me," and scurries out the door. Still boiling inside from my encounter with Donny, I stand in front of my desk and fold my arms. My students, all savvy survivors of raging parental emotions, pick up quickly on my mood and settle down. Straightening up the jumble of papers on my desk, I unearth a note from Marcy:

TALK TO JIMMY FELTHOUSE ABOUT SARA.

I crouch next to Jimmy's desk and whisper, "Do you know something about Sara Stepanek? Have you seen her?"

Jimmy tucks his stub of a pencil behind his ear and cracks his knuckles. "Yep, I seen her Friday night."

"Saw." I can't help myself.

"But you said 'seen.'"

Now is not the time for a lesson on helping verbs. "Just tell me what you saw."

"Well," he says, "I *saw* Sara during my break, proba- bly 'bout eight. I work at McDonald's, y'know. They can't never get along without me on the weekends."

I cringe but encourage him with a nonjudgmental "Uh huh."

"Anyways, I was outside havin' a smoke when I seen her go by in a blue Taurus."

"Driving or riding?"

"Ridin' shotgun. She was with some lady."

"Anybody you know?"

"Nope, but I know one thing: It wasn't Mrs. Hewitt."

I stand up and pat his shoulder. "Thanks."

Nick and I don't have a chance to talk until after school. The dismissal bell rings, and my students bolt, the scent of adolescent pheromones lingering in their wake. With a weary sigh, I slip off my shoes and plop down in my swivel chair. Nick straightens desks knocked out of alignment by the stampede while I fill him in on Jimmy's revelation.

Nick freezes. "He's sure it was a blue Taurus?"

"Come on, Nick. We're talking about Jimmy. He stole

cars for a living. So who drives a blue Taurus?"

He walks slowly to my desk. "Her caseworker, Peggy something, drives a blue Taurus."

"So she was with her caseworker Friday night at eight," I say. "Funny the Hewitts didn't mention it."

"Yeah," he agrees. "All the more reason we need to go to Better Buy."

Chapter 6

*B*etter Buy Auto Sales sprang up on a single, dusty lot in the area of town crowded with mattress factories, fast-food joints, and a cement plant. Multiple garish billboards and an aggressive television ad campaign by Guy Hornbuckle, its horse-faced owner, have won the hearts and opened the wallets of Vista Valley folk. Better Buy's ads feature Guy atop a real horse against a background of purple sage and the immortal words "If you're tired of horse *bleep*, come see Guy at Better Buy."

Now resplendent on an acre of land, the glittering L-shaped showroom might look inviting if not for the cluster of snappily dressed salesmen lurking beneath the "Grand Opening" banner.

A life-sized cardboard cutout of Better Buy Guy astride his steed graces the inside of one showroom window. A curtain, torn loose from its moorings and caught in an updraft, billows and flaps across his Stetson, giving him the appearance of a cowpoke moseying through an opulent Middle

Eastern harem.

Before I can turn off the ignition, one eager beaver peels off from the crowd and bears down on us. I reach for the lock. Nick flashes me a grin and bounds from the car, intercepting the salesman with "Hi. I'm Nick Dorsey. My mom's looking for a new van and, since she's real busy, my aunt brought me down to take a look."

Startled, the salesman reluctantly leaves my window and grasps Nick's diminutive hand in a hearty shake that almost topples the little guy. "Trent Maguire. Pleased to meet you, Nick."

I ease the door open and slip from the car. Big, buff, and tanning booth-enhanced, Trent flashes me a gleaming smile. His eyes do the up-and-down thing before he says to my breasts, "And you are?"

"My aunt," Nick says, "Allegra."

"Ah-LEG-ra!" he booms. "Beautiful name for a beautiful woman. All you need is a beautiful car. Right? What can I show you folks today?"

He gives me a seductive wink and rubs his hands together. *Lust or greed?* I ponder this mixed message before pointing at Nick. "Like he said, his mother wants a van. I'm just the chauffeur."

Trent's expectant gaze dims, and he turns to Nick. "Whatcha looking for, kid?"

"A Dodge Caravan like the one Dwight and Patsy Hewitt bought. They told me they got a real good deal here. Were you the salesman?"

Trent holds up a finger. "Just a sec."

He trots away to interrogate the others.

I'm in the middle of an exasperated sigh when he

reappears. "Lou sold it to them. He's off today."

Nick says, "I want to test drive a Grand Caravan. You know all about financing . . . right?"

Trent stares at Nick, brows gathered in suspicion. "You old enough to drive?"

"I'm small for my age." Nick digs out his wallet and flashes his Washington state limited driver's license. "I can drive with an adult but not with other kids in the car."

Trent squirms. "The boss doesn't like us to let kids drive. Maybe your aunt should drive—take 'er for a spin, see how she handles. Whaddaya think, Ah-LEG-ra?" He waggles his eyebrows.

I ignore the innuendo. "How's this for a plan? School's out for the day, and the student parking lot's empty. You drive to the school and let Nick try 'er out in the parking lot, see how she handles."

Nick grins. "Sure you don't want to go, Aunt Ah-LEG-ra?"

"I'll pass."

"Alrighty then." Trent points at the showroom. "There's a waiting room inside—TV, coffee, whatever you need."

I meander back to my truck feeling righteous. I'd make good use of my time and correct the math papers I stuffed in my bag. Reaching for the door handle, I hear, "Ms. Thome! Ms. Thome! It's me . . . JJ!"

I shade my eyes against the late afternoon sun bouncing off a sea of chrome and spot Jeremy Jones heading my way. Dressed in crisp, blue coveralls, lank brown hair pulled back in a neat ponytail, he seems delighted to see me—typical with former students who've given me the most grief.

"JJ!" I extend my hand. "Good to see you."

He looks at my hand with horror, as if shaking it would

break some cardinal rule of teacher-student interaction. Finally, he wipes his hand on the leg of his coveralls and gives mine a delicate squeeze. Pulling a towel from his pocket, he flicks a bit of dust from the Ranger. "I'm working here now, Ms. Thome. My PO got me the job. I detail the cars, keep 'em looking good."

Wow. This is cool: JJ proud of his accomplishments and gainfully employed. Not bad for a kid who came to class high and resisted my efforts to provide him with basic skills.

"Nice of Mr. Hornbuckle not to hold your past . . . er . . . indiscretions against you."

"Yeah, he said he'd kick my ass . . . oops . . . be disappointed in me if I let him down."

In his criminal days, JJ was the king of smash and dash. Astride his bike, he'd swoop down on a parked car, smash the window, grab the goodies, and disappear like a phantom in the mist. The twisted logic of a car dealer employing JJ appeals to my sense of whimsy.

"Lookin' for a new car? We got some sweet rides." JJ is coiled and ready to sprint off to fetch me a salesman.

I shake my head. "I'm waiting for somebody."

A shrill whistle splits the air. "Hey, kid, get your butt over here. We need you to make a run for us."

The summons comes from one of the salesmen: short guy, crew cut, cocky stance.

"Just a sec, Dave," JJ hollers. "Gotta go, Ms. Thome. The guys order take-out from the El Taquito. I walk over and get it for them."

"Walk?" I ask before realizing my mistake. "Oh, sorry, guess you aren't driving yet."

He flushes. "Not 'til I get off probation."

I feel bad about embarrassing him and a little pissed off at the men who treat him like their personal lackey. I motion at Red Ranger. "Hop in. I'll drive you."

A smile blooms on his thin face. We pull up to the men. JJ collects their money. As we pull away, Crew Cut winks at JJ. "Hurry back now, stud."

Under the guise of adjusting my sunglasses, I resort to immature behavior and flip him off. Crew Cut's mouth drops open. He grins and salutes.

Later, in El Taquito's parking lot, JJ and I sit at a picnic table munching on tacos and dishing the dirt. I get caught up on all of JJ's criminal buddies and fill him in on the latest school gossip, omitting any mention of Sara's disappearance.

But, hold the phone! I'm missing a golden opportunity here. JJ's a smart kid in a felonious sort of way. "Hey, JJ," I say. "If I wanted to buy a car and needed financing, who would I talk to?"

JJ dabs at the hot sauce running down the front of his coveralls. "Ms. Sawatsky. She's the old biddy who takes care a that. Why? I thought you wasn't looking for a new car?"

"I'm not, but a friend of mine is. She wants a van like the Hewitts bought and is wondering how they financed it."

"Oh, yeah, I remember them. Sweet van—if you like that kinda thing. Which, a course, I don't."

He glances at his watch and munches thoughtfully. "Ms. Sawatsky'll be gone at five then Rosie comes to work. We can ask her."

"Rosie?"

"Yeah, you remember Rosie . . . the one with all the kids."

"*My* Rosie? She works here? In the finance department?"

I'm astonished. Rosie created quite a stir at last year's

graduation. Hugely pregnant, she walked across the stage to shake hands with a school board member and receive her diploma . . . and then her water broke.

She screamed, "Oh, shit!" frightening the school board member so badly he took a startled step backward, slipped in the puddle, and fell on his butt. That night, Rosie was blessed with a diploma and a set of twin girls.

"Yeah," JJ says. "Welfare-to-work program. She comes on at five, works 'til nine. Ms. Sawatsky leaves a bunch of filing for her to do. But she knows how to work the computer. She has to 'cause sometimes the salesmen have questions, ya know?"

I nod. With two of my former students employed at Better Buy, clearly I'd have to rethink my opinion of Guy Hornbuckle. If he was kind enough to hire them, I sure didn't want to screw it up.

"Hey, JJ," I say. "Just forget it, okay? I don't want to get you or Rosie in trouble."

A crafty gleam appears in JJ's eyes. He stands and gathers up the take-out bags. "Don't worry about it, Ms. Thome. You won't."

We get back a little after five. JJ points out a dusty Toyota Tercel with two baby seats in the back. "Rosie's car. And there goes Ms. Sawatsky."

The salesmen part and fall silent as a tall thin woman in a pink pants suit throws open the door and marches to the parking lot, where she slips into a sensible beige sedan. After she pulls out, JJ sidles into the building while I wait in the truck.

Moments later, an electric blue Dodge Caravan pulls to a stop in front of the showroom, and then out pop Nick and Trent. After a few minutes of circling the van and looking thoughtful, Trent pumps Nick's hand once again and glances my way. I slump down in my seat and avoid eye contact.

Nick climbs in the Ranger, one corner of his mouth turned down.

"Struck out, huh?"

He shrugs. "Trent said he couldn't tell me how the Hewitts paid for their car. It's confidential. Told me if we want to finance, we need to go talk to some woman, a Mrs. Sa—Saw—"

"Mrs. Sawatsky." I smile smugly.

Nick starts to answer but, instead, sniffs the air. "It smells like tacos in here."

I reach behind the seat and hand him a take-out box from El Taquito. He mumbles his thanks and digs in. "How do you know about her? Mrs. Sawatsky?"

I see JJ pop out a side door. I twirl an imaginary mustache and say, *"Uno momento, ma petite chou."*

Two years of high school French were hardwired into my brain before mating with the Spanish I hear spoken every day, resulting in a bizarre *argot* my friends call *Franco Con Carne*.

Nick looks up from his tacos. "Hey, there's JJ."

I turn on the engine and zip the window down. After greeting Nick, JJ whispers a single word in my ear.

JJ and I exchange thanks—his for the food, mine for the information—before Nick and I hit the road.

"Well . . ." Nick demands.

"Cash," I say. "The Hewitts paid with cash."

"The deluxe model is over $20,000. That's a big wad

of cash."

"Maybe somebody died and they inherited money. Maybe they won the lottery."

"Maybe somebody paid them to keep quiet about something," Nick says.

"What could the Hewitts possibly know? Or who? They don't exactly hang with the rich and famous of Vista Valley."

"Not the legitimate ones anyway," Nick says.

He looks out the window and slaps his forehead. "Oops, I forgot to tell you I'm not going home. You can drop me at the Church of the Holy Light. Mom's picking me up later."

I brake, pull over to the side of the street, and turn off the ignition. "This truck doesn't move until you tell me what's going on. The whole story. Sara. Her big secret. All of it."

He stares at me, unblinking, eyes owlish behind round glasses. Finally, he sighs. "Sara told me not to tell anybody, even you, or she wouldn't be my friend anymore." His voice cracks, and he lifts his glasses to rub his eyes.

My sense of unease grows. Kids keep dangerous secrets, even smart kids like Nick. Especially like Nick. Pint-sized and frail, he struggles to find his niche in a world that prizes athletic prowess and "hotties." Sadly, few of his fellow students have taken the time to know and value him for his giant brain and wicked sense of humor. Until Sara.

Nick says, "Remember when the class studied birds?"

"Yeah, Sara's report was on magpies." *Oh, duh,* I think. *Magpie.*

"We were at the library looking up stuff for her report. She found out magpies steal eggs from other birds' nests

49

and even kill the baby birds. She started to cry and said she was worse than a magpie."

I'm still trying to fit the pieces together when Nick takes a deep breath and the story pours out. Sara was twelve when her home blew apart. Placed with a foster home in a neighboring town, she was scared and lonely, easy prey for a teenage gang. It took a year, but she finally gave in to the gang's promise to be her family. She then faced an ordeal so horrific that Nick looks everywhere but in my eyes as he relates it.

"Sara had to prove she was tough enough to be in the gang. They call it 'jumping in.'"

He glances up at me, eyes foreshadowing the revulsion he feels. "She had to fight all the girls and have sex with all the guys."

I shake my head, unable to speak past the lump in my throat.

"She got pregnant," he continues. "When she started throwing up in the morning, her foster mother found out. Sara had an abortion and was moved to Patsy and Dwight's."

Nick pauses again to wipe his eyes. I try to keep my tone neutral when I say, "Was it Sara's choice to abort the baby?"

Nick bristles. "Yeah, but it wasn't her fault. She was only thirteen."

"When did she tell you about the gang thing, the abortion?"

"Ages ago. Before Christmas."

"But she didn't seem upset until recently?"

"The Hewitts started taking her to church. At first it was okay, but then she started private counseling with the pastor. That's when she changed."

"You're sure this personality change happened after

she started going to the Church of the Holy Light?"

He shoots me a disgusted look. "Of course I'm sure. The minister screwed her up."

"So you think the minister has something to do with her running away?"

"She kept saying she had to get right with God," Nick mumbles, staring at his feet.

"Praying? Meditating? How was she going to get right with God?"

"I—don't—know," Nick gasps, his thin body overtaken by a spasm of coughing. Breaking his promise to Sara had cost him.

I grab his hand and hold on as if, by osmosis, I can infuse Nick with my healthy cells. "You're making yourself sick over this. Look, she loves her dad. She's probably . . ."

He raises his head, and I see his eyes flash with anger. "Oh yeah? Then what about Patsy and Dwight? They couldn't wait to bring her stuff back to school. Now, suddenly, they have a new car and TV?"

He wipes his mouth with a tissue and stares out the window.

Sara's phone call is heavy on my mind. She'd sounded so . . . What? Panicky? Desperate? Or was I putting my own spin on it?

"Wednesday's youth night at the church," Nick says. "Thought I'd check out Pastor Hunt."

In spite of his light tone, he looks at me as if he expects an argument. I keep my mouth shut. Nick's painful quest for the truth about Sara's disappearance is *his* journey. Unless he puts himself in danger, I have no right to interfere.

"Your mom okay with this?" I ask.

He nods. "Yeah. She thinks, you know . . ." His voice trails off. "The CF and all."

Susan knows kids with cystic fibrosis often die before the age of thirty. Perhaps she thinks he's looking for answers she can't give him. Maybe he is.

"You know where it is?" Nick asks.

"Sure. Who could miss it?" I start the engine, make a U-turn, and head for the Church of the Holy Light.

Minutes later we turn in to a curved drive, pass a reader board proclaiming "Sinners are welcome at the Church of the Holy Light," and pull to a stop in front of the soaring stone edifice. Glass double doors stand open, presumably to welcome the aforementioned sinners.

Nick opens the door then pauses. "Call tomorrow, and make an appointment with Sara's caseworker. Okay?"

Without waiting for an answer, he slams the door and merges with a group of sullen-looking teens recently disgorged from an enormous black SUV.

Then I remember. Every spring, the spacious grounds of the church are filled with tiny pink and blue crosses and a sign proclaiming, "ABORTION IS MURDER."

Chapter 7

I head toward home deep in thought. This whole Sara thing is making me crazy. It's as if there's a giant, electric Scrabble board with SARA flashing in the middle and all we can come up with are lame words like *is, am, or,* and *as,* leading to a dead end.

I pull into my driveway. No unidentified cars parked nearby. So far, so good. I find Grandma Sybil snoozing in her recliner, Vlad curled up in her lap next to the open volume of *Best Loved Poems.* When I asked her about the book, Grandma told me Sara borrowed it six months ago. "You weren't home, Allegra," Grandma said. "Nick and Sara dropped by for a visit. I never thought to mention it to you."

Both Grandma and Vlad snore, emitting dainty purring sounds, similar in tone and volume. Today is Grandma's day for personal enhancement. Her red hair is tightly curled, her fingernails freshly painted bubblegum pink and jewel embedded. I glance down at her toenails, visible through the tiny sandals she special orders from petitefeet.com. The butterflies have been replaced by tiny ladybugs.

I peek in her daybook lying open on the end table. Stanley is penciled in for 8 p.m. No wonder she needs a nap. After an exhausting session at the day spa, she's resting up for her night job. *Don't go there, Allegra,* I tell myself as I tiptoe away. *Everyone needs a hobby.* The *snap, snap* of Grandma's recliner, followed by a surprised hiss-meow-growl from Vlad as he's dumped onto the floor, stop me in my tracks.

"Oh, Allegra!" Grandma lifts her glasses to rub the sleep from her eyes. "How are you, sweetie?"

"I'm fine, Grandma. I was about to change clothes and go for a run."

"Take Vlad with you. He needs the exercise."

Vlad glares at me sullenly, no doubt blaming me for slumber interruptus. It's useless to point out cats don't jog, so I nod and head for the stairs.

"I almost forgot," Grandma calls. "That nice Mr. Sloan stopped by."

I stop in mid-stride. "Was it about Sara?"

Grandma giggles. "I think it was more of a personal nature. Check your phone messages."

I scamper upstairs and, sure enough, the message light is blinking. I punch *play* and hear a familiar growl. "Al. Friday night. Dinner. Pick you up at six."

"Oh yeah?" I yell at the phone. "I'm busy Friday night!"

I slip out of my work clothes and into shorts and a tee shirt. Who the hell does he think he is with his verbal shorthand and assumption I have no social life?

I reach for the phone. When voice mail kicks in with its long list of options, I jab *0* so viciously I break the nail on my pointer finger. A generic male voice tells me I've reached the central Washington office of the Drug Enforcement Agency.

"I want to talk to Sloan."

"I'm sorry, ma'am, he's in the field."

"Yeah, right," I snarl. "Is this Ernie?"

"No ma'am. It's Chuck."

"Chuck. I've got a message for Sloan."

"Who's calling, please?"

"He'll know who it is. Tell him . . ."

"Could you hold, miss?"

Before I can respond, I hear a series of beeps and clicks. Chuck returns, sounding like he's at the bottom of a well. "Go ahead with your message, please."

Speakerphone. *So this is what you've come to, Allegra. Entertainment for the friendly folks at the local DEA office. Might as well make the most of it.*

"In your dreams, Sloan!" I shout into the phone.

I hope people are wincing and covering their ears. "I am *not* available Friday night. I have a previous engagement. Unless, of course, you'd like to share information about my missing student. By the way, you may have charmed my aunt and grandmother, but you didn't fool *me*. You're just in it for the pie. And forget what they said about me needing *therapy*. What a crock!"

I probably shouldn't have mentioned the pie and therapy bit. But after listening to Dodie and Grandma, Sloan probably thinks I'm so desperate for a man I'll be waiting at the curb, sans panties with *mucho gusto* panting. I pause and take a deep breath. Do I hear muffled laughter?

"Anything else, ma'am?"

"No, Chuck. That will do it."

I'm still fuming moments later when I cut across the lawn and begin jogging down the sidewalk with Vlad at my heels.

I wave at Noe Maldonado, who is heading to our backyard, hoe in hand. Noe and his extended family are our neighbors to the north. Their big old house takes up most of the city lot. What's left provides parking for Noe's extended family, which can vary on a daily basis from eight to twelve, leaving Noe without space for a garden. Years ago, Grandma offered him a garden plot in our backyard. He insists on sharing the vegetables. And each week, he sends over a different son, grandson, daughter, niece, or nephew to cut our grass.

"Lettuce be ready soon," Noe calls with a gap-toothed grin.

"Looking forward to it." I holler, watching Vlad bound ahead of me. I know what's coming. After Grandma had him neutered, Vlad refocused his sex drive into three main objectives: (1) attacking my ankles, (2) lying in wait for the mailman, and (3) lurking under the bird feeder hoping for a slow, fat one.

At this moment, he's bounding ahead of me, searching for the perfect shrub in which to hide. As I jog by, he'll leap out, wrap both front paws around my ankle, and—depending on his mood—inflict damage, or not. Outsmarting Vlad lends an air of excitement to my exercise routine. Probably why I fail to notice the presence of Donny Thorndyke and one of his pals.

When the rumble of a V8 engine finally penetrates my brain, I glance over my shoulder and see Donny's red Firebird cruising slowly behind me. I slow to a walk as the car pulls up beside me. I keep walking. It keeps pace. Finally I stop, hands on my hips, and turn to face the car.

The passenger window slides down. I recognize Donny's companion. His name is Kelvin Koenig. A few years ago he'd been a linebacker on Donny's state championship team. Thugs are Donny's specialty. He seeks out and recruits the worst bullies in school then brags about how he's turned their lives around. Unfortunately, most of them, Kelvin included, return to their thuggish ways shortly after graduation. Since his divorce, Donny frequently hangs out with his former students, guys like Kelvin, who will do anything for Coach Thorndyke.

I lean over and peer in the window. "What's up, Donny?

He gives me his *aw, shucks* grin and says, "Me and Kelvin were in the neighborhood. Just being friendly, you know, after our little misunderstanding."

I narrow my eyes at him. "Funny, I've never seen you around here before."

Kelvin runs a hand over his shaved head and fingers the tattoo of a dagger dripping blood etched on his thick neck. He lowers his sunglasses and looks at me with cold, dead eyes. "You heard about my brother, right?"

I gulp and nod. Kelvin's brother, Dallas, just received a life sentence for a brutal murder he committed as part of a gang initiation.

"So what if I have?"

"We're real tight, and we've got lots of friends."

My heart's pounding in my throat, but I glare at him. "How nice for you."

Donny revs up the engine. Kelvin points an index

finger at me, cocks his thumb on top and mouths the word *bang* before they peel out on squealing tires.

A bit shaken, I resume my jog and ponder the surreal encounter. Who could I tell? What would I say? Coach Thorndyke stopped to say "hello"? Kelvin filled me in about his family before indulging in a gesture I'm sure he'd describe as a friendly wave? It all sounds perfectly innocent. Yet the menace behind the words and gestures was unmistakable. I'd keep it to myself for the time being and try to be more aware of my surroundings.

As if testing my resolve, a flash of orange hurtles from a nearby bush and Vlad pounces, capturing one of my ankles in mid-stride.

"Nice kitty," I murmur, trying to ignore the needle-like claws digging into my flesh. I rub rhythmically behind his ears and feel his claws retract. He releases me and flops onto his back, giving me access to his big, furry belly. After giving him a few tickles on the tummy, I tiptoe away, leaving Vlad snoring in the late afternoon sun.

Later that evening, I stand at the dormer window in my apartment and watch the cars zip up and down our busy street. When I'm sure no red Firebirds lurk in the shadows, I get on the phone to track down Sara's caseworker.

I strike gold with Evelyn, mother of Cody, a former student. A long-time secretary at the local Department of Social and Health Services, Evelyn is positive my Peggy with the blue Taurus is Peggy Mooney. After some polite chitchat about Cody now being gainfully employed at a video store, I thank her profusely and hang up.

I dine on Top Ramen, closing the door to keep the aroma from Grandma Sybil, who doesn't approve of processed food unless it's KFC, which she eats religiously every Friday night. Ignoring the stack of papers waiting to be checked, I paw through the desk drawer until I find a pad of sticky notes. Using a separate sheet for each incident, I write down what I know of Sara's disappearance: the bizarrely written note, her father's sudden reappearance in her life, the hidden notebook and Bible, the Hewitts' odd behavior and sudden influx of cash, and the fact that Sara was seen with her caseworker the night she allegedly ran away from home.

I put the bits of information onto the table and move them around, looking for some sort of pattern. When the clarity I hope to gain eludes me, I shove back the chair and pace, pausing now and again to rearrange the notes. Finally, guilt settles like a velvet shroud, and I reach for my red pencil and a stack of papers.

While my mind is busily engaged elsewhere, the answer pops up. It niggles at my mind until I set my pencil aside and pick up the paper that says "hidden notebook and Bible." Why did Sara copy poems from Grandma Sybil's book? Odd behavior for a girl for whom writing poetry is akin to gum surgery.

I need to check out the things I found hidden by the furnace. Maybe I'll notice something Nick missed. Right on cue, the phone rings. Nick. Filling me in on his session of religious enlightenment.

"Did you meet Pastor Hunt?"

"No, the youth pastor was in charge." His voice brightens,

and he says, "But I met a girl named Willow who knows Sara. She said Sara was spending a lot of time with Pastor Rob—it's what the kids call him—Pastor Rob. He'd show up during youth group, and Sara would take off with him. Sara told Willow she was having problems and Pastor Rob was helping her with them."

Helping her. A sick feeling creeps into my stomach, mingling unhappily with the ramen noodles. *Don't be such a cynic, Allegra. Men of the cloth are supposed to counsel troubled teenage girls.*

After quizzing Nick about Sara's notebook—he has no clue—I click off and glance at my watch: 7:30. Grandma has a half hour before Whatsis arrives. Since she's already curled, curried, and combed, she'll have time to listen.

I find her outside on the veranda. She sits in the porch swing, her feet not touching the floor. Vlad crouches hopefully under the bird feeder. Dodie sits in an adjacent wicker chair, glass of wine in hand.

I plop down beside Grandma and give the swing a gentle push. "Do either of you know anything about the Church of the Holy Light?"

Dodie gives an unladylike snort. "Well, I guess *so*!"

Grandma becomes agitated, her hands flutter wildly. "Oh honey," she says. "Surely you remember my friend Ruth Willard?"

I have vague memories of a plump, sweet-faced woman with gold-framed eyeglasses peeking over the steering wheel of a black Lincoln Town car.

Grandma continues, "She and Harvey had boatloads of money. Her family owned some big distillery in Canada. When Harvey died she was beside herself with loneliness—

they had no children, no family to speak of. That's when she got involved with *him.*"

"Him, being?" I prompt.

Grandma's eyes narrow, and she snaps, "The fake preacher. The one who started in a raggedy-assed tent!"

"Wow!" I say, impressed by Grandma's fervor. "You mean like Brother Love's traveling salvation show? Are you talking about Reverend Hunt?"

"Reverend, my sweet patootie," Dodie mumbles into her glass.

"It was five or six years ago, Allegra. You weren't here then," Grandma says.

She pauses and pats my hand. "You were overseas with Harley."

I grimace but hold back a bitter response. Maybe I'm moving on.

"Anyway," Grandma continues, "It was quite the talk of the town. Ruth started going to services every night in that awful tent thing. I told her he was nothing but a flim-flam man and the place was a death trap. One spark, and it would go up like an inferno. But she wouldn't listen, and look how it turned out."

"How?"

"Well, how do you think he got a big, fancy church? Ruth's money!" Indignation burns brightly in her eyes.

"*Mon Dieu!*" I exclaim. "Holy *caramba!*"

"Holy, my rosy red rump," Dodie says, refilling her glass.

Grandma removes her glasses and dabs at her eyes with the tail of her *Sexy Senior Citizen* tee shirt. "He got his hooks in Ruth good. I tried to warn her, but she wouldn't listen. It was 'Rob this' and 'Rob that' and what good works he'd do with his new church. I'm ashamed to say I gave up trying."

She looks so sad I give her a hug. "Not your fault, Grandma. Maybe she'll come around someday."

"Fat chance!" Dodie says.

Grandma frowns at Dodie then tells me, "She can't come around, Allegra. She's dead."

"Oops. Did he get all her money?"

Dodie shakes her head. "Not all of it. Enough to finish the church and build the winery. The bulk of her fortune was in trust for some hospital charity."

"Hunt has a winery?"

Dodie holds her glass up until it catches a sunbeam filtering through the maples. She swirls and smiles. "A marketing wonder. You've heard the expression 'WWJD'?"

"Sure. You see the bumper sticker everywhere. *What would Jesus do?*"

"Hunt's winery specializes in sacramental wines. He calls it *WWJD Winery. What would Jesus drink?*"

A ladylike giggle bursts from Grandma accompanied by my snort of incredulous amusement. "Too weird. You've gotta be making this up."

"Nope. If you don't believe me, look in the Yellow Pages. He puts ads in the Seattle papers, appealing to wacko, liberal, vegan Christians. Dr. Myers says they come in by chartered buses every weekend and drop a bundle of money."

"Hmm," I muse, giving the swing another push.

Grandma's head snaps back, and she grabs the armrest.

"Call Susan. She'll know about it," Dodie says as a meticulously restored '56 Chevy pulls up to the curb. Out pops a jaunty-looking white-haired gentleman. The gleam of anticipation in his eyes is apparent even from a distance.

Grandma greets him with a coy finger wave. "Oh, goodie. Stanley's here."

I leap from the swing, causing it to yaw violently. Grandma shrieks and clings to the seat. "For pity's sake, Allegra!"

"Sorry," I mutter and grab the armrest to slow it down. Ignoring Dodie's rendition of a squawking chicken, I slink into the house.

Chapter 8

Susan and I sit at her kitchen table drinking diet soda and eating warm chocolate chip cookies. Ever vigilant, I'm careful to eat only the broken ones. Nick makes a brief appearance to give me Sara's notebook and Bible. He swoops down on the cookies, grabs a handful, and drifts away.

"So, you know about this place—the WWJD Winery?" I ask Susan.

"Yeah, I met the guy who runs it." She breaks a cookie in half. "Weird dude named Gordon Venable. He's a CPA. Doesn't know jack about vineyards."

"Why would Hunt have a guy like Venable running it? Tax write-off?"

"Could be, but they get lots of traffic on the weekends. I assume it's making money."

We both reach for the other half cookie. I back off.

"Maybe Reverend Hunt's using the profit for good works," I say.

"Possibly, if good works include living in a three-story

house on Paradise Point." Susan pauses and smiles. "And he's probably serving the poor and needy zipping around town in his Mercedes convertible."

I raise an eyebrow. "He sounds shady. As conservative as Vista Valley is, I'm surprised he hasn't been run out of town."

Susan's eyes gleam. "Apparently it doesn't hurt to have a police captain and three members of the city council in your congregation."

I shake my head in wonder. "How do you know this stuff?"

"Monthly wine tasting at Quail Hollow. The boss likes us all to show up. Folks under the influence of a fine cabernet tend to run off at the mouth."

"Except you, of course."

Susan grins. "Just a fly on the wall."

I take a couple cookies for the road, gather up Sara's stuff, and head for the door. Susan walks me to my truck, a worry line creasing her forehead. I feel a tingle of alarm.

"Is Nick okay?" I ask, sliding behind the wheel.

She braces one hand against the open door and leans over. "Now don't kill the messenger, but Harley called. He wants to talk to you."

"Harley? Why? I've got nothing to say to him."

Susan says sharply, "Maybe if you could stop being mad at Harley, you could move on with your life."

I stare at her in disbelief. Susan is my friend. She's supposed to be on my side. A bitter brew of outrage and frustration boils over into my words. "Move on? Are you saying it was my fault he hit me?"

She grabs my hand and gives it a squeeze. "Of course it wasn't your fault, honey. Harley should've had his ass kicked. God knows I've told him often enough. I'm just say-ing you brought some baggage into the marriage, too. If I'm not mistaken, you married Harley to please your mother."

"But she had cancer," I say. My voice is choked with tears. "I thought she was dying. I treated her like shit for so many years . . . I just wanted her to be happy."

I've poured so much energy into hating Harley it's un-thinkable to believe I deserve some of the blame.

"But she didn't die."

"Yeah," I say. "The nerve of the woman!"

We both giggle. I swipe at my eyes.

"Harley called last night," Susan says. "He's had some sort of epiphany and wants to see you when he's home on leave."

"What about Melissa or Melinda or Melody—or what-ever the hell her name is? The one who was going to be the perfect officer's wife?"

"Meredith is no longer in the picture," Susan says with a smirk. "Part of the reason for the epiphany, I think."

"I don't know, Susan. I really like it when Harley and I have an ocean and a continent between us."

"Think of it as a therapy session." She brings my hand to her cheek. "Surely you realize every time a guy gets close to you, you find a reason to break it off."

I bristle. "Like who?"

Without a moment's hesitation she says, "Jerry Hanni-gan. He's smart, good-looking, has a great job . . ."

"He chews like a rabbit. His nose twitches. He does other things like a rabbit, too."

Susan snorts. "You're too picky. We live in Vista Valley, for God's sake. What about Michael?"

I snatch my hand back. "Not my fault. If that jerk Sloan hadn't been fondling my underwear . . ."

Susan shakes her head sadly then leans over and pecks me on the cheek. "Love ya, sis. Just think about what I said. Okay?"

Not trusting myself to speak, I nod and try to swallow the walnut-sized lump in my throat. I pull slowly out of the driveway. Damn it, I know Susan's right. I should think about what she said, and I will. But not now.

Thursday

I pictured Peggy Mooney as a round-faced, amply bosomed, jolly woman who dispensed hugs and motherly advice to the foster kids in her care. The name probably fooled me.

Using my cell phone, I try all day to get through to her. She calls back just as the dismissal bell rings to say she's far too busy and, really, she has nothing to say about Sara anyway.

At 4:30, I'm in the waiting room of the Department of Social and Health Services, where a harried secretary guards an open door leading to a warren of offices. I've already spotted a blue Taurus in the parking lot.

"Is she with somebody right now?" I say to the secretary.

"Her last appointment just left. She's getting caught up on paperwork."

"I'll wait."

"But . . ."

I stand up and take a step toward the open door.

"No!" The woman shrieks and grabs the phone. The swivel chair spins around until her back is to me. She crouches over the receiver, and I catch "refuses to leave" and "uh huh."

I edge closer to the door and look down the hall. About a third of the way down, a woman's head pops out for a quick peek.

"Miss Mooney will see you now," the secretary announces, happily back in control. "Third door on the right."

I bound into Peggy's office like a frisky puppy then extend a paw to be shaken. "Hi, Ms. Mooney. Thanks for seeing me."

Frozen over her desk chair, she clutches her purse in one hand and briefcase in the other. She sets her purse down, takes my outstretched hand in her fingertips and gives it a teensy squeeze. I'd bet money she has a bottle of hand sanitizer in her desk drawer.

She sits and waves me into a chair, which I immediately pull up, cozy-like, next to her desk. She's a tall, spare woman; her short, brown hair is parted severely and sprayed into complete and utter submission. My fingers itch to tousle it. She's dressed in a charcoal suit that drains the color from her face.

"What can I do for you, Miss Thorne?"

Her tone is clipped and icy. Once again I feel a wave of pity for Sara.

"As I told you on the phone, I'm Sara Stepanek's teacher."

I wait and watch. Had something flickered in her cool gray eyes?

She nods. "You're aware she left a note when she ran away?"

"Yes, but I'm concerned about her, as I know you must be. Have you notified the police?"

She blinks slowly before replying. "Do you think a runaway teenage girl is high priority to the police? Especially a girl in foster care?"

"So you did inform the police?" I persist.

"It's our procedure." She stands. "Now, if you'll excuse me, I really must go. I have another meeting."

"I'll walk you out."

I hold the door open for her. "Did you know Sara was seeing her father?"

She stops and gives me an annoyed glare. "How did you come by that information?"

Peggy Mooney is very good at answering a question with one of her own, a skill no doubt honed from years of experience with impertinent clients.

"She told a mutual friend."

Pulling the door shut, she locks it then turns to face me. "Well, there you go. She's probably with her dad. End of story."

She pretends I'm not there as we walk through the waiting room. We exit the building, and I trail behind until she approaches the blue Taurus.

"Just curious, Ms. Mooney—when did you last see Sara?"

She heaves an exasperated sigh. "I'd have to check my daybook, but Sara and I had a standing appointment on Tuesdays. Why do you ask?"

Again with the questions!

"One of my students saw Sara in a blue Taurus last Friday night. You know, the night she disappeared. I thought maybe she was with you."

Two spots of color appear on her sallow cheeks. She snaps, "Well, she wasn't, and I resent the insinuation that I'm lying."

I give her a big, friendly smile and gush, "Oh, gracious, you're taking this wrong. No innuendo intended. I just assumed you'd taken her out for a bite to eat and she ran away later."

She makes no effort to hide the hostility in her eyes. "I don't take clients out to eat."

She turns and unlocks her car with a keyless remote. I watch her drive away and murmur, "I'll bet you don't, lady."

I drive home determined to put the frosty Ms. Mooney out of my mind.

Instead, I savor the gorgeous, early June weather knowing I shouldn't. Ask any teacher the ideal weather for the end of the school year and they'll tell you, "Cold . . . rainy . . . dismal." Kids, especially teens with rampaging hormones, go nuts as summer vacation approaches, especially if the weather turns hot. Attention spans grow shorter, along with the girls' clothing. The boys, dazzled by the smorgasbord of female flesh, find it even more difficult to focus, and worn-out teachers struggle to keep order. With *my* students—times ten!

But, for now, I revel in the brilliant azure sky and verdant hills surrounding Vista Valley. By mid-July, the sky will be a pale, washed-out version of today's exquisite color and the hills brown and sere, baking in the blast furnace of summer.

I pull into the driveway and groan. *Damn!* Lefty is back. In April, Vlad bounded through the cat door with a half-dead robin in his mouth. Grandma nursed the bird back to health in a shoebox. Though he was missing an eye and had a droopy right wing, Lefty, the one-eyed robin, was pronounced fit and set free.

Sadly, Lefty doesn't want to be free. He flies from window to window and flings himself repeatedly against the pane. After scrambling his tiny brain, he perches on the sill, head cocked, staring at us with his one good eye. Dodie claims he's in love with his own reflection.

In spite of his visual impairment, Lefty has pooped on my head three times. I run for the door, a newspaper covering my head, and find Dodie in the living room thumbing through Sara's Bible and notebook. She looks up when I enter. "So did super kid figure it out?"

I shake my head. "Sara doesn't like poetry but copied page after page from Grandma's book. There's nothing unique about the Bible. No inscription, no dog-eared corners, nothing written in the margin."

I take the notebook from Dodie and rifle through the pages. Each poem is neatly written and uniformly spaced.

"Beats the hell out of me. Maybe she was practicing her penmanship."

Dodie hands me the Bible. As I reach for it, Vlad leaps out from behind the couch with a hiss and a snarl. I shriek and fling myself backward into a club chair, raising my ankles skyward. The Bible skids across the hardwood floor.

"Damn you, Vlad!" I yell.

Mission accomplished, he plops down in a patch of sunlight and begins cleaning his whiskers. Keeping a wary eye on the beast, I pick up the Bible and start for the stairs when something falls to the floor with a *clunk*.

"What the hell?" Dodie says.

I bend over and pick up a piece of notebook paper folded around something hard.

"Must have been taped inside the spine," Dodie says.

I unfold the paper to reveal a small key. "It has a number on it. Forty-two."

Dodie looks it over. "Not a safety deposit box key. Could be to a storage unit."

"Maybe it's not about the Bible," I muse. "Maybe it's about the key."

Dodie shrugs. Clutching the key, I head upstairs.

Halfway up, I hear Dodie say, "Almost forgot. Michael called. He said he'd be at the club."

"Did he say what he wanted?"

"No, but he sounded uptight."

I rack my brain in search of a reason Michael might be calling. I haven't seen him or spoken to him since the underwear fiasco.

The message light's blinking on my phone. I press play and hear Marcy's chirpy voice telling me she won't be at school tomorrow. She's exhausted and taking a personal day, but she'll meet me at Brewski's Pub tomorrow night for dinner at six sharp. Marcy likes Brewski's and its abundance of horny softball players who flock around her like yellow jackets at a picnic. She occasionally tosses one of her rejects my way.

I tuck the mystery key in my jewelry case and jot down the details on a sticky note, adding it to the others. Before I can talk myself out of it, I call Michael at his club.

Michael had the foresight to start one of the first wineries in our area that, geographically, matches the wine-growing regions in Europe. When a huge wine conglomerate offered to buy him out, he jumped on it. Consequently, at thirty-eight, he's joined the idle rich.

He answers on the third ring. "Hey, Michael, it's Allegra."

A brief silence is followed by a noncommittal "Hi. How are you?"

What am I doing? He probably thinks I'm calling to grovel and beg his forgiveness.

"I'm okay. Dodie said you called."

"Listen, I'm sorry I got so bent out of shape the other day. I'd like to see you again."

"You would?" I blurt.

"Yeah," he says. "But what about the DEA guy?"

Good question. What about the DEA guy?

"There is no other guy. Sloan was returning my—er—the stuff he'd impounded from my car."

"Can I call you?"

"Sure," I say. The silence grows.

"Is there something else?" I ask.

Dodie's right. Michael sounds uptight.

"Uh, not really. I heard one of your students ran away. I'll bet you're worried about her."

Since when did Michael give two hoots about my students? "Who told you?"

"A guy in my foursome. You don't know him."

"How did this guy in your foursome, who I don't know, figure out Sara is one of my students?"

"For Christ's sake, Allegra, I'm trying to be nice. What difference does it make who told me?"

"Sorry. It's just seems a little weird."

"So, has she turned up?"

"Not yet," I say. "Gotta go. Grandma's calling."

Damned if I'd tell him anymore.

After I call Nick and tell him about the key, I stretch out on the window seat and stare at the water spot on the ceiling, the one shaped like a question mark.

Michael wants to see me again. I'm sure his sudden change of attitude has nothing to do with my innate charm. At someone's behest, he must have been pumping me about Sara. When I pushed him about the person's identity, he lashed out, typical Michael style, to discourage further discussion.

He's fishing for information. No problem. I'll play the game. And in the process, maybe I'll find out why Michael LeClaire's mystery friend is so interested in Sara.

Chapter 9

*A*fter a night of jumbled dreams, I'm finally sleeping soundly when I should be up and in the shower. A phone call from Dodie jolts me from dreamland.

"You better get down here."

Startled, I throw on a robe and dash downstairs imagining the worst. Had Grandma Sybil eloped with the bright-eyed Stanley? Had her night of therapeutic bliss triggered a medical condition? Had Stanley died in the saddle?

I find Dodie at the front door talking to Noe Maldonado. Grandma, looking to be in fine fettle, stands behind her, clutching a steaming cup of coffee.

"What?" I ask, trying to clear the fog from my sleepy brain. "What happened?"

"Your truck." Dodie points at the driveway. "Noe spotted it when he was leaving for work."

I step out on the porch, and my heart sinks. My pride and joy, my precious baby, Red Ranger, has been vandalized with black spray paint by someone who thinks I'm a

NOSY BITCH and **NARC** times three.

"Oh, shit!" I yell.

"Who would do such a thing to you?" Noe asks. His soft brown eyes are full of concern. "You nice lady. You have rotten gang kids at school?"

I nod. "Only the semi-rotten ones. The really bad ones get kicked out."

I try to remember recent confrontations with kids who might wish to do me harm. Then I recall my encounter with Donny Thorndyke and the odious Kelvin. Hard to believe a colleague could sink to that level, but Donny is not noted for mature behavior. He's become increasingly unstable since his wife left him. He wouldn't have to do the deed himself. Any number of his hoodlum friends would be happy to help him out. Yes, it had to be Donny.

"You call police?" Noe asks. He shakes his head in disgust. "Damn *pendejos*! Gang bangers—no good! You should call policeman."

"Nothing they can do now," I say. "Whoever did it is long gone."

"If you want your insurance to pay, you'll have to file a police report," Dodie says. "I'll call them for you."

"You can't drive it to school that way," Grandma says. "Take the Olds."

"Isn't it Senior Day at the casino? Just drop me off at school. I'll catch a ride home."

"Melba can drive. Don't argue."

In truth, my heart beats a little faster at the prospect of driving the Olds. When Grandpa Mort shuffled off to the big auto parts store in the sky, he left behind a pristine 1968 Oldsmobile Delta 88. Pale turquoise with a white vinyl top, it boasts a 455 Rocket engine that springs to life on the first turn of the ignition and rumbles happily as it guzzles gas. Driving the Olds is like being aboard an untamed stallion. I'm never sure which one of us is in charge.

After Grandpa's death, Grandma gamely learned to drive, taught by our steadfast neighbor, Noe, who turned prematurely gray as a result.

After a quick shower, a cup of Earl Grey, and string cheese, I grab my bag and hurry downstairs to find Grandma backing the Olds out of the garage. She sits behind the wheel, head cocked, listening to the roar of the engine as she pumps the foot feed. She sees me approach and rolls the window down. "Mort always said it's important to warm up the engine. Be sure you remember that, Allegra. You're always in such a hurry."

As we exchange places, I assure her I'll care for her baby as if it's my own. I depress the clutch and shift into reverse. With a mere tap of the gas pedal, I shoot backwards out of the driveway and land in the grassy median that separates the two sides of our street, missing a giant maple tree by inches. The Olds growls ominously as I ease it off the curb and onto the street. I risk a glance at Grandma, who stands in the driveway with one hand clapped over her mouth in horror.

Dodie emerges from the house. "Hey, Earnhardt Jr.! Hold on a sec."

I roll down the window as she walks to the car.

"I called a guy I know who has a car painting business—Buddy. He'll get it done for you over the weekend. I need your keys."

"Bless you!" I dig the keys out of my bag. "Did he say

how much?"

She takes the keys and gives me an enigmatic smile. "We're going to dinner tonight."

"So my credit's good?"

"Oh, yeah," Dodie says, backing away from the car.

I shift into first and give her some gas. The tires screech, and I lurch down Maple Street like a robotic monster caught in the throes of a seizure. Noe's extended family stands on his front porch, cheering and waving. I roar into the teachers' parking lot a scant eight minutes later. Jimmy Felthouse stands across the street puffing one last cigarette before school starts.

"Hey, Ms. Thome! Sweet car!" He put out his cigarette and saunters across the street.

I pull out a five and give it to him. "Make sure nothing happens to it, and you'll get another one after school."

"No problem," he says. "You want me to stay out here all day?"

"Nice try," I say. "See you in class."

I've already made up my mind to talk to R.D. about Donny, even though I have no proof of any wrongdoing. During the lunch break, I lurk in the mail room until Sally scurries off to the copy machine, and then I pop through R.D.'s door. He stands in front of a mirror straightening his tie. Catching sight of me in the mirror, he turns. "Do we have an appointment, Miss Thome?"

I confess my visit is spontaneous, and promise to be brief. His eyes are wary, but he nods and retreats behind his big desk.

As my story pours out, I soon realize it's not going well. R.D. begins to swell up. His face turns fiery red, a color that doesn't go well with his burgundy jacket, pink shirt, and damask rose tie.

I pause for breath, and he springs to his feet. "Be careful what you say, Miss Thome. Donny Thorndyke has dedicated his life to this school. Do you know how many championships he's won?"

I zip my lip, though I long to say, "So what?"

"Furthermore," he continues. "Donny's been a guest in my home. My wife and I had him over for Sunday dinner just last weekend. Accusations like this could ruin the man's career. Is that what you want?"

I feel the heat rise in my cheeks. Why am I suddenly the guilty party? "Look, R.D., you're the principal. Donny's a letch. I don't trust him around female students. As far as his problem with me, don't worry about it. I'll take care of myself."

Before he can answer, I bolt, closing the door a little harder than necessary.

The bell rings as I dash down the hall to my room. As my students straggle in, I announce, "Time for SSR. Get your books."

Twenty minutes of silent, sustained reading helps them decompress and settle into classroom mode. However, for a handful of rebels, SSR means sniveling, snarling, and refusing. I finally give in and toss a *Teen People* magazine on Crystal's desk, which—thank you, God—shuts her up.

"Got another one at a yard sale, Ms. Thome. Only cost me a quarter." Arnulfo Vasquez, his moon face wreathed in smiles, holds his book up for me to see.

I smile and give him thumbs up. During his incarceration for almost beating a rival gang member to death, Arnie fell in love with the *Flowers in the Attic* series. If any of his classmates think it's odd, they keep it to themselves.

Well over six feet tall and weighing 350 pounds, Arnulfo Vasquez is regarded with awe by the rest of my petty criminals. Against all odds, he and Nick have formed a bond and often eat lunch together. Since Arnie's release, he's been a model citizen, only losing his cool once.

When a couple of my students started mouthing off to each, while I stood between them trying to cool the hostilities, Arnie stood up and slapped his desk. "Some of us are trying to learn. You two, shut the fuck up!" They did. Furthermore, nary a word was uttered about Arnie's profanity, a no-no in my classroom.

Arnie keeps the peace, which, in turn, allows me to teach.

"Very good!" I enthuse after twenty semi-silent minutes have elapsed. "Paper and pencil out, please. This next assignment is a culmination of all you've learned about essay writing."

I ignore the chorus of groans. "I've compiled a list of fascinating topics to choose from. Or, if you have one of your own, feel free to use it."

Oops. How could I have forgotten a recent student essay on "How to Grow Your Own Pot"?

"Run it by me first, of course."

Someone demands, "Why?"

Crystal sniggers. "She doesn't want you to write about no bad stuff, dummy, like drugs and erroneous zones."

"Any bad stuff, erogenous zones," I correct, once again on autopilot.

"What's erogenous zones, Ms. Thome?" Wesley (window peeping) asks.

"She's talking about your pencil dick, you dickhead," Crystal says.

I quell the uproar that follows Crystal's remark, for which she profusely apologizes when I threaten another visit to Sid's Gas and Grub, and peace reigns until the 3:05 dismissal bell.

I collapse in my chair and nibble at a slice of cold pizza, the lunch I didn't have time to eat.

Nick hovers over me, looking anxious. "Did you look at Sara's stuff?"

I tell him about the key, and he brightens momentarily, but it doesn't last.

"Damn!" He slams his fist against my desk. "We're missing something. And it's probably right under my nose."

Nick removes his glasses and polishes them with his shirt tail. The dark shadows under his eyes are in stark contrast to his pale, almost transparent skin. He rakes his fingers through his fair hair until it stands up in spikes. His eyes are huge, his forehead furrowed with worry lines. *Woodstock.* He looks so miserable I want to hug him but know better.

I rummage through my bag, pull out the key, and hand it to him. He examines it carefully.

"Gotta be a storage unit. Now all I have to do is find it."

"What's your plan? Skulk around storage facilities and try to unlock number 42?"

"You got a better one?"

I shake my head.

"Sunday," he says. "Pick me up at 10:30."

Nick thinks we need to go to Sunday services at the Church of the Holy Light.

Before he goes home, Nick retrieves the contents of my mailbox. I unfold a note written in Sally's precise hand. "A Mr. Sloan called to remind you about your 6 p.m. meeting."

Oh, so now we have a meeting? Dream on, Sloan.

Chapter 10

*I*t's Friday night and time to buy Marcy dinner for covering my class. I try not to think about Sloan as I slip into my best jeans and a pink V-neck sweater and then quickly attempt to tame my curly hair. Spraying and spritzing fail miserably. I finally give up and gather the whole mess into a ponytail with a hair clip made of fake amethyst hearts and flowers.

Knowing Grandma won't want her car in Brewski's lot, I dash off a quick note promising to park it across the street at the power substation, deserted after five o'clock. I leave the house well before six. My plan is to drive around until it's time to meet Marcy, even if it means taking out a loan to buy gas for the Olds. After rumbling up and down Vista Valley Avenue four times, my curiosity gets the best of me. At 5:45, I ease the Olds down the alley behind the house, roll down the window, and cut the engine. At 5:55, I hear a car door slam and allow myself a tiny evil chuckle. *Take that, Sloan!*

My chuckle turns into a gurgle of alarm when I hear Grandma Sybil's voice. Although I can't make out the words, the tone is unmistakable. Clearly, she's delighted to see Sloan. But why is Grandma home? It's Friday night. After a madcap day playing the penny slots at the Indian casino, she and Melba always stop for supper at KFC. *Damn!* Never trust an old lady.

I groan as the scenario plays out in my head. By now, Grandma will have read my note and will soon be blabbing my whereabouts. I fire up the Olds and bump down the alley.

"You told him you had plans," I mutter aloud. "If he can't take no for an answer, that's his problem."

Then why am I sneaking down the alley like I'm casing the neighborhood? I drive aimlessly for a while before cruising through Brewski's parking lot, where I spot Marcy's car but no black Lincoln Navigator.

Walking through the front door of Brewski's is always a surreal experience. The main room features a sports bar with a large-screen television positioned at each end. To the left is a family dining area where the kiddies can order off the half-pint menu and score chicken nuggets, French fries, and a mug of root beer. Never too early to hook 'em on greasy grub and suds.

A right turn leads to the area euphemistically known as Hookup Heaven, Vista Valley's excuse for a singles' bar. I spot Marcy alone at a booth. Definitely strange. Especially with three softball players sitting at a table nearby.

I slide into the seat across from her. "Lost your touch?"

Marcy grins. "Hardly. Blame it on your hunky, though menacing, new boyfriend." She shakes a finger at me.

"Naughty girl! Why didn't you tell me you had a date?"

"What? Sloan's here?" I rise to a half crouch, and just then the man himself sits down and pins me to the wall. He has two glasses of white wine in one hand and a beer in the other.

I scoot into the corner. "Grandma, huh?"

He nods and distributes the drinks—wine for Marcy and me, beer for him. He shoots a look toward the softball players who've been following the action. They suddenly get busy watching the Mariners lose to the White Sox.

"This isn't a date," I tell him.

"Not what I heard," he says, raising his beer mug toward Marcy. "She told me the umpire gets to call it."

"You told him about that?" I hiss at Marcy.

"Why not?" she says. "It applies. If one of us gets a date, the person who's stood up gets to decide if the other person can go or not."

"That's not how it works," I protest.

"Here's the set-up," Marcy says. "You're on third. The batter hits a pop fly to right field. You tag up and head for home. Since I'm without a date, that makes *me* the umpire. So I get to call it."

Marcy stands and crosses her hands in front of her, the umpire's signal for "safe" and says, "Go. Enjoy!"

"No way! You don't know the rules."

"Well, smarty pants, the runner on second is advancing, so you have to run, too!" She gives Sloan an appraising glance and adds, "At your own risk, of course."

"Who says there's a runner on second? That's not your call!" My voice is shrill. I can't believe how she's twisting our time-honored tradition.

I hear a little grunt of amusement from Sloan. Momentarily distracted, Marcy gives him a curious look. I know what's coming. "What about you, big, scary man? You married?"

Sloan holds up his left hand and displays a naked ring finger. "Not anymore."

His expression grows more forbidding. Marcy, however, is undeterred. "What happened?"

"She found another guy."

Do I see a flash of emotion in his frosty blue eyes? Is it possible Sloan is a member of the human race?

Marcy murmurs sympathetically before asking the big one. "Any kids?"

"She didn't want them." He downs the rest of his beer and sets the bottle down carefully. "Interrogation over?"

He flashes his shark grin.

"Just one more," Marcy says. "Sloan. Last name, I assume?"

I roll my eyes but lean forward in anticipation. He nods.

"Your first name is?" Marcy prompts.

"You said one more question. That's two."

He stands up and looks at me. "You ready to go? Got reservations for seven at the Lakeside."

Marcy gives a little hoot of appreciation. "The Lakeside, huh? Wow! See you Monday, Allegra."

"Sloan." I use my teacher voice. "I left a message at your workplace telling you I was busy tonight. I owe Marcy dinner. She covered my class."

"For Pete's sake, just go!" Marcy sounds exasperated.

She makes the sign of the cross in the air. "I absolve you of all guilt. Get this guy out of here. He's scaring my fans."

She looks over at the three guys with a big, encouraging smile. Taking care to avoid eye contact with Sloan, they grin back.

Still annoyed, I inch slowly across the bench seat. "Just remember," I caution Sloan, "this isn't a date."

Marcy tosses her head and laughs. "Yeah, right. Sloan's just looking for a buddy, somebody to talk baseball with."

"Oh, shut up, hot pants," I tell her.

Sloan clasps one hand around the back of my neck and guides me toward the exit.

I try to act cool, but the warmth of his hand sends a rampaging horde of neurons zinging through my body straight into the aforementioned "erroneous" zones. My knees wobble, and it has nothing to do with my shoes, even though they are attractive slides with cute little pink bows and two-inch wedge heels.

As we head toward the door, I ask myself, *Why?* Why is Sloan pursuing me? Why am I letting him march me through Brewski's like a border collie bringing in an errant sheep? Even more horrifying, what will we talk about at dinner? Suddenly, I foresee the awkwardness of the evening laid out in graphic detail: me throwing out conversational gambits, the monosyllabic Sloan grunting non-answers.

We charge through the door and start for the parking lot. I stop suddenly and "Why?" bursts from my lips. My abrupt halt causes Sloan to make full-body contact on my rear flank. I pull away and turn to face him.

"*Why* what?" he says.

"Why did you ask me out?"

"Maybe I like you. And your underwear's hot. Is that a crime?"

I feel my face heat up. "Yeah, uh, well, that wasn't my everyday underwear. I had a special night planned with my ex-boyfriend. Which you spoiled, by the way."

Sloan ignores my last comment. He takes my hand, and we head for a black Nissan parked away from the others. "My car's over here."

No wonder I hadn't sniffed out the fact he'd been lurking inside Brewski's.

I open my mouth to hurl a caustic comment—but then a speed bump looms up and snags the toe of my right shoe. With a little shriek, I lurch forward, bracing myself for a painful collision with the unforgiving pavement.

Quick as a big cat, Sloan whirls and catches me midtumble. Somehow, I end up astride his upper thigh, my arms wrapped around his body, a position that once again sets my naughty parts atingle. Wow! Not only am I tingling, but Sloan's body parts are answering.

With a look of regret, Sloan sets me on my feet and reaches into a pocket for his vibrating cell phone. He flips it open and growls, "Yeah, Sloan here."

I retrieve my shoe and try to make sense of his end of the conversation, which consists mostly of "uh huhs and yeahs."

He snaps the phone shut and mutters an unintelligible oath before saying, "Gotta go. How about tomorrow night?"

"Can't make it."

"Oh, right," he says. "Karaoke at Serenity Bay."

It's then I decide to follow him—admittedly not my finest moment in the logic department, but curiosity trumps caution. *Where does Sloan go when he's in the field? Inquiring minds want to know.*

He drops me off at the edge of the substation parking

lot. After killing the engine twice, I grind the Olds into first gear and give it some gas. The engine responds with a throaty growl, and I rocket out into the street.

Feeling clever and spy-like, I hang back so I can see around the giant SUV separating me from Sloan's car. I'm surprised when he passes the street that houses the central Washington DEA office. He and the SUV plow straight ahead. I run a red light and keep pace. After a quick left, right, right, we're back on the main drag. When Sloan suddenly turns onto my street, I know I'm busted.

He parks in front of my house, strides to my car, and yanks the driver's door open. "Out, Sherlock. You're going with me."

I smile sweetly. "Are we going to dinner after all?"

He grabs the car keys out of my hand. "No."

He crosses to the front porch and hands the keys to Grandma, who's standing at the front door.

She beams and trills, "You kids have fun now."

"It's not a date!" I yell as I slid into Sloan's car.

"For once, you're right," he says, jamming his foot to the accelerator.

"You probably think I was trying to follow you, but actually I was just heading home."

"You thought I wouldn't notice a '68 Oldsmobile Rocket?"

Wisely, I keep silent.

"Where's the Ranger?"

"Paint shop." Part of me wants to unload the whole Donny Thorndyke thing, but I don't know Sloan well enough to trust him. He'd probably think I'm a hysterical female with the vapors.

"Cherry car. Grandma's?"

I nod.

He makes a U-turn and heads north on Maple. A quick right on the one-way heading east leads us to the edge of town.

"Where are we going?"

"To the river. Local boys found a body. Someone you might be interested in."

A stab of fear shoots through me. I swallow hard. "Not Sara." I breathe the name like a prayer.

After a quick glance at my face, he says, "No, not Sara. Possibly her dad, Joe Stepanek. They want me to ID him."

"But if Sara's with her dad, and he's dead, what's happened to her?"

Sloan eases the car onto a rutted dirt road that winds around a saw mill and ends abruptly in a makeshift parking lot bordered by a thick grove of cottonwoods. An ambulance is backed in between two police cars. A young patrolman strings yellow crime scene tape around the perimeter. Two other cops are talking to a tall, skinny guy, who's leaning against a beat-up '70s vintage Bronco. He's got a greasy ponytail, and his face has a greenish tinge. A fourth officer sits in a patrol car working the computer. A gray sedan with county plates is nosed up against the Bronco.

Sloan shakes a finger at me. "Stay put."

He starts to get out and sighs. "Hell, I know you won't."

Reaching into the back seat, he grabs a pair of leather running shoes and thrusts them at me. "Put these on. The body's down by the river. I don't want to have to pack you out of here with another broken ankle."

After a tentative sniff, I say, "They smell, and they're too big. My shoes are fine."

Sloan curses and scrabbles around in the glove box. He

pulls out a pair of handcuffs. "I don't have time to argue. Put the shoes on, or I'll cuff you to the steering wheel. Your choice."

"What a grouch," I mutter. I slip into the clodhoppers and step out into dappled sunlight. A slight breeze flutters through the cottonwoods, clad now in brilliant spring foliage. The sound and smell of the river brings back a flood of childhood memories greatly at odds with this scene of death.

"Al!" The burly cop emerging from the patrol car is Marty Montgomery, a guy I've known forever. He envelops me in a bear hug. "You working for the DEA now?"

I grin up at him. "Good to see you, Marty. Not exactly working for them. I'm more like a consultant." I glance at Sloan, who rolls his eyes in disbelief.

"This girl used to beat me up in the fifth grade," Marty says.

"What a surprise," Sloan says.

I glance at Sloan. "That's because he called me Al."

Sloan asks Marty, "Whatcha got?"

Marty gestures at the civilian. "Guy was headed for his favorite fishing hole. He stepped off the trail to take a piss and tripped over the body. Fell right on top of him. Shook him up bad."

"Area sealed off?"

"Yeah. We did a quick search. Looks like an overdose." He gazes toward the river. "You wanna go down there?"

"M.E. here?"

"Yeah. They'll be bringing the body up in a minute."

Right on cue, two EMTs emerge from the trees lugging a body bag. An older gentleman dressed in khakis and a tan polo shirt trails behind them. I recognize him as the county's longtime medical examiner, Sherman McIntyre. As the techs place the body on the waiting gurney, he acknowledges Sloan with a grunt. "Want to take a look before we load him up?"

Sloan says, "How ya doin', Sherm?" and walks to the body.

I follow, sliding my feet through the dirt to keep the oversized shoes from falling off. I peer around him. *Do I really want to do this?*

As if he's reading my mind, Sloan growls. "I'm not catching you if you faint."

I gulp and say, "I'll be fine."

Sloan unzips the bag. Clad only in jeans, the dead man is sprawled on his back, face frozen in a permanent grimace. His right arm is bent and curled tight to his body. His left arm is extended, revealing the tattooed initials *UAO* on the inside of his wrist. His skin is pale, almost translucent in the fading sun. Slender and of average height, the man has the tough, stringy look of a street fighter. His light brown hair is chopped short, a homemade job. Blood has oozed out and congealed beneath his head.

Okay, I tell myself, *I can do this.* Then I look at his eyes. Dark blue. Luminous. Fixed on a distant horizon as if he sees something wonderful known only to him. Sara's eyes. I inhale noisily and look away.

Sloan glances over his shoulder. "You okay?"

"It's Joe Stepanek. Right?"

"Yeah, it's him."

McIntyre holds up a baggy with a hypodermic needle inside. "Found this under the body." Sloan slips on a pair of latex gloves and leans over the body. He smooths a finger over the exposed left arm. "Just the one puncture mark.

92

No needle tracks. Weird, huh?"

McIntyre shrugs. "We'll know more after the post."

"But he didn't use drugs," I blurt. "Sara said he wouldn't touch the stuff."

The three men regard me with varying degrees of skepticism. McIntyre looks puzzled; Marty, quizzical. Sloan reacts with his typical patronizing manner. "Yeah," he says, "I'm sure he was the pillar of the community."

"I'm not saying he was great guy," I protest. "Sara knew he sold drugs. Her dad told her, 'Users are losers, but they're going to buy it somewhere, and it might as well be from me.'"

"And let wifey take the fall when the family business gets busted," Sloan adds.

"Well, yeah," I admit. "I only got Sara's version, but she was adamant about her dad not using."

Marty peers over my shoulder. "But look at him, Al. Those are prison tats. White supremacist stuff, isn't it?"

"Yeah," Sloan says.

He picks up Stepanek's left hand, enclosed in a plastic bag, and points out the ornate spider web tattooed between Stepanek's thumb and forefinger. "Could mean a number of things. Used to be earned by killing a minority. But now the white cons are outnumbered, and they band together for protection. Hard to say if he's the real deal."

We study Joe Stepanek's body. A crude Celtic cross adorns his right bicep, now flaccid in death. The number 5 is inscribed on his right wrist. His chest is the canvas for a choppy sea into which the sun is setting, its beams bisected by three flying gulls. Its message is simple and uplifting, the workmanship starkly beautiful in contrast to the prison body art.

"The one on his chest is quite good," I say, my voice choked with emotion. I clear my throat. "Doesn't look like the rest of them."

"Freedom," Sloan says. "It symbolizes freedom. Probably done after he got out."

A wave of sadness sweeps over me. Whatever this man was, he had hopes, and dreams and at least one person loved him unconditionally. I blink hard, determined not to weaken my position with unseemly girly emotion.

Marty points at his wrist. "What about the *5*?"

"Symbolizes the white supremacists' code of silence," Sloan says. "The *5* stands for 'I have nothing to say.' The boys know their rights."

"And *UAO*?' I ask.

"United as one," Sloan says. "Another biggie for the Brotherhood."

He turns to Marty. "It's our boy, all right. Joe Stepanek. Case closed."

For Sloan it's simple: another case closed.

"What about next of kin?" Marty asks.

"His daughter, Sara, is one of my students," I say before Sloan can answer. "Sara has a little brother in a foster home somewhere. I'm here because Sara's missing. It's been a week now, and nobody cares!"

The words come out hot and angry. Marty squirms but, to his credit, gives me his full attention. "Anybody report her missing?"

I fight back tears. "Possibly her caseworker, Peggy Mooney. Sara left a note, so everybody thinks she's a runaway. But things don't add up."

I soften my tone and place a hand on Marty's arm. "I'd appreciate it if you'd check for me."

Sloan looks at my hand on Marty's arm and seems to grow larger, not unlike Vlad in his pre-neutered days. Marty sees it too. "You two seeing each other?"

Sloan nods. I shake my head.

Marty grins. "Nice to get that cleared up. I'll check on the Stepanek girl and let you know, Al." He glances at my shoes. "If I don't, you might stomp the shit out of me."

Chapter 11

Sloan and I sit on the porch swing, swaying to and fro in companionable silence. Sloan is being Sloan, and my normal chattiness has been stifled by sudden death. I sip a glass of Dodie's best Pinot Grigio. Under the circumstances, she'll surely understand. Sloan holds a can of Budweiser. As he takes a swallow, his stomach growls loudly.

"We never got dinner," he says.

"You can't be hungry."

He looks surprised by my comment. "A man's gotta eat."

Grandma would be only too delighted to feed him, but she's vanished. Dodie is dining out with Buddy the car painter and, I hope, working on my discount.

"Grandma Sybil has leftovers."

Sloan springs from the porch swing and stops it so I can climb out. Nice to know chivalry is not dead. I follow him to the kitchen and open the door to the fridge. "House rules: Top shelf, off limits. Second shelf, help yourself. Third shelf, eat it quick before it goes bad."

I sit at the kitchen table and watch Sloan off-load last week's meatloaf, leftover green bean casserole, and a slab of pound cake from the third shelf. Declining my offer of microwave warming, he digs in.

Finally, he comes up for air. With quick, precise movements, he rinses the dirty dishes, loads the dishwasher, and then walks to the table. He sits down, reaches over, and turns my chair sideways, yanking it close to him until our knees touch.

"How about it, Al? You're holding out on me," he says.

It? What it*? Ohmigod! Does he think we'll have sex on our first non-date?* I leap from my chair. "I told you this isn't a date. Sex is out of the question!"

Sloan stares at me thoughtfully then chuckles. "Sex, huh? I was talking about Sara. You remember Sara, your missing student?"

"Oh, Sara," I say in a small voice, flames licking at my cheeks. I sit down and look everywhere but at his face.

He leans over and puts his hands on my thighs. "You told Marty things don't add up. Maybe I can help."

"Will you let me know what you find out?"

His hands tighten. "If I can."

"The other night you told me you wouldn't share information."

"That was before we found Joe."

"After you left that night, Sara called me. She sounded scared. Somebody took the phone away from her before she could tell me what she wanted. I pressed star sixty-nine but got the 'party is unavailable' message."

"I'll have it traced. What else?"

I fill him in on some of it: the Hewitts and their new

lifestyle, the discrepancy in Peggy Mooney's story, the note-book of poems. I tell him about Nick: his illness and crush on Sara. Sloan listens carefully, but I can see the skepticism on his face. It does sound a bit silly, so I hold a few things back: Sara's abortion, her recent plunge into depression, the mysterious key, the Church of the Holy Light.

Sloan tips back in his chair, folds his arms . . . and shoots me down. "Tough situation. Kids run away all the time. Overloaded case workers are too tired to care. As for the Hewitts, who knows? Maybe somebody died and left them some ready cash."

I try not to show my bitter disappointment. Why did I think he'd be different from the others? "Just let me know about the phone, okay? I'll get you the number."

I trot up the stairs, Sloan at my heels. But wait! Do I really want Sloan in my private quarters? If I don't let him in, he'll think I'm hung up on the sex thing again. I open the door to my apartment and flick on a light.

Sloan looks around and points at the phone. "Messages."

"I'll get them later."

"Might be important. Maybe Grandma had an acci-dent."

I know he's manipulating me, but what if he's right? Praying the message isn't too personal, I press the *play* but-ton and hear, "Hey, Ah-LEG-ra. It's Trent . . . you know . . . from Better Buy. Your nephew gave me your number. Just wanted to tell you I felt something hot between us the other day, and I think you felt it, too. Maybe . . ."

I hit the *stop* button and groan. *Note to self: Yell at little rat-fink, Nick.*

"Trent from Better Buy, huh?" Sloan says. "Want me

to kill him for you?"

"I can handle it," I say and then add hastily, "Not the killing part, of course."

I dig through a jumble of paper, unearth the mystery phone number, and hand it to Sloan.

Sloan tucks the slip of paper into his shirt pocket and takes a step toward me. "Bet you'll never forget this date," he challenges. "Dead body and all."

"Not a date," I say.

He comes closer. His pale eyes are intense, focused. The image of a snake charmer and his asp comes to mind. I back slowly away until the backs of my thighs hit the desk.

"Not a date," he repeats. "And I'm not going to kiss you now."

He cups my face in his hands and leans into me, his lower body pressing against mine. Sloan's lips are surprisingly soft and warm as he touches them to mine, setting off a firestorm of sensation that leaves me gasping. His tongue, hot, silky, and talented, slips into my mouth.

My brain checks out and hovers somewhere near the ceiling, clucking its disapproval as the rest of me reacts to the delicious things Sloan is doing to me. Acting entirely on its own, my right foot slips out its shoe and coils around Sloan's leg, pulling him in closer. My hands—bold little creatures—grab his and place them on my butt before sliding sinuously up his body to snake around his neck. A slight tilt of the head gives him better access to my mouth. My ears are even getting into the act. Someone's moaning. Surely not me. And the thudding of Sloan's heart. Wow!

No wait—too loud even for Sloan's heart. In a flash, my brain flies back into my head, and I realize someone's pounding on the front door. *Bang, bang, bang.* Five-second pause. Repeat. A signature knock. I know it well.

Reluctantly, my leg disengages, and I let go of his neck. I pull back, pleased to see the dazed expression on the face of Mr. Stone Cold Sloan.

"It's Noe from next door," I croak. "I'd better see what he wants."

"Sloan," I say when he doesn't react. "I need to get the door."

He starts, as if waking from a dream. "Oh, sorry."

With Sloan trailing behind, I gallop down the stairs and open the front door.

"Oh, good. You here," Noe says.

As always, he refuses to come in the house, preferring to conduct business in the open doorway. When Sloan pops up behind me, Noe grasps the situation at once. He beams his approval. "Good. Very good," he tells me before turning his megawatt smile on Sloan. "Too many woman in theese house. Need man."

He thrusts out a right hand for Sloan to shake. Noe's life is written on his hands: thick, capable hands with ground-in dirt he can never scrub away. Hands that can thin apples, fix a balky tractor, or gently pat the back of a newborn grandchild. Noe and those like him provide the backbreaking labor that supports the agricultural backbone of Vista Valley.

"You Meese Allegra's new man, right?" Noe asks Sloan.

"No," I say.

"Yes," Sloan says and then speaks to Noe in rapid-fire Spanish.

A delighted Noe listens, nodding and murmuring his

approval. I hear my name mentioned frequently.

"What are you telling him?"

"How it is," Sloan says and falls silent.

"And how is it?"

Sloan ignores me.

Noe takes his hat off and scratches his head. He looks at me and searches for the words. "I come over to tell you. Meese Grandma and I talk. All set. She park car in my garage. You put truck in hers."

"Oh, no, I couldn't," I protest.

Noe's face grows stern. "I telling you. All set. Those bastards come back, I shoot their asses."

I glance at Sloan, who looks amused. I have no doubt Noe would carry out his threat. With several shotguns in his arsenal of weapons, Noe has earned the respect of our neighborhood hooligans.

"Better take him up on it, or he'll be offended," Sloan advises.

"Yeah, I bet you know all about machismo."

"Should have told me your truck got vandalized. Noe thinks it was kids."

"It's possible," I say, not wanting to shoot down Noe's theory. "But I had a run-in with a colleague last week. He's got a hair-trigger temper and some nasty little friends who like to terrorize people."

Sloan frowns. "Who is this guy?"

I have every intention of spilling the Donny Thorndyke story but stop short when a lavender, daisy-enhanced PT Cruiser pulls up to the curb. Grandma climbs out and scurries up the front walk.

"Good," Noe says, glaring at me. "Meese Grandma

here. She tell you garage thing."

Hoping to forestall a lengthy rehashing of his offer and my crass refusal, I quickly assure Noe I'll go along with the plan. Mollified, Noe greets Grandma and heads home.

"Back already?" Grandma chirps.

Before I can answer, Vlad pops out of the shrubs greeting Grandma with an inquisitive *rowwr?* After a half-assed swipe at my ankles, he trots to Sloan and twines his big orange body in and out of Sloan's legs, purring like a small gasoline engine.

"Oh, look." Grandma Sybil claps her tiny hands. "Vlad likes Mr. Sloan."

"No *Mr.*," Sloan says. "Just Sloan."

Vlad flops onto his back and waves all four paws in the air in ecstasy as Sloan rubs his belly. I see him bend over and take a closer look at Vlad's nether regions.

"Neutered, huh?" Sloan straightens up and looks at me. "Your idea?"

"Nope," I say. "Even though he blames me."

"It had to be done," Grandma says. "The other tomcats were beating him up."

"That happens." Sloan winks at me.

Grandma opens the front door. "Time for pie."

"Top shelf?" I ask.

"Allegra," Grandma scolds. "You know I wouldn't serve a guest anything but top shelf."

Sloan and I exchange a look. Maybe she won't notice the bottom shelf has been cleared.

Grandma wanders off for her nightly soak in the tub while Sloan downs his pie. I eat a few bites before setting down my fork, unable to shake the image of poor dead Joe Stepanek.

"You'll let me know about the postmortem?" I ask.

"I'm heading over there now. Sherm said it was a slow night and he'd get right on it. Unless, of course . . ." He points at the ceiling, my private quarters, his meaning unmistakable.

"Dream on, Sloan."

He flashes his *who do you think you're shittin'?* grin and says, "Yeah, damn shame you're so frigid."

"Oh, that." I make a dismissive gesture. "You caught me at a weak moment. It wasn't you, per se," I lie.

"We'll see about that."

Chapter 12

Saturday morning, I sit at Grandma's dining room table drinking coffee and filling out insurance forms, bummed to learn I have a $500 deductible. Lefty, looking dazed after an early morning round of window bashing, perches on the sill, a look of sympathy in his one good eye.

When Dodie returns home at 11 a.m. with Buddy in tow, I discover how things work in my aunt's world. Clad in a light brown leisure suit, Buddy has a gold hoop in his left ear and a satisfied grin on his face. Dodie's personal polyester pirate.

Dodie tells me to give Buddy a check for $500 as a down payment. Buddy will hold my check until the insurance company pays him and then give me a five hundred-dollar "rebate." Convoluted? Yes, but who am I to question Buddy's largesse? Or, for that matter, who or what sparked this burst of generosity?

A phone call from Nick's mom, Susan, allows me to escape the billing and cooing.

"Guess how I get to spend my Saturday?" Susan begins.

I try to read her tone. Resentful? Cheerful? Anticipatory? I need more information. "Give me a clue."

"Key," she snaps.

Oops.

"And," she says, "We are in the process of visiting every storage facility in Vista Valley, where Nick attempts to open number forty-two. You know how he is."

"Want me to spell you off for a while?"

Susan sighs. "No, that's okay. We're bonding. He's talking about Sara, something he's never done before."

She chuckles. "Besides, don't you have to get ready for the big show tonight?"

"Grandma's getting our outfits ready as we speak. Tell Nick I'll see him in the morning. Wanna come along? Check out Reverend Hunt?"

"I'll pass."

Karaoke night at Serenity Bay Assisted Living passes as peacefully as its name implies. Our Pointer Sisters set brings down the house with canes thumping like boom boxes. Other than Mr. Rosenblatt grabbing my ass during "Slow Hand," the evening is a rip-roaring success.

Sunday, 11:10 a.m.

Once again the victim of panty hose, I'm late picking up Nick. Sloan didn't return the new ones I purchased that fateful day, forcing me to borrow a spanking new pair from Grandma, whose legs are a good six inches shorter than mine.

An usher, her face frozen in disapproval at our late arrival, leads us to the front of the church as the choir sings the opening anthem. Shuffling along with my knees bound together by the crotch of Grandma's heavy duty, steel-belted panty hose, I feel the curious gaze of those already seated as they follow my odd perambulation down the center aisle.

We slip into the second pew, empty except for an elderly man with double hearing aides who passes us a hymnal. Directly in front of us sits a woman with perfectly coiffed blond hair. A barely pubescent girl sits motionless to her right, a small boy to her left. Reverend Hunt's nearest and dearest?

As we settle into our seats, the boy whips around and scrambles to his knees, peering over the back of the pew to give us his undivided attention. I wink at him. He grins and waves.

The woman turns her head a few inches and checks us out with one eyeball before grabbing the kid and plopping his little butt back down on the bench. I feel bad when I see his lower lip tremble. The woman ignores the lad and keeps her eyes fixed on a pulpit placed to the front and center of a massive stained-glass wall backlit by brilliant morning sun.

The music swells to a crescendo and stops. I feel a stirring behind me and glance over my shoulder. The entire congregation is standing and looking back at the closed double doors that separate the sanctuary from the vestibule. The air is charged with the kind of tension that springs from anticipation, excitement, or dread; I can't tell which. I find it disconcerting. Nick catches my eye and raises a quizzical eyebrow.

When the silence grows unbearable, the doors swing open and the choir bursts into song. A tall man clad in a dazzling white clerical robe strides down the center aisle, one hand raised heavenward, the other clutching a Bible. His head turns to and fro, and he scans the crowd as if probing for secret sinners masquerading as the godly. I feel a flash of primal fear as his gaze flicks over me once before returning for a longer look.

But wait! Doesn't the reader board say "sinners welcome"?

With a palpable sense of relief, people settle into their pews and look toward the pulpit. I break the silence by noisily sucking in air, having lapsed into oxygen deprivation by unwittingly holding my breath. This act of vulgarity earns me another eyeball flick from the blond woman.

The deep sonorous tones of Reverend Hunt wash over us like rich dark chocolate as we bow our heads for the invocation. All except for me. I peek.

Robinson Hunt stands with his arms and face lifted toward heaven, imploring God to shower us, we who have sinned, with mercy. As he prays, the choir joins hands and sways silently. And who is front and center gazing adoringly at Pastor Hunt, her sallow cheeks aglow with religious fervor? None other than Sara's no-nonsense caseworker, Peggy Mooney. I scan the rest of the choir, but Peggy's is the only familiar face.

I extend my scrutiny—it's a long prayer—to the reverend himself. Not a bad-looking man. Longish blond hair swept back and ending in a cluster of curls at the nape of his neck. Teeth looking as white as Chiclets against a tan face. A hawkish nose. His eyes are a clear hazel green with piercingly dark pupils. And they're staring directly into mine! I slam my eyes shut and bow my head, my face uncomfortably hot.

After my faux pas, I attempt to draw no more attention to myself as the service follows its prescribed format. Hymn, announcements, another hymn, and Reverend Hunt's sermon.

I begin to sense the power of the man. Choosing words carefully, he delivers his sermon with style and grace, his tone alternately seductive and challenging. He uses his voice like an instrument, starting out sweetly *pianissimo*, lulling the listener into a cozy cocoon of happiness and well-being. I relax and snuggle back in the pew.

"Sinners!" He roars, scaring the shit out of me. "We're all sinners!"

I start so violently Nick nudges me with his elbow and whispers, "Close your mouth. You're drooling."

Reverend Hunt switches once again to *sotto voce* and soothes, "Redemption. It's so easy. Trust me. I'll show you the way."

I think about Sara, who said she had to "get right with God." The state of grace Sara was seeking sounds remarkably similar to Robinson Hunt's promise of redemption. Chillingly similar.

Finally, the closing hymn—and one I can get into. Good ol' *Amazing Grace*. Caught up in the familiar melody, I let my voice soar. Nick looks embarrassed, but the little guy in the front pew loves it. He turns around once again and claps his hands in approval when the hymn is over.

After the recessional, Hunt strolls back up the center aisle scattering his personal blessings. The blond, presumably Mrs. Hunt, grabs the kids, slides out of the pew, and scurries behind him. As Nick and I wait for the people behind us to exit, I begin to see the advantage of our ring-side seats. I can check out the crowd for familiar faces.

In biblical terms, they are legion, beginning with none other than my fearless leader, R.D. Langley, and his perfect family. Not only is R.D. meticulous in a navy blue suit and snowy white shirt—probably to indicate the condition of his soul—but his two sons are outfitted in suits identical to his. His wife completes the picture. A willowy brunette, she wears a powder blue tailored dress with matching bolero jacket. Though he must have seen my late arrival, he doesn't look my way. *Thank you, God.* Prayers answered. Perks of the churchgoer.

I continue my perusal and spot Gwen Thorndyke, Donny's ex, and her three teenage children, who smile and wave. Two city councilmen chat in the foyer with George Samuelson, a prominent businessman who owns three, yes three, McDonald's. We aim high in Vista Valley.

Other than the elderly man in my pew, I see few seniors, normally the backbone of any church. Maybe, like Grandma, they resent Robinson Hunt for spending Ruth Willard's money. I've seen nothing that bears Ruth's name, not even a plaque.

Nick and I wait our turn to press the flesh of the man who speaks so eloquently of sin and redemption. Flanked by the wife and kiddies, he stands in the open doorway.

As we inch forward, I watch him in action. Right hand down low to shake the hand of the next person in line, left hand reaching out to grasp the shoulder or arm of the one behind, pulling him or her forward and ending with a pat or hug. Shake, grasp, pull, pat. A well-practiced technique that keeps people moving.

When we inch to the front of the line, I stick my hand

out, but he pulls a switcheroo. He places his right hand on my shoulder and turns me with a powerful grip to face him while reaching for Nick with the other.

"Welcome." His hypnotic eyes stare into mine. "Ah, the young lady who sings like an angel. We need you in our choir."

I have a sudden visual: Peggy Mooney and I are locked arm in arm, swaying in silent sisterhood as Reverend Hunt makes his approach to the pulpit.

"Th-thanks," I stammer. "I'll think about it. What I'd really like to do is—"

My voice trails off as his fingers tighten on my shoulder. "Miss Thome, I won't take no for an answer."

Whoa. How does he know my name? Acting cool isn't my strong suit, but I give it a try. We trade phony smiles.

"I'm Sara Stepanek's teacher. Do you know she's missing?"

His gaze flicks to the left then back to mine. His hand on my shoulder feels like twenty pounds of trouble. With great difficulty, I stand motionless.

The cheesy smile is gone now, replaced by a brow-knitting frown of concern. "A troubled girl, Sara. She was very fond of you."

His use of the past tense gives me a chill, but now is not the time. I can feel the crowd behind me growing restive.

"I'd like to talk to you about her. I'll call first," I say as he releases me.

He nods and does some complicated teenagey high-five, low-five thing with Nick.

When he reaches for the person behind Nick, the sleeve of his clerical robe slides back to reveal his hand and wrist. Under the pretense of waving at someone further down the line, I take a gander at his exposed flesh. The webbing between his thumb and forefinger is etched with a series of faint hash marks, pearly white against the tan of his hands. Before his sleeve slides back down, I catch a quick glimpse of similar scarring on his inner wrist.

Admittedly, the memory of Joe Stepanek's prison art looms large. Also true, Robinson Hunt may have come to the ministry as a full-blown adult, scared straight after experiencing the seamy side of life. Not the usual path for a man of the cloth but possible, hence his fascination with sinners and redemption. Perhaps he thought it unseemly for a man in his position to sport tattoos and had them removed. A logical explanation.

Why, then, does it bother me so much that I've clearly seen the outline of a spider web on his left hand and the number 5 on his wrist? Why did he have tattoos identical to those of Joe Stepanek?

Questions Nick and I ponder while I drive him home. Intrigued, Nick plans to fire up his computer, poke around in Robinson Hunt's past, and see what he can find. I hand him Sara's Bible and notebook when he climbs out.

Later, released from my panty hose prison, I flop on the bed and listen to my phone messages. Marcy, wanting the details from Friday night. My future soul mate, Trent, the car salesman, suggesting in a voice ripe with innuendo that we go for a ride in his new car. Michael, yes, *that* Michael, telling me he'll call back. Finally, Sloan rattling off a number and the terse message "Call me."

I stare at the phone. Why am I suddenly so alluring to the opposite sex? I think about Buddy's obvious fascination with Dodie. I think about Sloan. Michael. Harley wanting to see me again.

Of course! It has to be Grandma Sybil and her diligent efforts on the behalf of faulty male plumbing. Our household is tossing on a sea of powerful pheromones, attracting men like heat-seeking missiles.

I prioritize my callbacks and decide to start with Sloan, especially since I don't have to go through voice mail hell to reach him.

He answers on the first ring. I wait. He waits.

Finally, he says, "Yeah?"

"Damn it, Sloan, you called me! Are you aware of your limited social skills?"

"Uh huh."

He lapses once again into silence.

"Well?"

"Stepanek had a note in his pocket from the kid. Sara. Said not to worry about her, that she ran off with her boyfriend."

"No way," I say. "Sara doesn't have a boyfriend."

"That you know about."

"No. She doesn't have one."

"Yeah, whatever."

"Was the note handwritten?"

"Word processor."

"Did she sign it in longhand?"

"Nope."

"Then she probably didn't write it. Don't you see? Somebody wants us to believe she's run away. Hence, the note planted in her dad's pocket. Whoever killed Joe put it there."

"That's a reach."

"But he was murdered, right?"

"He had enough heroin in him to kill him. A few things don't add up. Sherm said he'd been dead at least forty-eight hours. Looks like he shot up, died, and somebody dumped him there," Sloan says.

"So what are you going to do about it?"

"Local guys are looking into it. Smells like a drug deal gone bad. They won't waste a lot of manpower on it."

"I said what are *you* going to do about it?"

"Give me a break. Joe was a wanted felon. Now he's not."

"But if Sara was with him, she could be in danger."

"Or, like the note said, she could be off screwing her boyfriend."

I bite back an angry response and take a deep breath. "Guess I'll have to prove you're wrong. What did you find out about the phone Sara used?"

"Dead end. Woman had her cell phone stolen at the mall."

"What's her name?"

Sloan gives an exasperated sigh. "Al. You've been reading too many mysteries."

"Just tell me her name."

I hear papers rustling. "Geneva Decker."

"Okay, thanks. Gotta go."

I click off before he can give me grief.

The phone rings immediately. Before I can speak, Sloan says, "I find out you're bugging Ms. Decker, you and I'll be having a serious talk."

"You? Talking? I'll look forward to it. Anything else?"

He growls, "That's it."

"I'll let you hang up first. Male ego and all that."

"Jesus Christ, woman, you're impossible!"

Chapter 13

Sunday night

Michael has been a busy boy. Unable to reach me, he's conned Grandma Sybil, most unfairly, I think.

"But, sweetie," she says as we cruise down Maple Street in the Olds. "He's Vista Valley's—"

"Most eligible bachelor," Dodie and I say together.

We wave at Noe, who sits on his front step watching a half dozen grandchildren ride their bikes up and down the sidewalk.

Yes, that's right. The three of us are heading for a late supper at Michael's club.

"But why now? Why so late? What does he want from me?" I wail from the back seat.

"Allegra, you ask far too many questions." Grandma's voice is calm and reasonable. "Obviously, he's had time to think it over and realizes he's acted hastily. We're eating late because he couldn't tee off until three."

She turns and frowns at me. "Personally, I think it's

very sweet of him to include Dodie and me. I haven't been to the club since Morty died."

I swallow my protest because, obviously, I'm a selfish bitch. A suspicious, selfish bitch. Yes, I'll keep my selfish, suspicious, bitchy thoughts to myself. Like, *Why the sudden interest in Grandma and Dodie when, in the past, Michael wouldn't give them the time of day?*

He meets us at the door. I'm relieved to see he's still dressed in his golf duds. Against Grandma's wishes, I refused to stuff myself back into her teensy panty hose. Instead, I'm bare legged and dressed simply in a sage green sundress with spaghetti straps and a pair of open-toed backless heels that match the dress perfectly.

After greeting Grandma and Dodie, Michael pulls me in for a hug. He smells of fresh air and expensive booze. Snuggled against him in full body contact, I feel a little surge of heat. Recalling my up close and personal inter-action with Sloan Friday night, I'm chagrined. Am I so desperate for a man that any man will do? To test my theory, I conjure up an image of Robinson Hunt complete with shiny white teeth and X-ray vision. To my great relief, the incipient spark dies aborning.

Michael murmurs in my ear, "I've missed you."

Instead of answering, I pat his cheek and pull away.

A waiter hovering nearby leads us to a table covered with crisp, white linen, the sight of which fills me with trepidation. I have a tendency to spatter colorful food stuffs. The table cloth looms like an empty artist's canvas waiting for the first brush stroke. I pray I can get through the salad without embarrassing myself. *Order Roquefort, hold the tomatoes.*

The waiter removes a bottle of champagne from a silver ice bucket and looks quizzically at Michael. "Now, sir?"

Michael nods. Four champagne flutes are filled with bubbly. The waiter steps back, discreetly out of conversational range.

"Are we celebrating something?" I narrow my eyes at Michael.

"I hope so," he says.

His teeth are bared in a frozen grin, an expression similar to that of a trapped wolverine I once saw on a nature show. His left eyelid begins to twitch. Not exactly the demeanor of a man reunited with his beloved. More like a man facing a firing squad.

"Here's to us." He raises his glass.

"Us?" I repeat, blinking rapidly to hide my surprise.

Grandma kicks me under the table. Hard. She stares pointedly at my champagne glass.

"Here's to the possibility of us," I amend with an insincere smile of my own.

Michael looks relieved as we clink glasses. He tosses back his champagne and signals the waiter, who trots after the requested bourbon on the rocks. When he delivers the drink to Michael, Dodie beckons the waiter. He scurries to her side, and she murmurs behind an uplifted hand. The waiter says, "Certainly, Madame. Red?"

Michael looks at her curiously. "Something special from the bar?"

"Possibly," Dodie says.

The waiter returns and thrusts a bottle of wine in front

of Dodie for her inspection.

"Will this do, madame?"

Dodie fishes her glasses out of her purse and examines the label. "Yes, thank you. Could you open it, please?"

I finally get a look at the label. *WWJD. What Would Jesus Drink?*

The waiter enthuses, "The owner is a member here. Robinson Hunt."

"I thought he might be." Dodie says. She takes a sip, makes a face, and sets the glass down.

Michael's expression has changed from mild disinterest to befuddlement. Two furrowed lines appear in his forehead, and his twitch increases in intensity. I'm looking at a man whose evening has spun out of control.

"Oh, really," I chirp. "Is he a golfer?"

"Indeed, he is," the waiter says, making a move toward Michael's wineglass. Michael snatches it away.

I let out a snicker, the first and last laugh of the evening. I take a sip of the wine and shudder. "I hope he's a better golfer than winemaker. Do you know him, Michael?"

Grandma Sybil and Aunt Dodie lean forward in their chairs.

"I've seen him around," Michael says. He grabs his menu. "Ready to order, ladies?"

Clearly, the subject of Robinson Hunt is off limits.

Dinner passes slowly as we churn out dutiful conversation on neutral topics, i.e. the weather and how it will affect the cherry crop, the Seattle Mariners and whether they will suck as bad as last year . . . Safe, boring topics unlikely to arouse passion of any sort, which accounts for my place at the table remaining pristine. No gravy stains propelled by a fit of spontaneous laughter. No shriek of dismay at some outrageous comment resulting in a chicken leg skittering across the table after an errant stab of the fork. No spillage. No broken crockery. Nothing at all, until the blueberry cobbler. Fortunately, I'm able to conceal the hideous blue blot with my napkin.

The interminable evening draws to a close with the requisite round of decaf coffee. Dodie spots the Myers clan and slips away for a quick word. Grandma excuses herself to go to the restroom, leaving me alone with Michael, who squirms in his chair.

"What's going on, Michael?"

"I, uh, well . . ."

A heavy hand falls on his shoulder, and his voice trails off. I look up to see George Samuelson, the McDonald's mogul, looming over Michael.

"Hey, buddy, I'd like to meet your pretty lady."

Though he holds a drink in one hand, his words are clearly enunciated, his eyes watchful, his expression serious.

Michael reddens and jumps to his feet to make the necessary introductions. Mr. Samuelson looks me over carefully. Can he tell I'd rather have a BK Broiler than a Quarter Pounder?

After he and Michael swap golf stories, Samuelson wanders off to rejoin his cronies. Grandma returns, giving me no further opportunity to question Michael. We collect Dodie and split, our night of mingling with Vista Valley's rich and famous mercifully at an end.

Michael walks us to the Olds. Grandma Sybil strolls slowly while throwing out numerous conversational gambits much like a biblical fisherman casting a net in the Sea of Tiberias. She's after the big one. Michael. I suppress a grin as she comes up with a list of creative reasons why I should invite Michael back to the house. I say nothing to encourage her.

A few steps away from the car, subtlety forgotten, she says, "Michael, dear, I wonder if you'd mind following us home. I need a hand with something."

Who can refuse Grandma Sybil without looking like an asshole? Certainly not Michael. "Sure, Mrs. Thome, what do you need?"

Under the cover of darkness, I reach over and pinch her, but she shakes it off. "We have a window that's stuck. Upstairs, in Allegra's apartment. None of us girls are strong enough to open it."

I say, "No, really, Michael. It's not necessary. Isn't Sunday your poker night?"

"Maybe he can kill that spider you've been bitching about for days," Dodie adds.

Yeah, I have a little thing about spiders. Actually, I have a big thing about spiders, and Dodie, who's fearless, loves to point it out.

"I'll get Noe to do it," I say.

"You know Noe won't come past the front door," Dodie says.

"I'll follow you home," Michael says.

Even in the dark, I can see Grandma's smile of triumph.

Grandma ignores my bitching and moaning on the journey home. As it turns out, I could have saved my breath.

When we turn right off Vista Valley Avenue, I spot the patrol cars, light bars flashing in brilliant syncopation.

"Oh my," Grandma says. "Is that our house?" One bejeweled hand leaves the steering wheel and flutters in alarm. Her eyes look big and frightened behind her glasses, her complexion a ghastly shade of gray as the flashing blue lights bounce crazily off the windshield of the Olds.

"Maybe not," I say. But I know it is. My stomach lurches in alarm even while I murmur a prayer of thanks that my family is safe.

One police car sits in our driveway; another is parked at the curb. Noe, his wife, Lorena, and at least eight members of their extended family mill around the front yard. Noe is speaking Spanish to a Hispanic policeman, gesticulating wildly. Spotting Grandma, he breaks off the conversation and hurries over to us. "Guy break in your house. I chase away but no catch. Lorena call policeman."

He shakes his head in regret. "I catch, I shoot his ass."

Grandma has pulled herself together. She pats Noe's arm. "I appreciate the thought, sweetie, but we have a house full of things. Things can be replaced. A neighbor like you is priceless. You did the right thing."

Noe flashes his gap-toothed grin and returns to the policeman to finish his story. Dodie wanders toward the front porch. Another policeman hurries up to Michael, apparently assuming he's the man of the house. I see him shake his head and point at Grandma. I hurry after Dodie, who's reached the front door.

"Make sure it's okay to go in." I caution her.

"The cops have been all through the house. Whoever

it was is gone now."

The place was hastily tossed, the intruders interrupted before they could cart away our valuables. Other than books pulled out of the bookcase and the contents of Grandma's desk drawers dumped on the floor, the damage is minimal.

My apartment is a different story. The tiny kitchen is a mess. Silverware is strewn across the floor, flour sits in snowy drifts on the countertop, and coffee beans litter the sink. Desk drawers hang askew, their contents scrambled and spilling out on the floor.

After the initial shock, I manage to rein in my emotions, at least until I see my bedroom. Every dresser drawer has been emptied, the bed torn apart, the mattress heaved to one side, my jewelry box upended. My lingerie has been flung with reckless abandon, seemingly over the thief's shoulder while he pawed through dresser drawers, looking for . . . what?

A black lace bra dangles from the ceiling light fixture. Pink panties grace a bedpost. The remainder has been dumped on the mattress, lacy underthings mingling unnaturally with flannel pajamas and a jogging bra. It's simply too much. I stamp my foot and screech, "Son of a bitch!"

I pick up an overturned chair and sit down amidst the panty storm bawling like a two-year-old whose older brother has trashed her Barbie collection.

When I stop howling, I hear male voices and heavy footsteps on the stairs. I leave the bedroom as one of the cops and Michael step through my broken door.

The cop dodges a toaster lying on its side in the middle

of the living room. He shakes his head and studies the devastation in my kitchen. "Looks like he took his time up here. Lucky your neighbor chased him off before he could do much damage down below."

"Is anything missing?" Michael asks.

Still fighting tears, I shake my head.

"Probably looking for cash and small valuables to fence. Most likely a junkie needing a fix," the cop says.

Michael slips an arm around my shoulder and squeezes. "I'll help you clean up."

Michael being nice. It's more than I can take. I feel my lower lip quiver again. *Damn, Allegra, don't start.* I pull away from Michael. "Thanks for offering, but I know Grandma and Dodie will help."

Michael looks relieved. "Okay, then, if you don't need me, I'll take off."

He leans over and pecks me on the cheek. "I'll be in touch."

Belatedly I remember my manners. "Thanks a lot for dinner. Grandma really enjoyed it."

He waves a hand in acknowledgement and heads for the open doorway. A doorway suddenly filled by Sloan.

Michael throws on the brakes and spins around to face me. "I thought you said you weren't seeing . . ." he begins, casting nervous glances at Sloan.

After a cursory glance around, Sloan crosses his arms and leans against the wall like an extra kitchen appliance. "Back with the boyfriend, huh?"

My angst stemming from panty drawer violation disappears, vanquished by mind-blowing rage.

"Shut up, both of you!" I shout. "I don't have time for this shit. Just get the hell out of here, and leave me alone!"

Neither man moves. I retreat to the bedroom and slam the door. Is it was too late to become a lesbian or, in Grandma's vernacular, Lebanese?

Chapter 14

$\mathcal{I}$ turn the radio on, crank up the volume, and begin setting the room to rights. I'll need Dodie's help putting the bed back together, but my undies are back where they belong, sorted by color and function. This small accomplishment quells my seething emotions. I open the door twenty minutes later to find my living quarters thankfully man-free. I go to the window and see that the police have split. Michael as well. Sloan's car is in the driveway.

I cross to the desk and begin replacing the drawers. Is the cop right? Was the thief looking for something to fence? Why, then, did he spend so much time in my apartment when clearly the valuables are downstairs? Michael's bizarre behavior throughout the evening adds another layer of confusion.

What about Donny Thorndyke and his creepy friends? Is this another warning? But why? R.D. dismissed my accusations as spiteful, albeit harmless, ranting.

If I eliminate Donny Thorndyke and the junkie-looking-for-valuables theory, one option remains: Sara. Her Bible. Her notebook. Her key. All of which have been in my possession until recently. But who would want or need the teenager's meager possessions, and for what possible reason? While poking around looking for Sara, have I stirred up something nasty?

In search of answers, I pick up the jumble of papers on the floor, looking for the hot pink sticky notes I stuck together and placed under a coffee mug on top of my desk. I go through my papers three times, examine each drawer, and crawl around on my hands and knees to search under the desk.

My notes are gone. What kind of a thief ignores an opportunity to steal my identity, my checkbook, my few decent pieces of jewelry, and makes off with scribbled sticky notes?

I stretch out on my back to stare at the ceiling while I ponder these questions. Michael has to be involved. I tick off the reasons in my head.

His phone call saying he wants to see me again and his not-so-subtle reference to my missing student.

His duplicity in avoiding me and making arrangements with Grandma Sybil to get us out of the house tonight.

The odd disconnect between his actions and demeanor. To wit, toasting the renewal of our relationship while looking like a man with a gun to his head.

His obvious discomfort at the mention of Robinson Hunt's name, as well as the fortuitous arrival of one of Hunt's parishioners when Michael and I were alone.

Damn, but I hate thinking such evil thoughts about Michael! This is a man I almost slept with, even thought about marrying.

If the break-in has something to do with Sara's disappearance, how did the thief know I had her things? I sneaked them out of the Hewitts' house, and Sara had taken great pains to hide them.

I sit up and reach for the bag of chips the thief conveniently tossed on the floor. I munch and muse. The rhythmic crunching works its magic, calming my fevered brain, which is reeling from data overload. I suddenly remember why I'm looking for the sticky notes. I need a visual, the reassuring sight of pencil on paper.

I sit down at my desk with a blank piece of paper. In the center of the page, I print *SARA* in block letters and draw a circle around it. From the circle, I draw a series of straight lines pointing outwards like bristles on a cactus. Each line leads to someone or something connected to Sara. Each person or event gets its own circle with more lines shooting outward.

The Hewitts occupy one small circle; Peggy Mooney, another. Beginning with Peggy's circle, I draw a line and print "RH" to indicate Peggy's connection to Robinson Hunt. On two other spokes, I write, "Last person to see Sara" and "lied about Sara."

The Hewitts are next. Nick said Peggy Mooney told the Hewitts to take Sara to church. Does that mean they're part of the congregation? Their circle fairly bristles with information: "Access to Sara's personal belongings." "Recipients of farewell note nobody has seen." "New car purchased with cash." "Expensive television set." "Hostility when questioned about Sara."

I start Nick's circle, carefully printing my own name on one of his extensions. If not for Nick, I'd have written Sara off as another runaway, certainly a common trait among my students.

I stare at my handiwork and, on a whim, draw a circle around Robinson Hunt. An errant thought lurking in my gray matter bobs to the surface. I print "DT?" next to Hunt's circle. Donny Thorndyke. His ex-wife, kids, and bosom buddy, R.D. Langley, are among Hunt's flock. Presumably, so is Donny. And if Donny and Hunt have a connection . . .

I think about Donny and Kelvin warning me off. And then about the words "nosy bitch" spray painted on my truck. Then the break-in. My missing sticky notes. Whether Donny knows something about Sara's disappearance. Whether the implied threats are about more than our recent spat. If I am so spooked by recent happenings that I'm seeing a conspiracy theory where none exists.

I reluctantly pull my mind away from Donny Thorndyke and finish filling in Nick's circle. Suddenly I'm struck with a stab of nausea-inducing fear. If this break-in is triggered by our not-so-subtle inquiries, then, thanks to my sticky notes, the perpetrators now know about the notebook, the Bible. And suddenly I realize Nick could very well be in danger. As a precaution, I tear up the paper and flush the pieces down the toilet.

I pick up the phone just as Dodie pops in armed with a broom and dustpan.

"Came to see if you need any help."

She crosses the kitchen and looks through the bedroom door. "Maybe we need to get Sloan up here to put the bed back together."

"No!" I set the phone down. "I'm sure we can manage."

Dodie smirks. "You sure? He looks like he'd be a big help in the bedroom."

"Yeah, yeah. Speaking of helpful, when's Buddy bringing my truck back?"

"Tomorrow."

She scoops flour from the counter into a garbage can.

We tackle the mess together, and I pour out my suspicions about Michael. Dodie's a good listener. She looks thoughtful and occasionally murmurs an affirmative. More importantly, she accepts my conspiracy theory with nary a lifted eyebrow or gasp of disapproval.

When I wind down, she says, "That's why I ordered the WWJD wine. I wanted to see Michael's reaction."

I feel giddy with relief. My practical aunt is a staunch ally. Nick's too emotionally involved, and Sloan . . . well, Sloan would probably blow off the sticky note incident, take the Michael incident seriously, and offer to kill him.

"I need to call Susan. She'll think I put Nick in danger," I say.

"I'll take care of it. You'd better get downstairs. Your grandmother has the picture album out."

Few things frighten me more than Grandma Sybil entertaining gentleman callers with the picture album. Not that Sloan is my gentleman caller. More like a giant irritating moth attracted by the flashing blue lights, bashing into things until somebody whaps him with an enormous rolled-up newspaper. Even though I feel guilty about leaving the dirty work to Dodie, I dash out of my apartment.

Halfway down the stairs, I pause to eavesdrop. I gather from their voices that Sloan and Grandma share the living room couch while they peruse my bare-assed baby pictures.

"Oooh," Grandma trills. "Look at that angry little face! But isn't she adorable in her tutu?"

I know the picture they're talking about. A head taller than the other little girls, I stand frozen in first position glaring angrily at the camera. After my numerous threats and bribes, Grandma relented and removed it from its place of honor on the mantle.

I clomp down the remaining stairs and say, "I'd just fallen on my butt for the third time in ten minutes. That's why I look mad."

Sloan and Grandma turn at the sound of my voice. They sit side by side on the couch drinking coffee and chatting amiably as they pore over my lurid photographic history. Empty pie plates sit on the coffee table. All traces of the break-in have been cleared away. I shake my head in wonder. It's like the burglary is a wonderful excuse for coffee and pie.

"Allegra didn't take to ballet," Grandma says. "It was her mother's idea. You've heard of Allegra Kent, the famous ballerina?"

Sloan shakes his head.

On dragging feet, I join the party. I plop down on an overstuffed ottoman and watch Grandma do her thing. She glances at me then leans toward Sloan. "Allegra's mother, Diane, is my daughter-in-law, not my daughter."

She waits for Sloan's nod.

"Diane saw Allegra Kent dance when she was a little girl and was determined to make our Allegra into a ballerina. Well, obviously . . ."

I grit my teeth as the familiar story of my rebellious childhood unfolds. The story ends as it always does. "My son, of course, realized Allegra was miserable."

"Not until I was ten." I'm surprised to feel the resentment still simmering beneath the surface.

Sloan gives me a quizzical look. "No brothers or sisters?"

"Mother didn't want to risk another disappointment."

"Allegra! How can you say that? You've never been a disappointment." Grandma puts the album aside, bounds off the couch, and gathers me into a hug before disappearing into the kitchen. Sloan raises an eyebrow and pats the spot Grandma abandoned. I shake my head and stay put.

"Scared to get too close to me, huh? Don't blame you. Can't deny the chemistry."

I roll my eyes.

After a lengthy pause, Sloan says, "So, about your date tonight . . ."

"It wasn't a date," I protest. "He wanted to take all of us to dinner."

"Not-a-date." Sloan gives me a frosty smile. "You have a lot of those."

Remembering Friday night and my parsing of words, I have the good grace to blush. "Oh, it wasn't like that at all."

His grin grows warmer.

"Why are you here anyway?" I ask.

"Saw the lights."

"That's it?"

"Yeah." He looks thoughtful. "Weird break-in. Nothing of value gone."

He moves to the ottoman, nudging me with a hip to make room for his big frame. I scoot over to the edge. He puts an arm around my shoulders and hauls me back. He puts his lips to my ear, and I give a little involuntary shiver. "Spill it, Al. What were they looking for?"

I try to ignore the heat rising between us. "I think it's

related to Sara Stepanek. I made some notes about the stuff we found. The burglar took them. It's the only thing missing."

I purposely omit my suspicions about Michael and the key. Searching for the storage unit has given Nick a sense of purpose. I voice my concern that Nick might be in danger now that the thief has my notes.

Sloan's grip tightens. "Does he have Sara's things?"

"Yeah, that's why I'm worried."

He releases me and stands. "Take me there."

I hear Dodie on the stairs. "Nick wants to talk to you," she calls.

I hear him wheezing before I put the phone to my ear. "Guess what I just found out?" His voice is shrill with excitement.

I glance at Sloan and go into the kitchen. I want to know what Nick's found but not how he found it. Nick amuses himself by hacking into so-called secure sites. I don't think Susan knows, and I sure don't want Sloan to know.

"I checked out Robinson Hunt's Social Security number. He died in 1992 at the age of thirty," Nick tells me.

"So our Robinson Hunt . . ."

"Stole his identity."

Chapter 15

*W*hile Nick and I talk, Dodie tells Sloan she'll pick up the stuff and lock them in the Myers' Clinic safe. Unable to buck the tide that is Dodie on a mission, Sloan agrees. With Dodie gone and Grandma having her nightly bubble bath, Sloan and I are alone.

"Need any help up there?" He points toward my apartment. Trust Sloan not to miss an opportunity.

"I'm good," I say, walking him to the door. It's late, and the last week of school's a doozy. I need sleep.

"You sure?" He moves in close.

"Positive."

He runs a finger across my lower lip. I shiver. He looks triumphant. "See ya," he says.

"If you're lucky."

"Oh, I have a feeling I will be."

With a mixture of relief and disappointment, I watch him drive away.

𝄞

Monday

Thankfully the weather gods cooperate, and our string of warm, sunny days ends. I rejoice in the dark, scudding clouds and gusty winds that blow through Vista Valley. My female students, yielding to the rainy weather, abandon their skimpy summer clothes in favor of sweatshirts and jeans. My guys, without the titillation of exposed female flesh, toil over their final essays, busy as little worker bees whose queen is unavailable.

After school, I've just finished reading "What I Learned in Juvie," by Jimmy Felthouse, and started on Janie Morrison's epistle, "Why I Hate My Mother's Fourth Husband," when I remember Sara's essays.

I drop what I'm doing and retrieve the plastic tote that holds Sara's work. Each folder is neatly labeled by quarters. The first-, second-, and third-quarter folders are plump with completed work; the fourth quarter, light by comparison.

I open the first-quarter folder and thumb through the contents, pausing to read through Sara's essay on the Westward Expansion.

During the first quarter, I scrawled a big red "A+" and "Well done!" at the top of Sara's essay. Using tidy, perfectly formed penmanship, she'd written an informative, well-organized essay complete with drawings of covered wagons and attacking Indians.

I pick up the fourth-quarter folder and pluck out an essay dated April 18. Because we added several bird feeders outside our classroom windows about that time, the topic is now backyard birds. Sara's grade slipped to a B-. The title's scrawled in jagged, gothic letters: "Magpies: Baby Killers of the Bird World."

I groan and rub my suddenly aching temples. Why didn't I pick up on Sara's emotionally charged language, the deterioration in her penmanship?

The essay starts in an ordinary fashion but quickly morphs into something quite different. Her points are poorly organized, her thoughts disjointed. The writing is ragged and uneven, some words so faint I can barely read them, and others so heavily scored they look etched with a sharpened dagger. Sara's fragile emotional state is splattered across the white paper in lurid purple ink.

After a brief description of the bird's habitat, Sara launches into the magpie's reputed penchant for robbing other birds' nests. The words "destroys eggs" and "kill nestlings" are written in large print and underlined with a vivid slash.

The last paragraph is the most disturbing.

Sara wrote, "By learning about the black-billed magpie, I discovered something very important about myself. Everybody hates magpies because they raid the nests of other birds, killing the babies or eating the eggs. Could anything be worse? Yes! It is far worse to destroy a life because it is merely inconvenient. Such an act is evil. Magpies are following their instincts. But people have the ability to make choices. A person who commits a grave sin must seek redemption."

One last sentence, "I hope it's not too late," is scrawled at the bottom of the page like an afterthought. The words are poorly formed, the *o*'s and *a*'s open at the top. Sara embellished her essay with a sprinkling of tiny teardrops that rained down the left margin and merged into the last sentence. A trail of tears. A blurred smudge appears below the final *I,* as if a real tear fell to the page. Like an epitaph.

I stare at the words I wrote across the top of the page. "Not your best work," and I'm ashamed. Sara was literally crying out for help, and I missed it.

A sudden gust of wind throws a spattering of rain across the windows. A tiny whirlwind sweeps down the sidewalk, picking up pebbles and discarded candy wrappers. The birds have abandoned their feeders and taken shelter in the row of flowering plums that stand as a living barrier between the school yard and the bus garage. The treetops whip back and forth violently. I hope the birds are safely tucked away from the storm.

Where did Sara go for shelter? Is she outside shivering in the rain? Shacked up with her boyfriend, as Sloan suggests? Seeking redemption for what she feels is an unforgivable transgression?

My thoughts lead me back to Robinson Hunt.

I've just clicked my cell phone off after making an appointment to see Reverend Hunt when a burst of static comes through the intercom.

Sally screeches, "Miss Thome! Are you there?"

"Yes, Sally."

"Dr. Langley would like to see you immediately."

I feel a little thrill of alarm, a reaction dating back to my rebellious youth and frequent trips to the principal's office.

Steady, girl, I think as I trot down the hall. R.D.'s my colleague, not a daddy figure waiting to give me a chewing out. I hope.

Sally is crouched over her computer, fingers flying, bun bobbing. She glances up at me, bares her teeth in a brief smile, and waves me into R.D.'s office.

Sally smiling? I have to know why. I return her phony smile and stumble into her desk, dislodging a stack of papers that tumbles to the floor.

"Oops, sorry." I move around the desk to help her.

She hisses, "Leave it!"

The smile disappears, replaced by the pinched frown of disapproval she normally wears. When she bends over to pick up the papers, I cop a look at the computer screen and see the reason for her glee. She's imputing a "plan of improvement," the euphemistically titled document resulting from an unsatisfactory teacher evaluation. The last step before a teacher is terminated. "Not a team player" seemed to be the predominant theme. Sally's head pops up before I can find the name of the poor sap about to be canned.

"He's waiting," she barks, jerking her head toward R.D.'s door.

R.D. sits behind his desk, resplendent in a plum-colored V-necked sweater over a lavender dress shirt and gray slacks. His hands grip a personnel folder, presumably mine. I feel a prickle of apprehension even though I've had nothing but glowing evaluations from R.D. in the past.

Each year, in fact, R.D. tiptoes into my room, spreads his handkerchief on a chair before he sits down, and leaves after five minutes of observation. He's happy as long as I keep my hooligans under control and away from public view. Why would this year be any different?

"Close the door, and have a seat," R.D. says, flipping

open the folder. Frowning, he bends over it, examining the contents. I swallow hard and sit down.

After a significant pause, he looks up. "We need to finalize your evaluation. Look this over, and sign it."

He slides the evaluation form across his desk, folds his arms, and swivels his chair around to gaze out the window.

I read through the document quickly. The words leap off the page and punch me in the gut.

In part, it says, "Ms. Thome must address some serious issues if she is to continue as a teacher at Vista Valley High School. Her room is messy, and her students are often rowdy and out of control. Because our community expects results, test scores are of the utmost importance. Her students consistently perform at an unacceptable level."

I stare at R.D.'s back and let my fury build.

"This is bullshit, R.D., and you know it!" My voice is shrill with rage.

R.D. swivels around. His brow is knit in consternation. "Language, Ms. Thome. You're not exactly improving your position here. I'm your superior, and I'd appreciate a civil discourse."

"I can't believe what I'm reading," I say. "My room is messy? What does that have to do with my teaching methods?"

Without breaking eye contact, I toss the form back on his desk. "I'm not signing this. Last year you gave me the highest marks possible. What's changed?"

R.D. starts to answer, when, after a discreet tap on the door, Sally enters and hands him a sheet of paper. Omigod! The "plan of improvement." The poor sap is me!

I spend the next twenty-four hours in a blue funk, reeling in disbelief, avoiding my friends and family. Something in R.D.'s message sends me spinning back in time.

In high school, I honed my reputation as a rebel, mostly because it gave my mother screaming fits. Dad, a pharmaceutical salesman, was away for days at a time. He'd return home to find the two women in his life slamming doors and hurling verbal firebombs. Trying to placate his wife without alienating his daughter proved to be mission impossible. No wonder he looked so happy walking out the door, suitcase in hand.

It all changed my senior year in high school when my mother found a malignant lump in her breast. During one of our bitter exchanges, she said it was my fault—the cancer—that the stress I put her through caused it. What did I know? I was a kid. I thought she was going to die, so I believed her. Exit bad Allegra.

In retrospect, I know my mother did me a favor.

I buckled down, improved my grades, and was admitted to college. On the other hand, the guilt I took on has been my constant companion over the years. I even married Harley because my mother was impressed by his West Point credentials. And, oh, yes, Mom's alive and well, having vanquished the big C. She and Dad went to Marriage Encounter and travel the country in their humongous motor coach. And, according to Grandma Sybil, who knows about these things, they keep the big rig rockin.' *Eewww!*

Even though I know R.D. is pitching bullshit, I begin to doubt myself. Maybe I'm not cut out for teaching. Maybe I shouldn't have divorced Harley. Maybe my mom's right.

I deserve a great big kick in the ass for all the hell I put her through. Will my debt never be discharged?

Tuesday

Such is my screwed-up state of mind Tuesday night, when I attend Vista Valley's graduation ceremony. Though my heart is lifted by my seniors' joy on their special night, I can't shake the blues.

Traditionally, the staff gathers at Brewski's to celebrate the end of school, even though lower classmen will be with us for another day. Since R.D. never darkens the door of Brewski's, I allow Marcy to twist my arm.

"Just keep Donny Thorndyke away from me," I mutter as we pass through Brewski's main entrance.

"Ah-LEG-ra! Over here!"

Too late my brain screams, "Retreat!"

"Who's the hunk?" Marcy asks as Better Buy Trent trots over to us, a lascivious smile upon his face.

"All yours," I murmur, making the introductions.

After castigating me for not returning his call when we're obviously soul mates, Trent is placated by Marcy's promise to dance with him later. So much for devotion.

We join our colleagues in the lounge. Three long tables are pushed together. Donny and his pals sit at one end, Marcy and I at the other. As we settle in, Donny sets his beer down, points at me, and says something to his buddies who smirk and chuckle.

When our wine is delivered, Marcy lifts her glass and

whispers "Here's to Donny and his asshole friends. May they trip over their swinging dicks, crash to the floor, and scramble what's left of their tiny brains."

I grin in spite of myself and lift my glass in response. "One of your best curses ever."

We clink, then crisscross arms, and sip our wine. At last, I feel R.D.'s words lose their sting. It's so simple. He's wrong. I'm not. I vow silently to call my union rep first thing Wednesday morning.

When Trent and one of his friends track us down to make good on Marcy's promise, I beg off, claiming I have a pressing date with the ladies' room. Though my black mood has lifted, I'm not up for the traditional Brewski mating ritual.

I linger in the bathroom, checking the mirror to see if the hag-ridden creature hiding deep inside has made an appearance. When the song ends, I slip out the door and come face to face with Donny Thorndyke. Before I can react, he grabs my arm and pulls me into the alcove leading to the men's room.

I try to jerk away. "Let go of me, Donny! What the hell's the matter with you?"

His grip tightens, and he leans in until his face is inches from mine. His breath is hot and smells of bourbon.

"We need to talk." He peers at me through small, hate-filled eyes.

I will myself to be calm, to deal with Donny as I would Vlad's pursuit of my ankles. I take a deep breath and let it out. "So talk."

"I warned you, babe." He presses me back against the wall. "Who do you think R.D. needs more: a winning football coach or a ditzy do-gooder working with a bunch of retards?"

Offended on so many levels, I'm rendered speechless, my mouth opening and closing like a landlocked trout.

"Let me put it this way," he says. The corner of his mouth lifts in a jerky, humorless smile. "You're on a plan of improvement. I'm not."

I stomp hard on his foot with a spike heel. He swears and releases me. Raising his hands, he backs away. As he retreats, I advance, step for step. When he stops, I stab a finger in his chest. "Don't think you can bully me. I'm going to the union with this."

My voice, choked with fury and frustration, sounds like that of a stranger.

"About what, babe?" Donny says, examining his foot. "We never had this conversation. You're just a teacher with a bad eval who has to blame somebody. Maybe you hit on me, and I turned you down. 'A woman scorned' and all that."

"R.D. had no right to tell you about my evaluation."

"What evaluation?" Donny says with a wink.

With a two-fingered salute, he moves out of range.

"Donny!" I call loudly.

He turns to face me.

"I know your buddies spray-painted my car. Keep them the hell away from my family, or you'll be sorry."

Smirking, Donny says, "Your nuts, babe. You need a shrink."

I have nothing to lose, so I add, "Do you know anything about Sara Stepanek?"

Donny stiffens. "You mean the kid that ran away?"

"Yeah."

With a snort of disgust, he says, "Sure. Why not? Give the cops a call. Tell 'em I've got her locked in my basement."

He saunters away. I stand outside the men's restroom, hyperventilating and cursing under my breath.

I want to follow him, scream epithets, smash a fist in his face, and, when the cops haul me off to jail, rejoice knowing I'll be vindicated. But, of course, I do none of those things. Donny is a skilled liar and I, no doubt, would end up looking like a crazed female. But that doesn't mean this is over. I believe in karma. My day will come.

Chapter 16

S o, me and Arnie are thinking," Nick begins, his eyes wide and hopeful behind his glasses.

"Arnie and I," I interject.

"Whatever," he says with a dismissive wave. "Anyway, Arnie and I were thinking since today's the last day of school and we have early dismissal and . . ."

I knew what was coming.

"His essay's done, and he could drive me around to check some storage units, and it wouldn't be like skipping school if we had your permission, and I just know I'm going to find it," he says in a rush.

Images of Susan in a towering rage loom large. "Nope."

"But why? You know we won't be screwing around. Don't you trust me?" His voice is filled with righteous indignation.

"Nick," I say. "Think about it. You and Arnie are driving around during school time when suddenly a senile old man of forty runs a red light, hits you broadside, and sends you both to the hospital. My butt's on the line, not yours, my boy."

His lip curls in scorn. "That won't happen, and you know it."

"Could and might," I say. "Drop it."

With an eye roll and a snort of disgust, he looks at Arnie and shakes his head. Arnie sighs and returns to *Flowers in the Attic*. Nick slouches to his computer and continues inputting test scores.

After a breakfast meeting with Dorothy Simonson, mild-mannered school librarian by day and union rep extraordinaire on her own time, my attitude has improved. Dorothy assured me she would deal with R.D. In fact, she was so eager I believe she has an ax to grind. But, instead of dishing the dirt, she admonished, "Remember, *do not* sign that evaluation. If you do, you're agreeing with every bit of his twisted logic."

Now my main problem is keeping peace until noon when, after a quick lunch in the cafeteria, my students will be free of my daily aggravation. Most of them, behind in credits, will join me for summer school.

I dip into my bag of teacher tricks to fill the time. We play American history Jeopardy, guys against girls, a real fave with my crew. I throw out an answer: "The philosophy behind the Western expansion," and one of my bright little girls chirps, "What is Manifest Destiny?"

At 11:45, violence very nearly breaks out when Crystal, emboldened by the fact that she's not required to attend summer school, announces, "You guys are so flippin' stupid you couldn't find your peckers without a map."

I give the guys the last fifteen minutes to defend themselves provided it's done in a gentlemanly fashion. The dismissal bell rings just as Wesley crows, "If we're so flippin' stupid, how come you chicks are always making us go to dances and stuff?"

In my opinion, a fine rebuttal.

They pour from the room still arguing the fine points, though the heat has dissipated.

Without a fare-thee-well, Nick takes off with Arnie, who charges through the crowd with one enormous hand on Nick's frail shoulder. Big Bird and Woodstock on a mission.

Jimmy, usually the first to bolt, lags behind, opening and closing the rings in his binder to insert the work I returned corrected and graded. He looks up to make sure the room's empty before meandering up to my desk. Desperately in need of sustenance, my stomach growls angrily.

"Guess I'll see you in a couple of weeks," Jimmy says.

"You bet. Enjoy your time off." I sidle toward the door. Jimmy shuffles behind.

"About Sara," he says.

I stop and turn to face him. He snaps his mouth shut and looks at the floor. I wait, though I want to scream, "What?"

"I know what happened to her."

"You know where she is?" The words come out shrill and accusatory.

Jimmy flinches.

I inhale and let it out, willing myself to speak in calm, soothing voice. *My God, is it possible Jimmy knows Sara's whereabouts? After all, it was Jimmy who told me about Peggy Mooney.*

"Let's sit down, and you can tell me about it." I motion to the student desks.

Spooked by my initial reaction, Jimmy positions himself with two desks between us. "What I mean is, something bad happened to her a few years ago, and I thought maybe it has something to do with her disappearing and all. She was getting jumped into a gang and she got—she got . . ." His voice trails off, his freckled face glowing with embarrassment.

"Raped," I finish. My glimmer of hope flickers and dies.

He exhales noisily. "Yeah, that. You know about that, huh?"

I nod. "Do other people know about it? Here at school, I mean?"

His eyes roll wildly. "I ain't told nobody, Ms. Thome. Not even Sara. Honest!"

I bite back my usual response to bad grammar. "Nobody's blaming you, Jimmy. But it might be helpful to know who told you."

"A guy I work with. She used to go to his school. Sara came in one time. After she left, he told me about the—the—"

"Rape," I say. The word bounces around the silent room, harsh and ugly.

"So anyways," Jimmy says. "Ya want me to ask around? See if she's hooked up with the gang again? I miss her, ya know?"

His eyes finally meet mine, and it's like looking into a sea of raw emotion. I know the price Jimmy's paid to survive. Abuse by a stepfather, aided and abetted by his slut of a mother. Petty crimes leading to grand theft auto, followed by incarceration. But now, he's landed in a stable foster home with good, caring people. Perhaps in Sara he sees the reflection of his own life, her fragile beauty a subtle reminder of his lost childhood. Or maybe he's just a teenage boy with a crush.

"Can you ask around without getting too involved? I don't want you messing with gangsters."

He blinks hard and thrusts his chin out, arming himself for the world outside my classroom. "Don't worry about me. Nobody messes with the Jimster."

In truth, his words do little to dampen my concern. Jimmy isn't very tough. His big mouth and belligerent attitude attract bullies like metal filings to a magnet. Fortunately, he can usually talk his way out of trouble.

"Just be careful," I admonish as he heads out. He turns and gives me one of his rare smiles, his eyes squinting almost shut, his cheeks like sun-burnished apples.

"You're a case, Ms. Thome."

In a weak moment, I agreed to a mid-week karaoke performance at Mystic Meadows Retirement Home. I try to get out of it but Grandma insists, "Just a few moments of your time to give some oldsters pleasure before they pass on. That's all I ask."

Grandma Sybil's a dirty fighter. She knows how to push my guilt buttons even though my mother installed them.

Halfway through our routine, in walks Sloan. He stands, smirk firmly in place, at the rear of the ballroom. Bud, our host for the evening zeroes in on him right away. Pushing a snazzy red walker, he gives an officious blast on his bicycle horn and walks quickly toward Sloan. I continue singing "Midnight Train to Georgia." Sloan points at me.

Bud claps him on the back and grins.

I pause for a moment and glare at Sloan while Grandma and Dodie do the Pips proud, shaking their groove things in perfect rhythm. Sloan snags a folding chair, turns it around, and straddles it, never taking his eyes off mine. I suddenly feel like I'm showing too much skin in my short, black skirt, slinky off-the-shoulder top, spike heels, and big hair.

The oldsters take in our silent exchange and poke each other with bony elbows, silver heads swiveling to and fro. Never has there been such excitement at Mystic Meadows.

I decide to ignore Sloan and throw myself into the next two songs, vamping with the Pips until we have the crowd on their wobbly feet, arms in the air, swaying to the music.

Sloan hangs around for cookies and punch. I keep my distance under the guise of accepting accolades from my new groupies. He's attracted a few of his own. He's surrounded by Grandma and a cluster of sweet-faced old ladies offering him tidbits and sweetmeats. Sloan samples each offering before edging away. I see him coming, and I go in search of Bud, who's dismantling Mystic Meadows' amplification system and stowing it on an antique metal audio-visual cart.

"Can I help?"

Bud peers at me over the top of his glasses and then checks his watch. "It is getting late."

It's 7:55.

Bud fumbles in his pocket and withdraws a key festooned with a loop of red yarn. "Now listen, young lady. This key unlocks the storage room in the basement where we keep expensive equipment. It's been entrusted to me. When you get the stuff put away, return the key to apartment 310. That's me. Knock loud."

"I'm very responsible," I assure him.

Bud starts to hand me the key, but when I extend my hand, his fingers close around it.

"Really, Bud," I say. "I'll take good care of it."

But Bud's ignoring me. He looks over my head and hands the key to Sloan standing silently behind me.

"I'll just give it to your boyfriend here," Bud says. "That way, I know I'll get it back."

I should be mad at Bud, but he is, after all, from a generation that believes women to be ditzy little creatures incapable of handling keys and money. Sloan is another matter.

"Listen, Bud. This man is not my boyfriend. He follows me around for no reason. I think he has one of those tracking thingies on my car."

Bud winks at Sloan and says, "Way to go, man," before tooling over to the cookie table.

"Well, damn," I mutter, pushing the cart toward the elevator. Sloan trails behind.

"Nice outfit," he says. "Looks good from back here."

"Keep the sexist comments to yourself."

"It's always about sex with you, Al. Be nice to me. I'm your ride. The Pips have left the building."

He moves me aside and takes charge of the cart. "Man's work."

I look around for Grandma and Dodie. They have, indeed, vanished. Inside the elevator, I jab the *B* button and wait for the elevator, whose ominous grinding sound fills me with alarm. Sloan and I, the cart between us, make our silent journey to the basement. After an interminable pause, the doors grind open revealing a small foyer and double doors that Sloan, wielding Bud's precious key, quickly unlocks.

We enter a large, dimly lit room lined with rows of storage lockers. A Ping-Pong table and exercise bike sit at one end of the room, a sheet-draped gurney at the other. While Sloan stows the cart, I bounce a ping pong ball off the face of a paddle. I'm up to fifteen bounces when he steps up behind me. "Feel like a game?"

I turn to find we're standing toe to toe. Way too close. "Bud's waiting for his key."

"Bud's asleep in his recliner." Sloan takes the paddle and ball from me and sets them on the table, slides his hands around my waist, and pulls me against him. Soft lips brush my cheek. His tongue traces the outline of my lips before gliding into my mouth. He tastes and smells of sugar cookies and salted nuts. *Yum!* I respond like a starving woman dropped into a sea of chocolate and return his kiss with enthusiastic moans. His hand traces the length of my spine and dives under my mini skirt, where it creates sensations that leave me trembling and gasping for air.

I break the lip-lock and mutter, "This can't be happening."

"Al." He nuzzles the side of my neck. I shiver with anticipation. "You think too much."

He needn't have worried. My mind has, once again, gone missing. Sloan lifts me up and parks me on the ping pong table. I snake my legs around his waist and pull him in. I feel his smile against the sensitive skin beneath my ear. It feels so damn good I smile, too.

Suddenly, surprisingly, I'm airborne as Sloan whisks me into his arms and carries me to the other end of the room.

"Don't want our first time to be on a ping pong table."

He plops me down on the gurney. His words bring me down fast. First time? Do I really want to do this? And with a man I know only by his last name?

Yeah, I do.

He flips up my skirt and removes my panties in a smooth move that suggests many years of practice. Back in mindless mode, I'm busy unzipping his pants, gratified to hear the hitch in his breathing.

"Pill?" he murmurs, his breath hot against my cheek.

Desperate to feel his bare skin against mine, I hear the sound of his voice but don't comprehend the question. He grabs my hands.

"Allegra, focus," he wheezes. "Are you on the pill?"

"Damn!" I stop nibbling his lower lip and push him away. "I stopped after Michael."

"No problem."

He fishes around in a pocket, withdrawing a foil-wrapped packet. Part of me is pissed off that he arrived at Mystic Meadows thusly armed. The other part screams, *Idiot! If Sloan's little swimmers are as determined as he is, you'd better hope the dam isn't breached.*

Then, all that remains is the tactile presence of Sloan's warm body against mine, my sense of wonder as I revel in intense waves of pleasure, which were always tantalizingly out of reach with Harley the Horrible. Sloan knows exactly what to do and how to move, angling his body until the delicious friction has me panting and moaning. I'm jarred back to earth when the top of my head slams into something hard.

"Eeeeoww!" I scream, pleasure and pain mingling in a single, violent explosion. Oh, God! Will I now need to be struck in the head in order to achieve sexual satisfaction? I curse my memory of Abnormal Psych 401.

Sloan turns us sideways and gives me an affectionate noogie while our breathing returns to normal. I feel a rumble of laughter start deep in his chest. "Did you feel the earth move, Al? Look around."

Dazed, I push up on my elbow and try to get my bearings.

Like a faithful steed, the gurney has galloped across the room, coming to rest against the ping pong table. After a spate of giggling I gaze down at Sloan, who's observing me with an air of bemusement. Since denial is my best friend, I say, "Please tell me I didn't just have the best sex of my life in the basement of Mystic Meadows Retirement Home."

"The best, huh?"

"Well, maybe not the best," I hedge. No sense pumping up his already inflated ego. "It was over pretty fast."

"Easy to fix. Later." He touches my cheek with a tenderness I find surprising and pulls me back into his arms.

"We should go." Even as I speak the words, I snuggle into his chest.

"No hurry," he says. One big hand massages the back of my neck, the other works on my spine. I relax against him, lulled by waves of contentment, the rhythmic beat of his heart and gentle stroking hands. My eyes fall shut, and I drift away.

I awake to a buzzing sound, and reality bites me in the butt. *Big mistake, Allegra!* The voice in my head sounds like my mother's. *Such a romantic. You just had sex on a gurney. With a man you barely know. Who's snoring like a power tool on speed.*

I glance at my watch. It's 8:45, and we have yet to return Bud's precious key. When I try to untangle our legs, Sloan wakes with a startled cry and throws out his arms, causing me to fly off the gurney and onto the floor. Karma.

"Oh, shit!" Sloan scrambles off the gurney and picks me up. "Sorry, Al. Guess I was dreaming. You okay?"

"Just dandy," I mutter, rubbing one knee. Sloan helps me gather up my scattered garments. The postcoital glow dissipates rapidly when I push the gurney back to its starting gate and try to take the sheet stamped "Property of Mystic Meadows" home for laundering.

"Are you nuts?" he says, dragging me to the elevator.

Back upstairs, Bud takes in my disheveled appearance and flashes his snowy white dentures at Sloan in a knowing grin.

After a quiet trip home—hard to find words that pertain to our situation—I shoot from the car. Sloan looks disappointed. Whether the seconds he wants involve me or Grandma's pie is impossible to discern. Before I take three steps, the window glides down and Sloan says, "Hey Al."

I turn to face him. He says, "You're something else."

I smile and start for the house.

"Hey, Al," he says again.

"Yeah?"

"I don't like to share."

I'm too tired to get mad. "No problem," I say. "I'll stop sleeping with those other five guys."

He grins and gives me a mock salute.

As I trudge up the stairs on shaky legs, I recall Jimmy's parting comment. "You're a case, Ms. Thorne."

Right you are, Jimmy. That's me. A real case.

Chapter 17

Thursday

Nick is waiting outside my classroom door the next morning. I'm running late after hitting the snooze button once too often. Determined to put Sloan out of my mind, I attribute my deep sleep to the rigors of karaoke on a weeknight.

I hand Nick my tote bag and coffee and then unlock the door. He sets my things on the desk. "See the paper this morning?"

I reach for my coffee and shake my head. "No time."

He slides the section labeled "Local News" onto my desk. The bold print jumps out at me. "Local Woman Found Dead." I set the cup down and scan the article.

"The body of Peggy Mooney, a twenty-year employee of the Department of Social and Health Services, was discovered by police late Wednesday morning after concerned co-workers reported her missing."

The word *suicide* is conspicuously absent. But the words "car running" and "closed garage" leave no doubt as to the cause of death. The article has quotes from shocked colleagues, including her secretary, who said, "It doesn't make sense. She'd just received a promotion and was looking forward to serving in a supervisory position."

I set the paper down and stare at Nick. "Didn't seem like a candidate for suicide. She acted like the queen of the universe."

"Sara," he says. "She has a connection to Sara. Somebody wanted to shut her up."

"No. Gotta be a coincidence. Why would somebody go to that much trouble to off a mid-management civil servant? Maybe her boyfriend dumped her. Maybe her girlfriend dumped her. Maybe she didn't get to sing the solo at church. Maybe . . ."

"Maybe I'm right." Nick lifts his chin in defiance. "Call that cop you know, and see what you can find out."

As an afterthought, he adds, "Please."

Marty didn't call me after our chat at the river. Since he promised to check on Sara's disappearance, I have a perfectly legit reason to call him.

"Yeah, okay," I agree. "After we get these grades done."

Satisfied, Nick buckles down to work, and I tear into the last of the essays. I glance at the clock. "Remember we've got an appointment this afternoon with Reverend Hunt, or whoever he is."

"For sure, he's not Robinson Hunt," Nick says, without taking his eyes off the computer screen.

"I'd keep quiet about that if I were you."

Nick rolls his eyes but nods.

At 8:55, I send Nick to the office to pick up my mail.

At precisely 9:00, Dorothy and R.D. will meet to decide

my professional future. I hate the feeling of helplessness Donny's actions set into motion, and I want to make sure the meeting goes off as planned. I would check out the meeting myself but don't feel up to eye-to-eye combat with the formidable Sally.

Nick's childlike stature and innocent demeanor make him the perfect spy.

I stare at the wall clock as the minute hand edges closer to the twelve. The peripatetic second hand orbits in measured fits and starts like my discombobulated life.

Suddenly the door burst open and Sloan steps through looking smokin' hot and slightly dangerous in faded jeans, black polo shirt, suede boots, and a day's growth of whiskers. Did he even go home last night?

A little shriek of surprise bursts from my lips. "Why are you here? I'm trying to work," I huff, as if I don't want to yank him into my room, sweep the papers off my desk, and climb aboard for another thrill-packed ride.

He leans against the door frame, regarding me with a look of faint amusement. His eyes say, *I know what you're thinking, babe, and it ain't about work.* But all he says is "I came by to talk to your nephew."

"Oh." I feel my cheeks grow hot. "Why?"

"The missing kid, Sara, seems like he knows a lot about her."

I mumble an affirmative while I search my memory banks for the salient details I've neglected to share with Sloan. Nick wears his heart on his sleeve and would blab to the devil himself if he thought it will help find Sara. If Nick shares information about Hunt's stolen identity, he'll get himself in trouble for hacking into a secure site. I have to warn Nick before Sloan grills him.

I grab the newspaper and edge toward the door, uncomfortable that Sloan is blocking my escape route. "Listen, Sloan. Nick's not well. I don't want you upsetting him."

With a snort of disgust, he says, "Do I look like the type who scares little kids?"

Frankly, he does, but I hand him the paper and say, "Peggy Mooney's dead. Sara's caseworker."

He scans the article, his expression carefully neutral. "Suicide, huh?"

"Seems odd that two people with a connection to Sara are dead within a week of each other."

He hands me back the paper. "You know this woman?"

"I met her once. She couldn't get rid of me fast enough."

Sloan grins. "Big surprise"

"One of my students saw Sara with Peggy on the Friday she disappeared. When I asked her about it, she all but called me a liar."

Sloan stares at me for a long moment, his eyes cool and appraising. "Precisely how many hornets' nests have you been poking around in?"

"Not that many." I try to dart through the door.

He catches my arm. "I came to see you for another reason. Marta Stepanek, Joe's wife, somehow scraped up enough money to have him buried. The services are tomorrow at one, graveside at Mountain View. They're bringing Marta over from Pine Lodge."

My mind quickly sorts through Sloan's reasons for sharing this information. I can come to only one conclusion. "You think Sara will show up?"

He shrugs. "It's possible. You said she and Joe were tight."

159

"And if she doesn't, maybe her mom knows where she is?"

"The DEA has other interests. When we arrested her, Marta clammed up to protect Joe. Now that he's dead, she's got no reason to hold out."

Okay, so I'm wrong. Of course it isn't about a missing girl.

"Joe was smart, didn't live high on the hog," Sloan says. "Other people were involved. You don't have an operation that size without keeping records. Marta knows something."

I'm tempted to tell him about the key but decide not to. Missing girls are not a priority for the DEA. Sloan is all about drug busts and only too willing to believe Sara ran off with a boyfriend. No, I won't allow last night's intimacy to cloud my judgment.

As if testing my resolve, Sloan leans over and blows a lock of hair out of my face.

"Whatcha thinking, Al? About last night?"

"Hardly," I say with a sneer. *Damn! The man can read my mind.* I pull away. "I'll get Nick for you."

I hear Nick's raspy breathing before I spot him, motionless, halfway up the stairs, holding onto the railing.

"You've got an elevator key. Why don't you use it?"

I know why, of course. He wants to be like the other kids.

"Nah, I need the exercise," he gasps and begins to climb the stairs slowly.

I wait until his breathing stabilizes before I ask, "What's up in the office?"

"That librarian lady—you know, Ms. Simonson—she walked past Dr. Langley's secretary like she wasn't there. Then she went in his office and shut the door."

"Way to go, Dorothy," I say, pumping a fist in the air.

As we walk back to my room, I fill him in on Sloan and warn him not to mention the key or his cyberspace adventures.

We find Sloan sprawled in a student desk, munching the apple I planned to eat for a mid-morning snack. I make the introductions. Nick squares his diminutive shoulders and thrusts out a hand to be shaken. He grins up at Sloan, his look of hero worship unmistakable. "Pleased to meet you." His voice is a good octave lower than normal.

I hadn't given much thought to the void in Nick's life. With his father AWOL, Nick lives in world of women, surely a trial for a boy of sixteen. Sloan mentions breakfast, and the two of them are off like a shot.

I return to my essays only to be interrupted by Dorothy. Small in stature and soft-spoken, Dorothy is resolved to right wrongs. Anyone who underestimates her lives to regret it. A tiny dynamo, she has stylishly cut gray hair. She loves kids, books, and wine-tasting tours, not necessarily in that order. When she's amused, she belts out a hearty "ho-ho-HO," a laugh so infectious it seems to emanate from the soles of her feet. Many a staff meeting has been broken up when something has tickled Dorothy's funny bone.

Wearing a sly smile and without preamble, Dorothy says, "R.D.'s having some second thoughts about your evaluation."

I feel my stomach unclench for the first time in days. "How did you manage that?"

"Let's just say I'm privy to certain information he'd rather keep on the Q.T."

"So you blackmailed him."

"Ho-ho-HO!" Dorothy shouts, slapping my desk in glee. "Allegra, please. Doctor Langley and I are engaged in ongoing negotiations."

She wipes her eyes and rearranges her face until it looks properly sober. "You're not out of the woods yet. I'll be in touch."

She cautions me once again to sign nothing and slips out of my room to return to her precise world of books and periodicals. I wonder idly where she's hidden her cape.

Nick returns bearing foodstuffs in a grease-soaked bag. In spite of my probing questions, I learn nothing of their conversation other than the fact that he was allowed to see Sloan's gun. Furthermore, Sloan promised to teach him how to shoot. I cringe, graphic images of Mama Bear, Susan, on a rampage careening through my mind.

Greasy food and guns. What better way to ensure male bonding?

Nick and I arrive for our audience with Reverend Hunt twenty minutes early to allow plenty of snooping time. While Nick studies the brochures stacked neatly on a table in the foyer, I slip into the cavernous sanctuary. Without the sun glinting off the massive stained glass window, the room feels heavy and airless, as if it contains a malevolent presence. Not like a church at all.

Though I hate to admit my mother was right, enforced attendance at Sunday school smoothed away my rough edges and filled me with a sense of tranquility that lingered at least until Monday morning. Even as an adult, walking through the doors of a church always whisks me back to that time and space. I feel a lightness of spirit that otherwise eludes me.

But not here. Not in the Church of the Unholy Light.

Nick and I go in search of Hunt's office, wandering through a maze of corridors. We peek into Sunday school rooms filled with tiny chairs and felt boards. I have a sudden longing for cherry Kool-Aid.

The pastor's study, actually a suite of offices, is at the end of a long wing, far removed from the public areas. As I reach for the door, a woman bursts through, red-faced and breathing hard. I catch the sound of voices raised in anger as I stumble backward and land on Nick's foot. The woman's squeak of surprise, Nick's yelp of pain, and my muttered apology burst out simultaneously, adding to the confusion.

"If you're Allegra Thome, you're early," the woman blurts, firmly closing the door behind her.

"I am," I acknowledge and can't resist adding, "Is arriving early a sin in the eyes of God?"

Nick squirms in embarrassment, but my words have the desired effect. The woman winces. "I'm sorry. That was rude. It's just that today's been crazy. We need to reschedule your appointment."

"Sure," I say, starting for the door. She slides sideways and blocks me.

"Don't you want to check the calendar?" I ask.

She doesn't budge. "I'm in a bit of a hurry. I'll call you."

She stands at her post until we turn and start back down the corridor. When we round the corner, I hear her hurried footsteps behind us.

"Walk slower." I tell Nick.

"We're not leaving, huh?"

"No way."

When the woman, presumably Hunt's secretary, catches up with us, I say, "My nephew needs to use the bathroom."

Nick flushes but performs a convincing pee-pee dance. Without slowing down, the woman says, "In the Narthex, to the left of the doors."

We dawdle until the woman's out of sight, after which we reverse course and trot back to Hunt's office. We slip through the door into a reception area. A large desk sits between us and the inner office. The voices inside are muffled and seem to lack the heat marking the earlier conversation.

Nick flops down on a leather settee, and I wander over to the desk. The woman didn't take the time to shut down her computer. The cursor blinks patiently, awaiting her next keystroke. Assorted papers and memos lay in jumbled disarray across the surface of the desk. I spot the appointment calendar. As I reach for it, the door behind me opens.

Startled, I whirl to face the door and backpedal toward the sitting area. Robinson Hunt's wife, her face the color of parchment, hurries through the outer office looking neither left nor right. One hand clutches her purse; the other covers her cheek. She pauses when she reaches the door, her shoulders heaving with emotion. She takes a quick peek over her shoulder, and recognition blooms in her eyes. She lowers the hand that covers her cheek revealing the scarlet imprint of a recent blow, already purpling into an ugly bruise. Gone is the icy demeanor of last Sunday. Her gaze darts around the room like a cornered rabbit's. When finally she meets my eyes, she draws a deep, shuddering breath. After a long moment, she's gone.

Chapter 18

*L*ater, Nick would tell me I all but pawed the ground and snorted after Mrs. Hunt slipped through the door.

"Aunt Al," he says with that solemn look he gets when he's pulling my leg. "You spoke in tongues. Smoke shot out of your nostrils."

Yes, the sight of a recently beaten woman pushes all my buttons, transporting me back in time to an army base in Germany.

Filled with shame and self-loathing, I study my bloody face in the mirror and hate the fear in my eyes.

When Harley heads for the officers' club, satisfied he's corrected my errant ways, I launch into a series of actions that seems outside my consciousness. My trembling hands apply super glue to each and every fly of Harley's army issue skivvies. Moving in a robotic fashion, I go to the closet and stuff clothes and family photos into Harley's favorite backpack. I rummage through a pile of camouflage gear in Harley's footlocker and find the credit card he thinks I don't know about.

At the stroke of midnight, I slam the door on the past, trudge to the gate, and hitch a ride to the airport. Goodbye, Harley. May you rot in hell.

When I come back into real time, I'm in a half crouch, my hands in tight fists. Nick looks at me as if I might explode into a million tiny Allegra particles.

"I'm okay," I mutter, taking deep breaths.

I stand and stride to Hunt's door. I lift my hand to knock, and the door flies open revealing a tall, spare man with hunched shoulders and a bad comb-over. He stands in the open doorway and looks down at me through heavy, dark-rimmed glasses perched on his beak of a nose.

"And you are?" His voice sounds rusty, like he's suffered trauma to his vocal cords. The skin on his scalp is speckled from sun damage, giving him a reptilian look.

"Reverend Hunt's next appointment." I meet his unblinking stare with one of my own, still seething from my trip down memory lane.

He glances over his shoulder. I peek around him to see Hunt standing with his back to the door, gazing out the window.

"Just a minute," the geek says and tries to shut the door. I block it with my foot. Nick creeps up behind me.

"Maybe we better come back another time," he says.

"You can go wait in the car if you want. I'm not leaving," I say, a bit louder than necessary. Nick sighs but doesn't retreat.

After a hushed exchange, the pastor and his sidekick invite us in. Their resigned expressions clearly say, "Please, God, not another hysterical female."

I vow to be calm and focused. Now is not the time to

right domestic wrongs. We need to know about Sara, and accusing Robinson Hunt of spousal abuse will get us nowhere.

"Ms. Thome!" Reverend Hunt pulls himself together and walks toward me with both hands outstretched. "How wonderful to see you again."

After the laying on of hands, Nick and I are ushered to our chairs as Hunt braces himself on the corner of his desk and leans toward us, his face a picture of pastoral concern. His buddy plops down on a hard-back chair and drops his gangly arms between splayed knees. Behind the desk, a broken floor lamp tilts crazily toward the wall.

"Sorry to keep you waiting, my dear," Hunt says, staring intently into my eyes. "Did you meet my wife on her way out?"

When I nod, he continues with a condescending chuckle. "Poor Heather—a bit of a family crisis, I'm afraid—she slipped in the shower and struck her face on the fixture. With the women's luncheon tomorrow, she wants to look her best. Oh well, these things happen . . ."

Someone should tell Hunt the shower story's been done to death. I ignore his explanation and look at the geek. "We haven't met. I'm Allegra Thome. This is my nephew, Nick Dorsey."

Hunt springs off the desk. "Sorry. I assumed you'd met my colleague, Gordon Venable. Gordy's my business manager."

Venable stands, unfolding his gaunt frame in a series of awkward jerks, as if his movements are controlled by a puppeteer still learning his craft. "Ms. Thome," he says in his creepy voice, thankfully not offering to shake my hand.

"Mr. Venable," I reply.

I turn my attention to Hunt. "I didn't know ministers needed business managers."

He flushes and parks his butt on the corner of the desk again. "The church is involved in several business ventures that require his expertise."

"Ah, yes. The winery, What Would Jesus Drink."

"Yes, that," Hunt says as Venable snatches what looks like a computerized spreadsheet from the desk and begins poring over it.

Though it makes me uncomfortable, I let the silence build. Hunt glances at his watch and squirms. I smile pleasantly.

He gives me a grimace of a smile. "How may I be of spiritual assistance today?"

"Oh, my spirit's in fine fettle." I try to disguise my hostility with a hearty chuckle. "It's Sara Stepanek I'm concerned about. She's been missing almost two weeks. I know you were counseling her. Do you have any thoughts on her whereabouts?"

Hunt waggles his finger and scolds, "You know counseling sessions are confidential. I couldn't tell you even if I wanted to."

I shake my finger back at him. "Unless she revealed something that might put her in harm's way. Then, you're required to notify the proper authorities."

His studied expression of concern slips briefly, and I see something primal and savage flash in his eyes. "What makes you think I haven't done that?"

"So you have talked to the police?"

His eyes shift to Venable, who pauses, a bony finger marking his place, to stare at me, his eyes half hidden behind hooded lids. I curse myself for not taking the time to call Marty to see if anyone was concerned enough about Sara to report her missing.

Once again the jolly caretaker of souls, Hunt says, "I can tell you this much. Sara is a very troubled child. I did my best to offer her comfort. It's possible she may have run off with a boyfriend."

"She didn't have a boyfriend," Nick says.

Hunt gives Nick a conspiratorial wink. "Women have their secrets, son. That's what makes them so interesting." He stands and glances at his watch. "Now, if you'll excuse me, Gordy and I have a committee meeting. Sorry I couldn't help."

After assuring us he'll pray for Sara, Hunt ushers us out. We walk to the car in silence. When I pull up in front of Nick's house, he looks at me with pain-filled eyes. "We're never going to find her, are we?"

I grab his hand and squeeze. "Keep looking for that storage locker, bud. That's your job. I've got a plan."

He snatches his hand away. "You do? What?"

"Tell you tomorrow." *Maybe I'll know by then.*

I turn the car toward Paradise Point and drive to the home of Robinson Hunt. With no plan in mind, I hope my clumsy charm will prove to be the unlikely key to the Hunt family secrets.

The massive three-story house soars above its distant neighbors and is set well back from the street. I turn in to the long drive, round a curve, and stop at the massive iron gate that will swing open if only I know the code, which, of course, I don't.

Robinson Hunt has erected a veritable fortress. *Strange,* I think, *for a man of the cloth.* And why? Disgruntled elders?

Angry luncheon ladies? Or is there a more sinister reason? I rein in my overwrought flights of fancy, get out of the car, and look for a way in.

Mounted next to the keypad is an intercom. I press the button and call, "Hello? Anybody home?"

After a hiss and crackle, a woman's voice says, "Who there?"

"Flowers for Mrs. Hunt," I say, hoping her husband is a traditionalist, a batterer who follows up a beating with flowers.

After a brief pause, the heavily accented voice says, "*Sí*, yes. I open gate. You come in."

The gate slides open, and I drive through, dismayed when I glance in the rearview mirror and see it close behind me. Maybe this isn't such a good idea.

Flowers! I promised flowers. I hit the brakes and peruse the palatial grounds for signs of color. The lilacs are spent, the roses in tight bud, and the annual beds newly planted and bloomless. Uneasy, I glance over my shoulder at the gate and spot a scraggly rhododendron fighting for its place in the sun behind two tall arborvitae, its three puny pink blossoms my ticket into the mansion. Hoping I won't hasten the shrub's almost-certain death, I use my nail file to saw and hack the woody stems.

Looking like a prospective suitor with my hastily gathered bouquet hidden behind my back, I press my finger against the doorbell and listen to the chimes bong "Rock of Ages." The door flies open, and a middle-aged Hispanic woman, round and plump as a Bosc pear peers at me through dark, suspicious eyes. The small boy from church clutches the leg of her navy polyester pants and gives a gurgle of delight when he spots me. I grin back at him. I wave the flowers and step past the maid into the massive entry hall featuring two flights of stairs that I assume lead to different wings of the house. My actions result in a spate of furious Spanish I loosely translate to mean "Get the hell out!"

I lean over and speak to my only ally, hoping he's old enough to talk. "Hi, little guy. What's your name?"

"Mason," he says, holding up three fingers.

"Wow!" I enthuse. "You're only three? I thought you were at least ten."

He giggles and pats the maid's leg. "Lucita," he says.

Lucita gasps as if some sacred house rule has been violated, and begins berating the child. I recognize only the "No, no, no" part. Mason seems unperturbed.

"Where's your mommy?" I ask. "I have flowers for her."

Mason releases his death grip on the maid's trousers, puts his hand trustingly in mine, and pulls me toward the staircase. I feel a twinge of guilt at using an innocent child to achieve my ends, but then I remember why I'm here: another vulnerable youngster's strange disappearance leads straight to the door of this fortified parsonage.

Lucita springs into action and flies by us, ordering, "I check with Señora. You stay here."

We ignore her warning and climb the stairs as fast as Mason's chubby little legs can carry him. He tows me toward a closed door. Though I can't make out the words, I hear the muffled sound of female voices within.

"Mommy's room," Mason says with a proud grin.

Though I'm dying to ask if Daddy stays there, too, I thank him and pat the top of his head. He grins and scampers away.

The door's unlocked. I slip into the dimly lit room and find Heather Hunt seated at a vanity table holding an ice pack to her cheek. Lucita whirls around and flaps her hands at me like she's shooing chickens. "See what I tell you? She no listen!"

Heather stares at me through panic-filled eyes. Her face is ashen.

"It's okay, Lucita. Mrs. Hunt wants to talk to me," I say.

Lucita turns to her mistress, lifts her hands, and shrugs helplessly. I seem to affect people that way.

Heather thinks about it for a moment then nods. With one last suspicious look, Lucita vamooses.

I cross to the windows and pull open the heavy brocade draperies, revealing a sweeping view of Vista Valley. If I lived here, I'd never close the curtains.

I sit on the edge of the bed. "How long has he been knocking you around?"

She stares at me in the mirror. "You need to get out of here before my husband gets home."

"Committee meeting. Hubby and Gordy," I say.

She turns to face me, her face tight with anger. "How dare you barge into my home with your accusations? Everybody loves Rob. Get out before I call the police!"

Her words are filled with outrage, but her voice is soft, almost pleading. I understand the fractured nature of the conflict boiling within her. At the church, she let her guard down, an impulsive act as the result of rage, shame, or pain. But now, my arrival fills her with terror. To overtly acknowledge her abuse will break the code of silence that ensures her very survival.

I talk to her, keeping my tone low and soothing. I tell

her my name and that she doesn't need to say anything because I know what's happening to her. I watch her shoulders relax. She drops the ice pack to the floor, and I see the ugly evidence of her husband's brutality.

Still, she won't look at me but studies the items on the dressing table surface with a puzzled frown. She begins fiddling perfume bottles and squat jars of cosmetics, sliding them around into intricate patterns. Her fingers are long and graceful, but the nails are bitten to the quick. Faster and faster, her hands move, desperate to achieve some sort of order known only to her.

I dig around in my bag and pull out a business card. I step toward her, taking care not to enter her personal space. "Heather, please listen," I say as her hands flutter over the tabletop like frantic birds.

She turns to face me, her expression dazed and unfocused. Has she forgotten I'm in the room? Her hand closes convulsively around a bottle of Vera Wang for Women. For a moment, I think she might throw it at me or try to spray me to death. But she does neither. I hold out the card. She sets the perfume down, takes the card, and slips it into a pocket without looking at it.

"Think about your kids," I urge. "Do you want your son to think it's okay to beat up on women?"

She bites her lip and looks away.

"How old is your daughter?"

Her wary eyes slide back to mine. "Thirteen. Why?"

"I'm looking for one of my students. Her name's Sara Stepanek. She's sixteen, and your husband's been counseling her. Maybe your daughter knows her. Maybe you know her."

Her face tightens, and recognition flashes in her eyes before she turns her gaze downward. "I might have heard the name."

"Anything you'd like to tell me?"

"You need to leave. If Rob finds you here . . ."

I walk to the door and then give it one last shot. "Your daughter will be next, if it hasn't already started."

"No!"

She jumps to her feet, her hands curled into fists. "You don't understand. It's not like that. He'd never hit Brittany."

"I'm not talking about hitting."

We lock gazes, and I see awareness bloom on her face. My words hang in the air between us like a low-hanging cloud, redolent with unspoken truths. Splotches of red appear high on her cheekbones. She lifts a hand to her bruised cheek and whispers, "Brittany's not his daughter. She's mine, not his."

"Doesn't matter."

She advances toward me, her eyes wild and crazy. "Mine!" she affirms. Her voice is stronger. "Not his. Mine!"

I slip through the door and close it behind me.

I hear a shrill cry and the sound of something heavy crashing against the door. So much for Vera Wang.

Not wanting to wait around for the man of the house, I take the stairs two at a time. A frowning Lucita stands by the front door and throws it open as I careen down the last few stairs and into the cavernous foyer. I thrust the pathetic bouquet into her hands and ask how to open the gate.

She points down the curved drive and snarls, "You go! You go!"

To my relief, the gate's open, and I tool away without

incident. The bizarre encounter with Heather Hunt lingers in my mind. I've never been good at puzzles. Where other people see patterns, I see none. And now, faced with tantalizing clues to Sara's whereabouts, jumbled bits of information remain in chaos, swimming around in my cerebral soup like colorful neon tetras gamely trying to school up in a too-small tank.

At the bottom of the hill, I'm startled to see Hunt in a dark blue Mercedes convertible zipping by me toward the mansion. Must have been a short meeting. Or did Lucita call him when I showed up? Something akin to panic crashes over me as I imagine how it might have gone down if Hunt had caught me there, behind the iron gate. None of my nearest and dearest know where I am. I have no proof . . . but something in Hunt's eyes scares the hell out of me.

"Stupid, stupid!" I say out loud, gripping the steering wheel harder to stop my hands from shaking.

I glance frequently in the rearview mirror and think about Heather Hunt, alone and hurting. Trapped in her luxurious prison. A feeling of unease settles in and stays with me the rest of the night.

Chapter 19

Friday

After endless teachers' meetings and the official "turning in of the keys," I collect Nick and head for Joe Stepanek's graveside service. The inappropriately named Mountain View Cemetery has no view, situated as it is on bottom land. Not that it matters to its clientele. Massive iron gates stand open, a concession to those not planning a one-way trip. I steer the Ranger slowly down a drive that winds in graceful looping curves through the old part of the cemetery where elaborate above-ground headstones and majestic trees shelter Vista Valley's pioneers.

To the right, a long, sad line of white crosses marks the final resting place of soldiers killed in combat. Miniature American flags fly from each cross, fluttering in the gusting wind that always follows rain in our valley.

Abruptly, the lushness of the old morphs into the starkly new. Gone are the grand old markers of a time past, replaced by the flat, in-ground slabs suitable for gang mowers and other labor-saving devices. A row of trees lines the drive, spaced far enough apart for a riding mower to pass through. Progress is not always attractive.

Finding Joe Stepanek's graveside service is not difficult. From a distance, we can see the canopy covering an open grave and two short rows of white folding chairs, mostly empty. Drawing closer, I spot Sloan strolling around the hearse and pausing occasionally to peer in the windows and open doors. In honor of the occasion, he's thrown a leather bomber jacket over his tee shirt and jeans. His eyes are hidden behind a pair of mirrored sunglasses.

I pull in behind a half dozen cars parked haphazardly on the narrow drive. I've barely come to a complete stop when Nick hops out and heads for the small funeral party, hoping against hope that Sara will show up. As I walk toward Sloan, I take note of the gray van nosed in behind the hearse. Mesh-covered windows and the words "Washington State Dept. of Corrections" printed on the side tell me it's Marta Stepanek's ride.

Sloan carefully closes a door. "Thought you weren't coming."

"Looking for something?"

"Nah, I just like hearses. This one's a beauty. '98 Caddy. Leather interior, recessed crown molding, violet strobe light, stainless steel flagstaffs."

He pulls his shirttail out of his jeans and gently polishes a bit of chrome.

Startled by his enthusiasm, I say, "Wow! I had no idea."

"My family's in the business," he says then clamps his mouth shut as if he wants to take the words back.

Golly, gee. Is this Sloan cutting loose with personal information? "Oh, yeah," I say, fishing for more information.

"Sloan and Sons. I've heard of them."

"No. You haven't." True confession time is over. He grabs my arm and steers me toward the gravesite.

"Did you talk to Sara's mom?" I ask.

Sloan nods.

"And?" I prompt, wanting to shake him until his teeth rattle.

"She's an angry woman."

"That's it?"

He nods again.

"Can I talk to her?"

"Doubt it," he says, guiding me to the second row of chairs next to Nick. He moves behind me and remains standing.

"Abide With Me" blares from a boom box sitting on a rickety card table. A black-suited man—probably the funeral director—hovers nearby, finger poised and ready to pounce when the song finishes.

I'm seated directly behind a small, black-haired woman, who turns as I sit down and flashes me a look so filled with hate it feels like an electric shock. I recoil in surprise but rally quickly and give her a brief rapport-building smile. If this is Marta Stepanek, we need to bond. It doesn't work. She warns me off by narrowing her eyes before she turns to face the front.

Strike one. A swing and a miss.

I wonder if Marta can feel me studying her. Probably so, since she sits straighter in her chair. Her long, dark hair, fastened at the nape with a single rubber band, is tucked inside the white cardigan she wears over dark slacks. In a sudden, jerky move, she gathers up her hair and flips it back toward me before letting it fall down her back. Sort of a "take that, you bitch," gesture.

Low and inside. Strike two.

After sending me two messages only women understand, she reaches out with her left arm and gathers in the small, blond boy sitting next to her. He looks up at her with a sweet smile before snuggling closer, his profile a cookie cutter version of Joe Stepanek.

I feel a lump in my throat and swallow hard. Despite Marta's rigid posture, she lists slightly to the right. Her right arm is held low between the chairs and securely fastened to a correctional officer in full regalia. *Jeez,* I think, feeling bad for Marta. The least they could do is wear civilian clothes to a funeral.

The guard shifts in his seat, causing a domino effect that pulls Marta toward him. Her left arm tightens around the boy, almost pulling him off his chair. Marta turns her fierce gaze on the guard. He looks away and lifts a tobacco-stained hand, raking it through his hair in a gesture of supreme indifference. A blizzard of dandruff cascades from the man's head. In a convulsive sideways jerk, Nick narrowly avoids the fallout. I hear Sloan clear his throat and cough in an effort to disguise a chuckle of mirth.

When the music ends, an elderly man, presumably the minister provided by the funeral home, stands before us and does his best to eulogize a man he knows nothing about. From time to time, the boy glances at his mother, a puzzled frown creasing his brow. Marta remains stoic. Nick slumps in his chair. Since Sara's a no-show, he's quickly lost interest.

The painful service concludes with the internment of Joe's remains. Marta, still clinging to her son, is whisked off to the waiting van. I trail behind at a respectful distance, not wanting to interfere with their last moments together. Nick and Sloan come up behind me.

"Come on, Sloan," I say under my breath. "Make it happen. A little girl talk; that's all I want."

"Yeah, I can tell she really likes you."

"Please," I say, though it sticks in my throat.

"I'll have to pat you down, make sure you're not carrying any weapons," he says with a calculating look.

"What?" I yelp.

"Unless you want ol' Sheldon, here, to do it."

He points at the guard who stands outside the van smoking a cigarette and scratching his butt.

I shudder.

Sloan grins. "That's what I thought."

Chapter 20

*W*ho the hell are you?" Marta Stepanek snarls as I enter the van. "Another narc trying to figure out where Joe hid his stash?" With a bark of humorless laughter, she adds, "Why should I tell you anything? 'Cause you're a woman? Well, fuck that!"

She scoots away from me, her movement brought up short by an ankle hobble whose end is bolted to the frame of the van. She turns to stare out the window. Her shoulders heave as she fights for control over the emotional storm assailing her.

Marta's high cheekbones and flat intonation indicate she's at least part Native American. Hers is an institutional hatred, shaped and honed by tales of the not-so-distant past, a time before the reservation became their world and a generation was lost to drugs and alcohol.

What a relief! She doesn't hate me, per se.

Strike three narrowly avoided.

"I'm not a cop," I say quickly. "I'm Sara's teacher, and

I'm trying to find her. I hope you can help."

She turns to look at me. Unchecked, silent tears stream down her face, smoothing away the hard edges, though anger still burns in her eyes. "Damn bastards! Nobody told me nothin' until today, and it's like, 'Oh, by the way, Marta, your daughter's missing. Now, tell us all you know about Joe's drug operation.' Like I'd tell those assholes anything!"

I want to pepper her with questions. How does she feel about taking the fall for Joe? Does she know of a connection between Joe and Robinson Hunt? What about the key?

But I hold back. Sloan's interrogation gained nothing but Marta's undying hatred.

I settle on a simple question: "When was the last time you heard from Sara?" I wonder how much of the girl's painful past I should reveal.

Marta averts her eyes. "Not one word in four years. Joe, I can understand. He was on the run."

"Before she ran away, Sara was seeing her dad," I say. "For a while, we thought maybe they were together. We hoped she'd turn up for his funeral."

"If she knew about it, she'd be here," Marta says. "I carried that girl for nine months, but she's always been Joe's. But that one . . ." Her voice breaks, and she points to a car slowly pulling away, the one carrying her son back to his foster home. "He's mine. He's my baby."

The yearning in her eyes is almost too much to bear. I blink back tears and take a shaky breath.

"I haven't given up on my girl, though," she says softly, all traces of anger gone. "She'll come around someday."

In stark contrast to the soft words, her eyes are hard, like obsidian stone.

"Do you have family in the area? Someone she might have contacted?"

She looks at me with an expression of disbelief. "Are you stupid? If I had family, do you think my kids would be in foster care?"

Oops. Properly chastised, I bite my tongue and wait. Marta studies me through narrowed eyes. Since my friendly puppy dog approach hasn't worked, I try the opposite. I turn away from her and reach for the door.

Her barely audible words stop me. "Sara looks at me and sees the Indian part of herself. She can't get past it."

"Hard to take." I put my hand on the door handle.

Sheldon grinds out his cigarette. He and the driver are shifting restlessly, glancing from time to time into the windows of the van. They're ready to hit the road, and Marta knows it.

"It's not right. You know my girl better than I do," she says. Her tone is wistful.

I wrestle with my conscience. Marta deserves the truth, but I can't bring myself to cause her more pain. Already filled to the brim, she has no place to put it. As Sheldon prowls the perimeter of the van, kicking the tires, I make my decision.

The words fairly tumble from my lips as I fill Marta in on Sara's last few years, the abridged edition, emphasizing her scholastic achievement and plans to attend college. Without mentioning Sara's gang rape and subsequent abortion, I talk about Sara's recent mood swings, her involvement with Robinson Hunt, her letter to Nick, the mystery key. I ask no questions.

Marta listens without comment, her hungry gaze so

intense I feel pinned to the seat.

Sheldon jerks the passenger side door open. "Time to hit the road, Marta."

Marta has no choice, so I know the message is for me. I start to exit the van. I've learned nothing, but it doesn't matter. If my hasty oral history gave Marta a few moments of happiness, that's good enough for me.

I'd struck out. Period.

"Keep your damn shirt on," Marta yells at Sheldon. "Let the woman get out first."

"Yeah, yeah," Sheldon says with a dismissive glance over his shoulder.

When the driver opens his door, Sheldon asks him, "Wanna stop at Burger King for a bite?"

I'm halfway out when Marta plucks at my sleeve. "I like your earrings. Is that your birth sign?"

She checks the rearview mirror. The men continue to shoot the breeze as the engine roars to life. Marta stares into my eyes and then looks down at her hands resting in her lap. My gaze follows, and I see her index finger curl, inviting me back in.

"Yeah, it is," I say.

I scoot across the slippery vinyl seat to give her an up-close view of my left ear and its unremarkable earring. "Gemini, the twins," I say.

"Cool," Marta says. She leans in for a closer look and, in a breathy whisper, delivers the goods.

I slide back across the seat. "When's your birthday? I'll send you a pair."

"July," she says. "Thanks."

I hop out. Before I close the door, she says, "Tell that

big bastard to find my daughter; then we'll talk."

The heat is back in her voice. I presume Sloan is the "big bastard." I grin and assure her I will. In fact, I can hardly wait. The van pulls away, with Marta looking straight ahead. I wave at her rigid back.

I look around for Sloan and Nick. They're gone, along with my truck. The car keys are in my tote, and Sloan seized my tote after patting me down—an extremely thorough job I might add—on the off chance I harbored plans to stab the guard with my nail file and go on the lam with Marta.

I'm building up a head of steam when a window zips down on the only car left, the object of Sloan's affections, the hearse. Its driver, a beetle-browed man clad in a slate-gray chauffeur's uniform calls to me. "Sloan said he'd drop off your nephew and meet you back at the funeral home for debriefing. Hop in."

Debriefing? Fat chance! Sure, eventually I'll share Marta's revelation with Sloan, but Nick's first in line.

Back at the funeral home, the driver pulls behind the building and looks pointedly at his watch. Various and sundry folk dribble out of a private back entrance and head for their cars.

"Must be quitting time, huh?" I say in an effort to make conversation. *Damn you, Sloan!*

"Yeah. Night shift will be here soon."

"Night shift?" The very thought creeps me out.

"Viewings, body pick-ups. You know, stuff like that," he says.

Thinking to interject a bit of death humor, I say, "Well, I guess the grim reaper doesn't keep office hours. Hope he gets paid overtime."

I laugh hysterically. The man knits his hairy brows. "The grim reaper? Who's he?"

His stomach growls ferociously. Mine joins in. We lapse into uncomfortable silence.

Finally, I say, "Look, maybe you could drop me at my house."

He shakes his head. "No can do. He said to keep you here."

I draw an offended breath and swell up like a puffer fish in peril. Just then, Sloan zips into the parking lot, hops out of the Ranger and off-loads two pizza boxes. I exhale. Life's too short to be angry, and pizza sounds damn fine.

I exit the hearse. Sloan ignores me and trots around to the driver's side. The guy steps out, and the two of them confer in low voices. Sloan hands him a pizza box, and, if I'm not mistaken, money changes hands. Grinning happily, the driver wastes no time on farewells. He peels out of the parking lot in a dusty green Kia, one hand on the wheel, the other holding a giant slab of pizza.

"Let's go for a ride," Sloan says, opening the passenger door and guiding me onto the seat.

"Are you nuts? You want to go joyriding in a hearse?"

"You mean you've never had a pizza party in a hearse?"

He slides behind the steering wheel with a chortle of merriment and turns the key. I start to speak, but he holds up his hand for silence. He cocks his head to one side and listens to the big engine purr.

My jaw drops in amazement. Sloan caught in the throes of joy is a sight to behold. I've experienced the sneer, the smirk, and the teasing half grin, but for a man like Sloan, this is all-out, heel-clicking giddiness. Who am I to rain on his parade?

Ten minutes later, we're on a hilltop with a sweeping 360-degree view. Vista Valley is nestled into the rain shadow of the Cascades and ringed by gray, softly mounded foothills. Mount Adams looms to the south, Mount Rainier's snowy peak to the west. The few remaining orchards appear as lush green patches in our crazy quilt of a town, crowded out by tract housing with spotty green lawns.

The one exception is Robinson Hunt's neighborhood, Paradise Point. Verdant stands of trees shelter luxurious, multilevel homes cut into the hillside far above the common folks'. I think about Heather Hunt trapped in her expensive cage and hope all is well in her world, though I suspect it isn't.

Sloan turns the Caddy around and backs it within five feet of the cliff. Moving swiftly, he transforms the business end of the hearse into a makeshift picnic table. I keep track of his progress with surreptitious peeks over the seat back. He shakes out a pile of quilted pads and spreads them over the metal framework designed to hold the coffin in place during transport, and *voila*: Dining *alfresco!*

Because of the *ick* factor, I plan to hold out. But when he lifts the lid on the pizza box and releases the tantalizing aroma of Italian spices and herbs topped with bubbling mozzarella cheese, I all but leap out of the car and sprint to join him. He's thoughtfully included paper plates, a bottle of white wine, and plastic cups.

I've been to worse picnics. Sitting side by side in the open hatch of a hearse enjoying the view and eating pizza—veggie, topped with black olives, mushrooms, and fresh tomatoes for me; meat lovers' supreme for him—is not in my realm of experience, but the quirkiness is growing on me.

When I come up for air, I say, "You really know how treat a girl."

"Third date," he says. "Had to do something special."

"Third date? How do you figure?"

He wipes tomato sauce from my chin and raises a finger. "Number one: Joe's body at the river."

Another finger shoots up. "Number two: Karaoke night at Mystic Meadows."

He leans over and nuzzles my cheek. His breath is fragrant with pizza. "Don't tell me you've forgotten the galloping gurney."

I turn to look at him, my face hot with remembering. "Oh, yeah, that."

"Yeah, that," he repeats. "Makes this number three."

With hunger no longer my body's driving force, slumbering hormones awake with a gleeful cry and shout, *Hey, he's sitting right next to you, and he got us all riled up with that full body search. Why the hell not?*

I lick my lips and tilt my head. Sloan cups my face in his hands and stares hungrily at my mouth. He lowers his face toward mine. When our lips are inches away from touching, he murmurs, "What did Marta tell you?"

I roll my eyes, pull away, and reach for the wine bottle.

"Oh, she had a very special message for you." I repeat verbatim Marta's "big bastard" remark.

"Anything else?"

Sloan gazes intently into my eyes. Too intently. I sip

my wine and look out over the valley. A red-tailed hawk soars in the distance, scanning the earth below with its binocular vision. It's dinnertime everywhere.

"She wanted to know all about Sara. That's pretty much it."

He takes hold of my chin and turns me to face him.

"You sure about that?"

"Yes, I'm sure," I say with a snotty little huff of exasperation. "Oh, wait. She liked my earrings. I'm going to get her a pair."

I know he doesn't believe me, but, short of torture, he's not getting any more out of me.

"In that case," he says. "Consider yourself debriefed."

He sweeps the remains of our makeshift dinner into a garbage bag and tosses it into the front seat. Moving with an economy of motion, he plucks me from my perch, and I land, yelping with surprise, astride his lap. His hands slide down to clasp my buns, pulling me into full frontal contact. Unfortunately, I now face the long, long cargo area of the hearse. The abyss. My clamoring hormones note our surroundings and lapse into silent reproach.

Sloan's expression, however, is that of an astronaut climbing into a space shuttle praying for a successful launch. Totally focused on his yet-to-be-completed mission, the man is a sensual blitzkrieg, all warm, moist lips, and knowing hands. A firestorm of erotic energy. He knows what buttons to hit and how hard to press.

My perspective undergoes a radical change. Viewed through my lust-filled eyes, the back end of the hearse is now a cozy love nest. The quilted pads are down-filled comforters, the smell of pizza an aphrodisiac.

Still, a token protest is in order. "We can't do it in a hearse," I gasp.

"Why not?" says the ever practical Sloan as he unzips my pants. "It has curtains."

An hour later, we're in my Ranger and I wail, "Please tell me I didn't have sex in a hearse." I stomp on the accelerator, and Sloan's head snaps back.

He braces his legs and fastens his seat belt. "Last time, you said 'the best sex of my life,'" he says, gripping the door handle.

"Fine," I snap. "Please tell me I didn't have the second best sex of my life in a hearse."

"What the hell's the matter with you?"

"Think about it, Sloan. The last time was in the basement of a retirement home. What's wrong with us?"

"Spontaneous?" Sloan offers.

I shake my head. "Nuts. Creepy. Kinky." I shoot through an intersection as the yellow light turned to red.

"Pull over," Sloan orders. "I'll drive."

"Hell, no, it's my truck," I snarl.

Sloan's the kind of man who can't relax unless he's behind the wheel. When we returned the hearse—I'd insisted on opening the windows to blow out the smell of sex and pizza—I offered to drop him off. He dug my car keys from his pocket and headed confidently for the driver's side. I knew I'd lose a verbal wrestling match. Instead, I slipped between Sloan and my beloved truck and pulled him in for one last, lingering kiss, after which I snatched the keys from his hand.

He's still pouting. "You drive too fast," he grouses.

"You're just mad 'cause I wouldn't let you drive," I say. "What's your problem? Big, tough cop like you scared to let a girl drive?"

On that note, we part, Sloan stomping toward his car in the DEA parking lot, I heading home for a shower before sharing Marta's information with Nick.

Chapter 21

In Wakanda?" Nick shakes his head in disbelief. "All this time I've been looking in Vista Valley. No wonder I couldn't find it."

"Number forty-two, Wahconda" was Marta's hastily whispered message.

"Makes sense," I tell Nick. "Marta's Native American. Wakanda's on the rez."

Nick's eyes sparkle. He's ready to roll.

"We should probably wait until morning," I say in a halfhearted effort to head him off. Wakanda after dark is not the place for a white woman and her even paler nephew. But, with Joe Stepanek's funeral and Sara's fate weighing heavily on my mind, I'm also eager to discover the contents of the storage locker.

Susan is out, so I make Nick leave her a note. Wisely, he omits any mention of Wakanda and writes, "I'm with Aunt Allegra."

I'm curious about Susan's absence. "Your mom got

a date?"

"Nah, she had to go to Seattle."

"You want to stay with us tonight?"

"Oh, she'll be back later." His smirk is a carbon copy of Sloan's, and it makes me just as apprehensive.

"What's the big secret?"

"It's a surprise."

"Will I like it?"

"Dunno." He climbs into the Ranger and zips his lip.

At the edge of town, we head for an interchange that leads through a gap in the long, sloping ridge that separates the northern border of the reservation from the town of Vista Valley.

The lower valley is an olio of ethnicities that seemingly coexist peacefully on the reservation. Agribusiness—and its white owners—flourish on fertile Indian land that's been sold or leased. The hefty demand for day laborers has brought in Mexican farm workers who migrated to the valley and stayed on with their families. In the summer, roadside stands laden with fresh produce from Filipino and Japanese truck gardens attract our yuppie neighbors from west of the Cascades, locally known as "Seattle people."

Nick remains silent as I merge onto the highway known as Blood Alley. Dotted with white crosses, the route is infamous for fiery crashes involving Native Americans who refuse to wear seat belts. Their act of defiance, though deadly, is perfectly legal on their reservation, deemed a sovereign nation by our federal government.

It's fully dark when we turn off the highway at Wahconda's only stoplight and onto a main street lined with small, grubby markets catering to its mixed population. Equal opportunity vendors plaster their windows with weekly specials, featuring low-low prices on beer and *cerveza*.

I drive through the entire heart of the town, a distance of four blocks. Traffic moves slowly in Wauconda, most of it heading toward the highway in search of a livelier place to spend Friday night.

After a couple of wrong turns, we find the storage building, a shabby structure on the east edge of town. Several blocks of darkness separate it from its nearest neighbor. I pull up and kill the engine but leave the headlights on. A single bulb on the front of the building casts a sickly pool of yellow light.

Neither of us makes a move to get out as we check out the dimly lit facility consisting of two long buildings facing each other, the far end secured by a high concrete wall. Directly in front of us, the only attempt at security is a chain stretched across the opening, each end permanently affixed to metal posts and fastened in the middle with a combination lock. We can't drive in, but scouting out number forty-two will not be a problem.

"Looks like we're in luck. No bright lights, no CCTV," Nick says. He puts his hand on the door handle.

My skin crawls with apprehension. The place gives me the heebie-jeebies. "Wait." I start the engine. "Whatever's in there will wait until morning."

Nick gives me a look of supreme adolescent disgust. "I'm not scared. Stay here if you want."

He jumps out of the truck and slips under the chain. Caught between the headlights and the darkness that lies beyond, he looks like a frail soldier marching stoically into the unknown.

I kill the headlights, grab a flashlight, and catch up with him.

"In and out fast. Okay, bud?"

"Yeah, yeah."

The weather is still unsettled. A partial moon emerges from behind scudding clouds and bathes us in an eerie light. Gusting wind swirls through the long drive, picking up dust, dead leaves, and the detritus from dozens of fast-food meals. When the moon disappears, I feel the hair on the back of my neck stand up. Nick grabs the flashlight and checks the numbers scrawled in black marking pen over storage units that seem to march endlessly into the inky darkness.

Adding to my anxiety, we find number forty-two at the end of the line, flush against the concrete wall. As far away from my truck as possible. While I peek over my shoulder for shape-shifters lurking in the dark, Nick whistles through his teeth and digs the key from his pocket. Squatting, he works the key into the metal handle at the bottom of the roll-up door.

When it clicks into place, he looks at me and grins. "Yes!"

Vivid images of *Silence of the Lambs* and the grisly contents of a similar storage unit flash through my mind. I bend over to help Nick haul the door upward, my eyes squeezed shut. When I open them, I see only the sad remnants of Joe Stepanek's ruined life illuminated in the glow of the rapidly dimming flashlight. A dusty Big Wheel sits in one corner next to a baby swing and rusty gas barbeque.

"Oh," I sigh. The word, tinged with sadness, lingers in the gloom like a whispered prayer. The mundane nature of the items tugs at my heart. Joe had plans for the future.

Backyard barbeques. Another baby?

I remind myself that Joe, the drug dealer, is dead, his wife is behind bars, one child is unaccounted for, and the other is in foster care.

"Come on! Before the flashlight conks out." Nick's whisper is urgent.

I grab his sleeve. "Wait!" I take the flashlight and sweep its beam across the floor. Joe-sized boot prints are visible on the dusty floor. They lead to the half dozen cardboard boxes stacked against the wall.

"Joe must have been here not long ago. Don't step in the prints." An atavistic fear sweeps through me, probably imprinted in my DNA by some ancient ancestor shuffling along on all fours. Perhaps my recent experience hearsewise—lust in the presence of death—has left me open to the transient nature of life. Nick makes an exasperated sound but carefully avoids the footprints.

"Start with the bottom," I say. "Anything important will be hidden in the bottom box."

Nick ignores me, grabs the top box, and sets it on the floor. The box is crammed with old sweaters, unmated socks and musty-smelling bed linens, some of which are tossed aside as Nick scrabbles through the contents. With the top layer removed, Nick extends an arm deep into the box.

"Something's hidden at the bottom!" His voice shoots up a full octave. "Something hard. Gimme the light."

Before I can respond, he grabs the flashlight, its murky beam now stuttering in final death throes. With a cry of triumph, Nick pounces, withdraws a small wooden box, and hands it to me. He roots around some more and pulls out a file folder crammed with papers. Just then the flashlight peters out, and we're plunged into darkness. We step to the open doorway to examine the goods in the anemic light. The wooden box is a tiny cedar chest, its lid held in place by a metal hasp fastened with a tiny gold padlock.

"Oh, great," I say. "This time we have a lock but no key."

"Let's check out the rest of the boxes."

Feeling like we're on borrowed time, we ignore the footprints and drag each box to the light for a quick look. We find nothing but old clothes, rusty tools, and what looks like meth-cooking equipment. A sudden gust of wind rattles the door. I yip in alarm and pluck at Nick's sleeve. "Time to hit the road, big boy."

On the ride back, Nick snags a screwdriver from the glove box and tries to pry the box open. "We'll get it later," I say. "What's in the file folder?"

Nick withdraws a handful of papers and holds them to the window, trying to catch a glimmer of light as we speed down Blood Alley. "Marriage license, birth certificates . . . stuff like that. Oh, wait. Looks like he photocopied a page from some newspaper."

"Where from?"

"The Daily Bulletin. Ontario, California? Know where that is?"

"Yeah, close to L.A."

"Dated eight years ago."

He squints in the dim light. "Here's something. An article about three guys being released from prison in Chino. Sex offenders who refused treatment and are likely to re-offend. Pictures, too."

"Read me their names." Anticipation curls in the pit of my stomach. Is it possible the missing puzzle pieces are right here in the cab of my cherry red Ford Ranger?

"Clyde Snell," Nick reads. "Tyrone Dalrymple and Roy Harris."

"Check out Roy Harris's picture. See if he looks like anybody you know," I tell him. Roy Harris, Robinson Hunt. Maybe . . .

"Yeah, right," Nick says. "Like I'd know this guy."

"Just do it, okay?"

When he speaks again, his voice is apologetic. "He looks familiar. Do you think—"

"Later."

I stomp on the accelerator. I need light. Bright light. I need to put some distance between myself and the dark-shrouded remnants of a family torn asunder. I need to get off this ghost-ridden highway.

We're in Nick's family room examining our booty. Nick places the wooden box on the coffee table and works on the last stubborn hinge screw. Susan has not yet made an appearance. I study the newspaper article. "I'm sure it's him. Roy Harris is Robinson Hunt."

Nick looks over my shoulder. Roy Harris stares at the camera. His lips, curled in a sullen *fuck you* expression, reveal a crooked front tooth.

"His hair's darker, but that's easy to change," I say. "Picture him with blond hair and a thinner face. Fix his teeth, dress him in a snowy white robe, and you've got Pastor Rob. I'd bet money on it."

Nick nods slowly. "Yeah, could be. So that means . . ."

Silence falls while we think of all the juicy possibilities. I speak first. "It means Joe knew about Hunt's past. Maybe they served time together."

"Easy enough to find out," Nick says. "Ask Sloan."

I'm suddenly bombarded with images of Sloan. Sloan with his busy, knowing hands and tongue. I feel a rush of heat flood my cheeks. Nick gives me a curious look. "You guys seeing each other? You and Sloan?"

"No!" I bark. "And I'd rather keep Sloan out of it. As far as he's concerned, the case is closed."

"Okay, I'll hack into the California Department of Corrections. No problem."

The flush of erotic memories turn into a blush of shame. My refusal to involve Sloan will force my nephew into further criminal activity. "I could go visit Marta, now that we're buds," I offer. "She'll tell me."

"Nah, I can do it tonight. Don't worry. I won't get caught."

I hear the sound of a tiny screw hitting the coffee table.

"Got it!" Nick crows. He wrenches off the lid and dumps the meager contents of the box onto the coffee table. While Nick sorts bits of paper, I flip through faded Polaroid snapshots of a younger, buffer Joe leaning against a pickup truck. Joe holding a baby. Sara? Joe, grinning at the camera with a kid under each arm. No pictures of Marta. It's as if she never existed.

I look up to see Nick fingering a small envelope wrapped around a thin, square object.

"Looks like a—"

"Floppy disk," Nick says with a triumphant grin. "Don't get your hopes up. Could be demagnetized. Depends on how long it's been stored."

I look over his shoulder as he slides the disk into his computer. After a few keystrokes, we see a spreadsheet with four columns. Three are easy to understand: date, name and dollar amount. The fourth column contains only initials: M.H.C.

I feel a surge of excitement. "Gotta be Joe's drug sales. The initials should be easy to figure out. 'M' probably stands for meth . . . or maybe marijuana. Sloan would kill for this."

I scan the list and spot the names of several prominent Vista Valley citizens. "Joe was a busy boy."

"According to the newspaper article," Nick says, "Harris was released from prison April of 1998. Do we know when Robinson Hunt showed up in Vista Valley?"

"Grandma said three or four years ago."

"Okay," Nick says. "That would be around the time the Stepaneks got busted. But where does Harris fit in?"

Then it hits me. If Robinson Hunt, the charismatic saver of lost souls and crony to the rich and powerful of Vista Valley, is really Roy Harris, sex offender, Sloan isn't the only one who'd kill to get his mitts on the stuff we've found. I grab Nick's shoulder. "Give me the disk!"

Startled, Nick says, "Jeez, what's your problem?"

"Just do it." I find the newspaper clipping about Roy Harris, wrap it around the disk, and shove it under the couch. Something catches my eye in the jumble of papers.

"What's this?" I pluck an official looking document

from the pile.

Nick carefully unfolds another birth certificate, this one done in pink parchment paper. The name "Clementine" and a birth date of October 1, 1991 appear in the center. A Cabbage Patch logo decorates the bottom. I remember the dirty-faced doll in Sara's depressing bedroom.

I gasp, Nick gapes, and together we exclaim, "Clementine!"

Nick jumps up. "That's what she was trying to tell me in her letter. We gotta get that doll."

I retrieve the stash from under the couch and return it to the wooden box. We double wrap everything in two plastic grocery bags and stash them under the frozen peas in Susan's chest freezer. Tomorrow, I'll have Dodie lock them in the safe. I offer to stay until Susan returns, but Nick won't hear of it. I wait outside until he sets the alarm.

When I pull into my driveway, I'm rummy with fatigue. It has been a full day, what with teachers' meetings, Joe Stepanek's funeral, my interview with Marta, hearse-related activities, and a spooky visit to Wahconda.

Probably why I didn't have my guard up.

Chapter 22

Grandma Sybil's detached garage is vintage 1930s and set well back from the street. No remote control. Just two wooden doors secured in the middle by a padlock, requiring the driver—in this case a slow-footed and soporific driver—to exit the vehicle, unlock the lock, and open the doors.

Though our porch light burns and a light still shines in Noe's upstairs window, the garage is deep in the shadows. I leave the headlights on and trudge to the garage, key in hand. The rattle of a garbage can in the alley tells me Vlad is out and about. No longer a member of the dating pool, he often prowls the neighborhood looking for garbage cans with lids ajar. One swipe of his paw and Vlad will settle in for an all-you-can-eat buffet.

The men wait to jump me until after I pull the Ranger into the garage.

Later, I will look back and view my memories of that night like some horrifying PowerPoint presentation.

Allegra, closing the garage door, dreaming of bed. A silent foot-fall from behind. A dark looming figure. A split second of paralyzing fear before her arms are pinioned, her mouth covered with a brutally strong hand.

My aborted screams and flailing limbs have little effect on my attacker, who drags me toward the alley. I hear the sound of an idling engine and another man's hoarse whisper. "Get her in the car."

"No!" I yell from behind the gloved hand, my muffled voice little more than a squeak.

I kick hard, land a blow, and hear the man grunt with pain. Then he adjusts his hand so it not only covers my mouth but pinches my nose shut. Panicky and desperate for air, I bite at his gloved hand while my heart tries to hammer its way out of my chest. A car door opens. Sky rockets burst in my dimming vision. I redouble my efforts, even though my strength is fading fast. Trapped in the car, I'll be SOL. Maybe even DOA.

I decide to play dead, thinking I can lull them into complacency and then spring back to life and escape before they can load me in the car. Granted, I'm not thinking too straight since my brain is deprived of oxygen. But then I hear a sound that, even years later, will bring tears of gratitude to my eyes.

With a hideous *yowl*, Vlad lands on the back of my assailant's neck, fifteen pounds of enraged tomcat, an orange fury with razor-sharp teeth, unsheathed claws, and an overwhelming desire to inflict pain.

Grandma will say later that *I* am Vlad's own personal victim and, like Sloan, he doesn't like to share.

"What the fuck?" the man shouts, releasing me to swat

at the furry demon clinging to his head like a giant coon-skin hat.

Air—wonderful, glorious, life-giving air—fills my lungs, and I scream for Noe, Grandma, Dodie, and quite possibly Sloan while I run from the alley. I hear the sound of running feet and a squeal of tires. Noe, shotgun in hand, is first on the scene, followed by Grandma in her nightgown and slippers. A few seconds later, Dodie appears, clutching a pearl handled revolver and a butcher knife.

The next two hours are a kaleidoscope of images and words that bounce off my shocked and insensate mind, insignificant compared to my joy at being alive. When the police arrive—I've requested Marty if available—Grandma thanks Noe and ushers us into the house. Earl Gray tea and warm chocolate chip cookies on a china plate follow in short order. I'm shaking so hard I have to hold the mug with two hands.

Marty and his partner question me gently. "Can you describe your assailants?"

"It was dark. One was stocky and strong, about my height. The other guy looked tall and thin."

"Did you see their faces?"

I shake my head, not wanting to go there. "The guy grabbed me from behind. The other man was in the shadows. When they ran, they, they . . ."

The image flashes through my mind. Two dark figures running toward a car. Vlad flying through the air, hitting the side of the garage with a hiss and growl. "Ski masks," I say. "Their faces were covered with dark ski masks."

"What about the car?"

"Big and boxy. Maybe an SUV. A dark color, black

or maybe dark green. It happened so fast. All I could think about was getting away . . ." My voice breaks, and Grandma moves behind me. She wraps her arms around my shoulders and puts her soft cheek next to mine. Her gentle touch puts me over the edge, and I draw a shuddering breath.

She whispers, "My sweet, sweet girl. Thank God you're all right."

I pat her face and feel her tears. "Good old Vlad," I say. "First thing tomorrow morning I'll buy him a case of tuna. The good stuff. Albacore."

Grandma giggles, her good nature restored. She swoops down and picks up Vlad, who's popped through his cat door seemingly no worse for wear. She hurries off to find him a special treat. Dodie has vanished with her arsenal of weapons, clearly disappointed she wasn't able to use them.

"Any idea who might have done this, Allegra?" Marty asks.

I avoid his eyes and shake my head. My list of suspects is short. Though Donny is capable of vandalizing my car, I don't think he'd resort to kidnapping.

I know my attack is connected to Sara's disappearance. While Marty looks at me expectantly, I tick off the reasons in my mind. The Hewitts and their sudden influx of cash. Sara's letter. My stolen sticky notes. Robinson Hunt's phony identity and possible criminal past. The trail of bodies: Joe Stepanek. Peggy Mooney. Was I to be the third?

And yesterday, I poked hard at Hunt's hornet's nest. Did his wife tell him of my visit? In our search for Sara, we've found information people are willing to kill for. I look at Marty, open my mouth, and then slam it shut. I have no proof, just suspicions. He'll think I'm a nut job.

Marty and his partner exchange glances but wait while I muse. Finally, Marty tells his partner. "How about checking the alley for tire marks?"

When we're alone, Marty says, "What is it, Al? Tell me."

I swallow hard. "I've been meaning to call you. What did you find out about Sara Stepanek?"

Marty's demeanor changes. Shifting in his chair, he gazes into his tea. When he looks up at me, his expression is carefully neutral. "Case closed," he says.

Sloan's words. Words that unleash a firestorm of fury deep within me. When I speak, my voice is tight, controlled. "What exactly does that mean, Marty?"

He flushes. "Take it easy, Al. I'm way down in the pecking order."

"Who did you talk to?"

"You know about chain of command, right?"

I think about Donny Thorndyke and R.D. "Yeah, I know how that goes."

Marty glances at the door then back at me. "This is between you and me. Got it?"

I nod, afraid to speak lest he change his mind.

"I checked to see if the girl had been reported missing. Nope. So I ask the lieutenant if he's heard about a kid who went missing a few weeks back." Marty leans forward and lowers his voice. "Here's the weird part. He said, 'Oh, yeah, the Stepanek girl. Forget about it. That's the word from above.'"

"Just another throwaway kid," I say, bitterness creeping into my voice. "What's so weird about that?"

"But, Al," Marty says. "How did he know who I was talking about? I never said her name."

I sip my tea and think about his words. "So someone is stonewalling. Any idea who?"

But Marty is all done talking. He stands and gathers up notebook and pen. We walk to the front door. I thank him and pull an imaginary zipper across my lips, make a tiny locking motion, and toss the invisible key over my shoulder. I'm looking for a big Marty smile. All I get is a grim "See ya."

I go to the kitchen and kiss Grandma good night and then climb the stairs, toying with the idea of calling Sloan. My weak, girly part cries, *Do it. Maybe he'll come over, wrap his big strong arms around you, and make everything okay.* But my other persona, the one whose blood and bones are constructed of powerful DNA from generations of women like Sybil and Dodie, shouts, *Suck it up, you wuss,* so I resist.

Good decision, as it turns out, since my answering machine has a message from Sloan.

"Hey. Gotta go to D.C. Just found out. Be good. I'll dust you for prints when I get back. Ha."

I assume he tacked on the single 'ha" to let me know he's trying to be funny. So Sloan is gone. Not that I care. At least that's what I tell myself when I brush my teeth and examine myself in the mirror. I fully expect to see a wild shock of prematurely gray hair and a face frozen in horror like Edvard Munch's *The Scream*. I'm dismayed to see I look none the worse for my ordeal. I slip into my Tweety Bird jammies and hit the sack.

Saturday

I awake late the next morning. Anticipating nightmares the night before, I went over every possible horror-filled scenario in my head before sleep bore me away. The mind games have worked, and I awake demon-free, refreshed and with a ravenous appetite. The only dream I remember makes me smile: Clad in a chauffeur's cap and nothing else, I scampered through Mountain View Cemetery, dodging tombstones while Sloan pursued me with a fingerprinting kit.

Before I throw the covers off, I make a mental to-do list. First, a run with my new best buddy, Vlad. Second, shower, shampoo, and a stack of Grandma's blueberry pancakes. Third, a talk with Nick to see if he's figured out how to retrieve Sara's Cabbage Patch Doll. But "the best-laid plans," as they say . . .

I run a brush through my hair, slip into my jogging duds, throw open the door, and scream. There on my threshold, hand upraised to knock, stands my ex-husband, Harley the Horrible. Now I know why my sleep was untroubled. The real nightmare is standing right in front of me.

"Oh, shit!" I yell and try to slam the door. It bounces off his foot.

"Aw, come on, Allegra," Harley says behind the door. "Just give me a few minutes. No harm, no foul."

My affinity for sports analogies is the only thing I retain from our marriage.

"Maybe not for you," I hiss through the crack in the door. One hand drifts to my face, and I finger the scar left by his West Point ring. "Hold up your right hand," I order.

He puts his right hand through the crack.

"Take that damn ring off, and you can come in."

I watch through the crack as he puts the ring in his pocket. I know it makes no sense. If Harley wants to hurt me, he can do so with his fists. But stripping away the symbol that proclaims Harley to be an officer and a gentleman unveils his true identity: that of a wife-beating bully. Buoyed by this small victory, I open the door.

A worried looking Susan stands next to Harley. At least she has the good grace not to yell, "Surprise!"

"So that's why you went to Seattle," I say. "To pick up Harley."

"Yeah, well, remember I said he wanted to see you," she says, a trifle defensively. Then she sighs. "I know, I know. I should have called you first. But he asked me not to. After all, he is my brother."

Before I allow Harley into my apartment, I look for backup. Grandma Sybil and Aunt Dodie stand side by side at the bottom of the stairs. The high-beam intensity of their glares causes Harley to glance nervously over his shoulder.

"We're right here if you need us, sweetie," Grandma says. "Leave the door open."

Susan says, "I'll wait downstairs."

I step aside to let Harley in.

"Nice," he murmurs, looking around. "Susan said you're doing well."

While Harley checks out my apartment, I check out Harley. Lean and fit. Where once he was bulky and soft around the middle, he now sports washboard abs and a healthy glow. The buzz cut is gone. His light brown hair is long enough to part and comb to one side. Harley remodeled. Because I can't peek inside his soul, I assume the changes are cosmetic.

He makes a move toward the kitchen table. "All right if I sit down?"

"You won't be here that long. What do you want, Harley?"

He shifts a little and clears his throat. "Would you please look at me?"

When I meet his gaze, his eyes are soft, almost pleading. "I've quit drinking."

He pulls a folded paper from his pocket. I watch, astounded, as he unfolds it and reads, "Step Eight: Make a list of all the people I've harmed and become willing to make amends to them. Step Nine: Make direct amends to such people whenever possible."

He pauses and gives me a significant look. "That's where you come in."

"I'm part of your twelve-step program?"

"Yeah," he says with a sickly grin. "This is me making amends."

I rub my scar. "How do you propose to do that?"

I've thrown him a curve. Worry lines appear in his smooth, tan forehead, and his eyes dart across the page as he peruses his notes. The words "I'm sorry" have never been a part of Harley's vocabulary. When he looks up at me, I see flashes of the old Harley. "Dammit, Allegra, why are you making this so hard?"

I point at the door. "I think you've got some more work to do. See ya, Harley."

He looks like a kid whose brand-new skateboard was stolen the day after Christmas. I almost feel sorry for him. Almost.

"I really want to cross you off my list."

I give him a mock salute. "As they say in the army, tough titties."

He flushes and heads for the door.

"Harley," I say when he reaches the door. "Go ahead and cross me off your list. I crossed you off mine a long time ago."

He turns to look at me. I see the sadness in his eyes and feel ashamed.

"It doesn't work that way, Allegra."

I hear Harley descend the stairs, Susan questioning him, his muffled reply, the front door opening and closing. I think about my mean-spirited words. Words I've waited a long time to say. They haven't made me feel better.

I remember Susan's gentle remonstration. "If I'm not mistaken, you married Harley to please your mother."

Chagrined, I realize there's a distinct possibility I have some work of my own to do.

Two hours later, I've accomplished the first two items on my list. Feeling righteous after a forty-five minute run and replete with blueberry pancakes, I ponder my options for the third. I don't want to call Nick for fear Harley will answer.

I needn't have worried. The phone rings just before noon.

Before I can answer, Nick says, "I got it! I got the doll."

"How did you manage that?"

"I told Patsy my Boy Scout troop was having a toy drive and could I please have Sara's doll."

"Where are you now?"

"Home."

"Is your mom there?" I ask.

"Oh," he says with thinly disguised amusement. "You mean, is Uncle Harley here?"

I make a disgusted noise.

"They're visiting friends. Won't be home 'til later."

"I'll be right over."

Chapter 23

*N*ick and I rendezvous in the family room, and I fill him in on last night's aborted kidnap attempt.

"So you didn't see their faces?"

"No, but the guy who grabbed me seemed about my height. I only saw the tall guy for a second when he was running for the car. He ran funny, you know, flopping around like a scarecrow, and his voice sounded weird. It had an edge to it like . . ."

I force my mind back to that dark, scary place. The odd tonality. The awkward hitch in his get along. "Like a rusty gate," I finish.

I think about the jerky, ungainly mannerisms of Robinson Hunt's financial manager. Last night I was so terrified my mind slammed shut. "Gordon Venable. He sounded like Gordon Venable!"

Nick's eyes widen in surprise.

"Oh, my God!" I clap a hand over my mouth.

Nick's face drains of color. "If it was Venable, it

probably means they've got Sara."

"Maybe not," I say. "Maybe we have something they want. First, they break into my house. They find my sticky notes so they know about the key, our suspicions about the Hewitts and Peggy Mooney, and that we have Sara's note-book. And if Robinson Hunt really is Roy Harris—"

"He is," Nick says, his thin chest rising and falling in his effort to breathe. "I checked last night, and Joe Stepanek served time at Chino for selling drugs. His sentence over-lapped with Roy Harris'."

"So Joe knew Roy Harris in prison," I say. "Joe came back to Vista Valley and recognized Hunt, knew he wasn't who he said he was. Now Joe is dead."

I grab Nick's hand and squeeze it. "This may not be about Sara at all."

Nick looks grim. "There's more," he says. "I ran the Hewitts' name and got a hit in the archives of the *Vista Valley Tribune*. Three years ago, a foster child died in their care. A twelve-year-old boy."

"The year before I came back to Vista Valley. How did he die?"

"Head injuries. The Hewitts said he fell off the top bunk."

"Was there an investigation?"

"Yeah, sort of. The first article said the Hewitts heard a thump around midnight and found the kid dead on the floor the next morning. Two days later, a different story came out. Patsy and Dwight gave an interview, and guess who their spokesman was?" Without waiting for my re-sponse, Nick says, "Their family minister, Robinson Hunt."

I catch my breath. "How did their story change?"

"Hunt said the kid had night terrors. The Hewitts

heard a noise but thought he was having another nightmare. When it got quiet, they assumed he went back to sleep."

"Very handily giving them a good reason for not checking on the boy sooner."

"Yeah, and that's not all. Hunt said the kid was troubled and that he was working with the family. Counseling them."

My sense of dread deepens. "Troubled," I murmur. The same word he used to describe Sara. "I don't get it. What would Hunt have to gain by helping the Hewitts?"

He shrugs. "Dunno. But the same article said a lawyer had been retained for the family. Peter Ford."

I throw up my hands. "So the Hewitts, who don't have a penny to their name, have the support of a charismatic minister and a high-powered lawyer. Anything more?"

"Just one. The police cleared the Hewitts. Social and Health Services said they would continue to place foster children with the Hewitts."

"Peggy Mooney?" I ask.

"You got it."

"Damn!" I yell. Information swirls through my overloaded brain. Too many unconnected facts crackle and snap like crossed wires. The inside of my head is probably filled with blue-black smoke and noxious fumes. I can almost smell them.

Nick gives me a quizzical look. "You okay?"

"I can't think straight." I take a deep breath and blow it out. "Let's see what's inside Clementine."

The doll is as grubby as I remember. Her stringy blond hair has faded to the color of dirty straw, her little pink dress threadbare and worn. The doll's slovenly appearance is in stark contrast to the trademark Cabbage Patch moon face with its dimpled apple cheeks, innocent close-set eyes, and lips curled upward in an expression of perpetual joy.

I peek under her dress and spy a Onesie, that all-purpose garment babies wear instead of an undershirt. I press gently on Clementine's tummy and hear a crinkling sound.

"Paper?"

"Sounds like it," Nick says.

Feeling like a voyeur, I unsnap the Onesie, pull it up and discover Cabbage Patch dolls have belly buttons. Who knew?

But Clementine's belly button is unique. It's bisected by a crooked, crudely fashioned seam. Someone cut a three-inch slit in the fabric, overlapped the raw edges, and fastened it with snaps. I unsnap it quickly, reach inside the slit, and pull out a sheet of paper folded into fourths.

Nick leans close as I carefully smooth it out. It's written in purple ink and says:

> If anyone needs to know,
> my life is written between the lines.
>   Sara

Beneath the signature is the freehand drawing of a soaring bird, not unlike the one tattooed on Joe's chest. But this bird is rendered in elaborate detail, a glammed-up seagull complete with flaring tail feathers, curlicued wings, curved beak, fluttering eyelashes, and grasping claws.

"Oh, this is a big help," I say, blowing out an irritated breath.

"Hold it," Nick says, grabbing the paper from my hand. He holds it up to the lamp and studies it.

"Okay," he says. "There's an *S*. Look at the tail feathers."

He's right. A stylized *S* adorns the gull's fanny. I keep quiet and let Nick do his thing. He grabs a pencil and begins to write as the letters appear to him.

S-T-E-N-O-G-R-A-P-H-Y.

Nick dashes over to his computer. After a few key strokes, he says, "Stenography is the art of writing hidden messages in a manner that no one but the recipient can interpret. The message may be hidden in pictures, covered in wax or written with invisible ink."

"Huh," I say, still not seeing a connection.

I look at Clementine lying forgotten on the table, clothes in disarray, her chubby baby arms and legs splayed open and vulnerable. When I pick her up and reach under her dress to grab the end of Onesie and pull it down, I see something strange. Something is written on Clementine's back. Apparently I made a sound, because Nick grabs the doll out of my hands. He studies the words for a moment and then gives a yip of excitement.

"*Best Loved Poems.* That's what it says. *Best Loved Poems!*"

I stare at the words and try to wrap my brain around the concept.

Nick gives me a pitying glance. "You don't get it, huh?"

"Get what?"

"She copied the poems out of your grandmother's book. Right?"

I nod.

"I'll bet she's written her diary between the lines of the poems. In invisible ink."

"That's a bit of a reach."

He turns back to the computer. "It says here you can make invisible ink out of milk, diluted honey, vinegar, cola . . ."

I flash back to the bottle of cola under Sara's bed. I still think Nick's gone off on a wild tangent, so I don't mention it.

Allegra the smart-ass doubter says, "What do you write with? An invisible pen?"

He shoots me a disgusted look. "Of course not."

He looks at the screen. "Toothpicks, fountain pen, finger dipped in the liquid, feather quill . . ."

"Feathers!" I exclaim loudly. "Sara had a bouquet of feathers in her room and a bottle of cola under the bed."

"Why didn't you tell me?" Nick demands.

"I didn't think it was important."

My stomach feels queasy. I glance out the window, suddenly aware of every passing vehicle. Venable and his cronies must know where Nick lives. Whether they're after Sara's diary or Joe's information is beyond me, but I know we need a safe place for Nick to work.

Nick is studying Sara's message. The back of his neck is exposed. Pale, thin. Easy to snap. I shudder at the image. "We can't stay here."

Surprisingly, he agrees. "Maybe we should call Sloan."

"Gone to D.C." I think for a moment. "Sara's notebook is locked in the safe at Doc Myers' office. Nobody around on a Saturday . . . perfect place for you to work. I'll call Dodie."

"Call me when you're done, and I'll come back and set the alarm," Dodie says. "And, you, Ms. Nosy!" She shakes a finger in my face. "Don't touch the medical equipment. Remember the time you dismantled an examination room? Believe me, Dr. Myers does."

"*Moi?*" I put on an injured face. "How *muy absurdo*!

Besides, I was only nine at the time."

Dodie rolls her eyes and leaves.

Nick sits at a table in the employees' lounge, Sara's notebook in front of him. He's found out heat is required to activate the hidden messages. Susan's iron, set on low, is plugged in next to the table. I stand behind him and watch.

He gives me an irritated look. "I can't concentrate with you breathing on me. Go find something to do."

So, really, it's Nick's fault I stumble into the room that holds patient files. The file room has bright fluorescent lighting and a gaily colored filing system that intrigues me. Warm colors dominate the top shelf: reds, oranges, and yellows. Cool shades of blues and greens are assigned to the bottom shelf.

I'm in the yellow section. Since I find no mention of jaundice, I deduce the color scheme has nothing to do with diagnoses. My medical history is a real snoozer: childhood vaccinations, broken left arm when I fell off my bike, annual checkups, and a broken big toe when I worked for Grandpa Mort one summer and dropped a battery on my foot.

I replace my file and look for something juicier. In my own defense, I only scan the medical records of people I don't like. What I discover reinforces my belief in karma. My second-grade teacher, Mrs. Moats, who tied me to my desk with a jump rope, suffers from shingles. Makes sense. All that meanness had to go somewhere when she retired and quit tormenting little kids. And Sandra Boyle, the girl who stole my boyfriend in tenth grade? Ha! Genital warts!

"What are you doing?"

I shriek and drop a folder. Several loose papers flutter across the floor. Nick stands in the doorway, his face a mask of disapproval.

"Just checking my medical information. Patients' rights and all that."

Before I can pick it up, Nick snags an errant file folder. "Yeah, if your name's Donald A. Thorndyke."

"Guess I grabbed the wrong one. Thome, Thorndyke. Right next to each other."

I gather up the loose papers and take a quick peek on my way to the shelves. What I see stops me cold. The results of a CT scan. I stuff the folder back in the yellow section.

Nick is trying to be casual, but his face-splitting grin gives him away. "I was right! Sara's diary is written between the lines of poetry."

I put Donny and his medical problems on the back burner. "Yes!" I boogie across the file room and give Nick a high five.

I flip out the light and follow Nick back into the lounge. The room smells of scorched paper. He opens Sara's notebook to "Shall I Compare Thee to a Summer's Day?" I squint to read the message scrawled in messy, light brown script between the lines of the sonnet, the words activated by heat from the iron.

Feb. 15. Counseling with Pastor Rob. Asked me if I missed Dad. I cried. He hugged me. Said I could tell him anything. Don't want him to think I'm bad.

It still doesn't make sense to me. "Why go to all that trouble? The notebook was hidden by the furnace. It was written in invisible ink, for God's sake. Why would she think anyone would need to read it?"

Nick shakes his head. "She must have sensed something wasn't right. Guess we'll find out when we read her diary, huh?"

He's pale and trembling. It's as if he can't bear to know the truth.

"You okay?" I ask.

"I'm fine." He draws a deep, raspy breath and says, "It figures, you know? Sara loves puzzles. She and her dad used to write in code."

"It must have taken her forever to write her entries."

"Naw, she probably got pretty good at it. And she didn't write that much," Nick said.

A sharp pain shoots through my temples indicating one of two things: extreme information overload, or bad karma as a result of my snooping. I massage my temples. "How long will it take you to decipher her entries?"

"Activate," he corrects. "I'll work on it now." He reaches for the iron.

Big question marks bang around in my skull, the kind you see in the funny papers right before the lightbulb comes on. Unable to process as I usually do, by running my motormouth, I grab a pencil and make a list.

What was Joe Stepanek's connection to Roy Harris?

When did Roy Harris become Robinson Hunt?

How did Gordon Venable get involved with Roy Harris?

Who was Joe Stepanek's supplier?

I set my list aside and go in search of a phone book.

I find Gordon Venable's ad in the yellow pages under *accountants.* Venable Business Service, Gordon Venable, CPA. Good ol' Gordy offers financial management, full bookkeeping services, income tax returns, payroll, and business planning. Could it be his work for the church is pro bono? But Susan told me Venable manages the WWJD winery as well. Venable has his long, bony fingers in a lot of pies.

I've just checked my list again when the long-awaited lightbulb pops up in my head. It's a big one, maybe even a floodlight.

"Marta," I say with absolute certainty. "I need to talk to Marta."

Chapter 24

*a*fter a burst of static and a series of clicks, a recorded message informs me the call is from the Pine Lodge Correctional Center. Will I accept a collect call from— after a brief pause—"Marta." As she says her name, Marta's voice is flat, almost as devoid of emotion as the mechanical one preceding it.

"Yes, yes," bursts from my lips before she's done speaking.

Two hours have passed since my first attempt to contact Marta. After discovering my cell phone was dead, I dashed home and sent Dodie back to stay with Nick, who was still deeply engrossed in reading Sara's diary.

In my naïveté, I thought I could dial up Pine Lodge, ask for Marta, and have a friendly little chat. A surly matron told me prisoners could only call out, that it had to be a collect call and the time limit was strictly enforced.

Though Marta and I made a fleeting connection in the van, the memory of her hate-filled eyes lingers in my mind. To ensure a return call, I told the matron I had information about Marta's daughter. Okay, so I *need* information.

"Hi, Marta," I chirp.

"You found Sara?" Marta asks.

Her question hangs in the air between us, and I feel a twinge of remorse.

"Not exactly," I hedge. "That's why I'm calling. We found the storage locker and some information about Joe's drug business."

Marta gives a disgusted snort. "Joe didn't tell me nothing about that."

"That's not why I called," I tell her. "But I've got some questions I think you can help me with."

"Joe didn't tell me nothing," she repeats. "Said it was better that way. That big dude tell you to call me? You taping this?" Her voice is strident with anger and betrayal. I'm losing her.

"No, no," I assure her. "Look, Marta, I think we're getting close to finding Sara. Her disappearance could be connected to Joe's death. I think she's in danger. I need your help. Please."

The urgency in my tone results in a palpable silence that stretches between us like a shimmering filament, taut yet fragile, easily shattered by word or nuance. I zip my lip and hold my breath.

Finally, Marta sighs, a whispery sound that conveys a lifetime of broken dreams. "Okay, but like I said before, I don't know nothing."

Giddy with relief and oxygen deprivation, I exhale loudly. "You might know more than you think."

I reach for my list of questions.

For a woman who claims to know "nothing," Marta's

memory is undiminished by time. The words pour out in staccato bursts like pent-up birds seeking an open window. As she speaks, I grab a piece of paper and scribble notes.

Joe and Marta lived in California, "bumming around" as Marta put it. Joe was heavily involved in a biker gang and doing a lot of stuff he shouldn't. Like meth labs. During a bust, Joe's buddies left him to take the fall. Because of previous run-ins with the law, he was sentenced to hard time.

"Chino," I murmur.

"Yeah, Chino." She spits out the word as if it has a bad taste.

Alone with five-year-old Sara, Marta had two choices. Hook up with another biker or return to the reservation. She chose the latter and thumbed her way back home. She and Sara were taken in by a thrice-removed "aunty," and slept on the floor of a flimsy HUD-built house already bursting at the seams with extended family. Marta tried to figure out a way to feed her daughter. Her options were few. When a cousin offered to hook her up with "the Man" for some easy money, she jumped at the chance.

"The Man?" I ask.

"God, you don't know anything, do you?" Marta is clearly irritated with my interruption.

Chastened, I murmur, "Sorry."

"The Man, the Big Guy, B.G. That's what we called him," she says. "He ran things back then. Maybe he still does. Anyway, he didn't bother with the rez. Not a big enough return. That's where we came in. I made enough to get my own place."

"And that's how Joe ended up here after he got out?"

"Yeah, he wanted to put some space between him and

the gang. You know, make a fresh start."

Yeah, I think, *make a fresh start by jumping into the drug business with both feet.* "What year was that?"

"It was '97. Joey was born in '98. Joe was doing real good by then, and we bought a place west of Vista Valley. Out in the sticks. Joe liked it out there."

I check my watch. Only five minutes left. I broach the subject of Roy Harris.

"Oh, that guy!" Marta says with a bark of laughter. "Joe knew him at Chino. Called him 'Slick.' Said he could make people believe all kinds of shit. He told a guard he could read his mind. Spooked the guy so much they had to move him to a different unit."

"Did he come to Vista Valley after he got out?"

"He was going to," Marta says. "But he said he got a better gig."

"Know what it was?"

"Yeah, he turned into a fake preacher. Said it was a sweet deal and that people couldn't wait to stuff the collection plate with money. Some scam he had going, huh? A creep like that pretending to be religious."

"Do you know if he changed his name?"

"Might have. Joe never told me."

"Before you—you know—went away, did Harris ever come to Vista Valley?"

The silence grows as Marta mulls it over. Finally, she says, "Yeah, I think he did. I remember Joe laughing about it. I think he sold him some stuff."

"What about the drug guy, B.G.? Did he ever come to the house?"

A huff of disapproval from Marta. "Course not. Joe

didn't want him around the kids."

"I don't suppose you know his name."

"Joe slipped once and called him Jordy or Gary or Gordy, something like that."

I suck in my breath. The second hand on my watch is racing toward the finish line. "Joe ever say what he looked like?"

"No," Marta says. "But he called him the geek."

Bingo. Gordon Venable is the Man. B.G. The Big Guy.

"Why you asking about him? What's he got to do with my girl?"

Marta sounds peevish.

Torn between providing information and not causing Marta further pain, I share my suspicions about Roy Harris-slash-Robinson Hunt and his connection to Gordon Venable. In my highly edited version, I make no mention of Hunt's penchant for young female flesh, saying only that Sara underwent a religious conversion. Though I believe otherwise, I tell Marta that Sara could be receiving some sort of counseling, that she may be a willing participant.

I should have saved my breath.

"Bullshit!" Marta screams into the phone. "You know what Roy Harris was in for?"

She doesn't wait for my answer. "He's a God damn perv! That's why Joe hated his guts. If he's got my girl . . ." Her voice breaks, and she begins to keen, a sound so raw, so filled with primitive pain I feel her bleakness and sorrow pour into my soul.

"Wait! Marta," I shriek. "Please listen . . ."

I hear an ominous click. In the silence that follows, I can still hear the eerie sound of Marta's cry. Maybe I'll hear it forever. I pound my fist against my desk.

I made Marta cry. Tough little Marta with the "fuck you" attitude and the "don't mess with me" stare.

Nice going, Allegra. Hope it was worth it.

I'm still pacing and stewing two hours later when I hear the front door open and the tantalizing smell of deep-fried food wafts up the stairway and into my apartment. Dodie has returned with Nick. My stomach growls ferociously, reminding me that the blueberry pancakes are long gone.

Hmmm. French fries or onion rings? I can always count on Nick for junk food. CF kids have trouble keeping weight on, hence the high-fat diet. I trot happily toward the door. The ringing of the phone stops me in my tracks. I holler down the stairs, "Save some for me," and go to the phone.

"Allegra? It's Michael."

What the hell? First Harley and now Michael. Did the powers that be slip in a new holiday without my noticing? A Call Your Ex Day?

"We need to talk," Michael says.

"Go ahead."

"Look, Allegra. There's stuff going on you don't understand."

"Like how you had a sudden urge to take my family out to dinner and our place gets tossed while we're gone? You're right. I don't understand. So why don't you tell me?"

I wait for him to deny it. Silence hangs in the air between us like acrid smoke.

Finally, he sighs. "The kid you're looking for?"

"Sara."

"Yeah, Sara. You're making a lot of people upset with your accusations. Important people."

"What accusations?" I yell and hear him wince. "I haven't accused anybody of anything. I just want to know why nobody's looking for her!" My voice has shot up an octave. I half expect to hear wineglasses exploding in the cupboard.

"I gotta go, Al," Michael says. His voice is tinged with an emotion I can't identify. Regret? Sadness? "Just promise me one thing," he adds. "If you hear something bad about me, don't believe it."

Before he clicks off, I think I hear a soft "love ya."

I don't know what shocks me more, Michael uttering the *l* word or his bewildering message. I hang up the phone and head downstairs. A large serving from the grease group will help me focus. Rather than trying to stuff my brain with facts that make no sense, I stuff my face with onion rings.

Nick wipes his face with a napkin and noisily sucks in air, his lungs wheezing with the effort. His face has a bluish cast, a sure sign he isn't getting enough oxygen.

"You okay?" I ask.

"I read Sara's diary."

His pallor alarms me, but I know I need to hear him out.

"I screwed up, Aunt Allegra."

His chest rises and falls rapidly with the effort of breathing. "She thought we'd have the notebook *and* the doll. If I'd only remembered about the doll . . ." He doubles over, caught up in a spasm of coughing.

When he's able to breathe again, he reaches into his

backpack and pulls out a wad of papers. "I made copies for you. The original is locked in the safe. Get rid of them when you're finished."

He slumps back in his chair, his face pinched with exhaustion.

Dodie picks up her purse. "Let's go, Nick. I'll run you home."

Her tone is casual, but I see the concern on her face. I start to get up to go with them, but she waves me away. "Stay put. I'll visit with Susan a while." Flashing me a wicked grin, she asks, "Any messages for Harley?"

I bare my teeth. "Yeah, I can think of several."

This gets a weak smile out of Nick. "Any I can repeat?" he asks.

"Just one," I say. "Tell him I'll think about what he said."

Chapter 25

*R*eading Sara's diary is painful. I feel like a voyeur gobbling up words not meant to be shared. The entries clearly show that Sara's guilt and confusion began when she started counseling with Robinson Hunt. The casual cruelty of Hunt's seduction turns my stomach.

March 2. Told Pastor Rob about the gang initiation. Not the other thing, though. We prayed. Said God would forgive me.

God would forgive her? I curse out loud and think about how neatly Hunt made Sara believe she was responsible for the rape, thus giving him the power to grant absolution. I assume from her words she hadn't yet told him about the abortion.

I quickly scan some entries that make no mention of Hunt. Typical teenage stuff: school activities, ongoing frustration with Patsy and Dwight, her affection for Nick. Around the first of April the tone grows darker and Nick has suddenly morphed into Woodstock. I thumb through the pages looking for the first mention of magpies and find one dated the first week in April. Tuesday, the day before her weekly appointment with Hunt.

Library today. Research. Magpies eat other birds' eggs. Even kill babies. Am I a magpie?

The next week Sara unburdened herself to Robinson Hunt.

April 13. Told Rob I did bad thing. Asked him if he thought abortion was murder. He said yes but I could be cleansed. Let him know when I'm ready.

The black seed of suspicion sown earlier has lain dormant in my subconscious for days. Now, illuminated by the word "cleansed," the seed sprouts, sends out roots, and grows into a full-blown theory so tangled and noxious I can hardly bear to let it linger in my mind. Even before I find the entry, I know what it will say. I know how Sara will be cleansed.

May 4. Rob said I had to atone for the life I'd taken. That God will forgive me if I have another baby.

Even though I've been expecting them, the words are written with such innocence and trust that they take my breath away. Just for a second. Then a burning fury grips me, and I reach for the phone.

Who ya going to call, Allegra? says a mocking voice inside my head. *The cops? And tell them what? That the minister of a church thinks abortion is murder? Not exactly a revolutionary idea in Vista Valley. That he believes Sara needs to have a baby to achieve redemption?* In truth, her words lend credence to the theory that she's run off with a boyfriend. What better way to get pregnant?

What about Robinson Hunt-slash-Roy Harris? The cops already think I'm a bleeding heart whacko trying to make them look for a kid who doesn't want to be found. Marty is a great guy, but I can't ask him to challenge his superiors.

I know in my heart Robinson has Sara. I want to call him up, threaten him with bodily harm, and demand her whereabouts. But instead, I sip Diet Pepsi and keep on reading.

Joe entered the picture in May. Down and out and living rough in a makeshift shelter by the river, Joe got around on a bicycle. Joe and Sara wrote each other notes and left them under a rock in the alley behind the Hewitts' garage. They met at the public library in the evening, often walking the streets as they talked. Sara was clearly torn between love for her father and her desire to get right with God.

May 9. Dad saw big billboard of Pastor Rob. Asked me questions about Rob. Why?

I know that billboard. It features a giant-sized Robinson Hunt wearing his clerical gown and smiling his smarmy smile, along with the words "I am the light of the world."

No attribution follows the quote. Without book, chapter, and verse, it appears Robinson Hunt, not Jesus, is the light of the world. Probably not an accident.

Sara was clearly curious about her dad's reaction to the billboard. From her entries, I'm convinced Sara was unaware of her dad's history with Robinson Hunt. Reading between the lines proves to be more informative.

Joe was a quick study. By the middle of May, he told Sara he had something in the works, a big score. He'd be able to buy a car. They could be a family again. He knew where Joey was. They'd drive to the lower valley and pick up him up when he walked home from school. Head for Canada. Make a new start.

The pieces of the puzzle are coming together in my mind.

Joe was destitute. He had nothing, not even a roof over his head. But he did have proof Hunt was a pedophile.

By contrast, Robinson Hunt was at the top of his game. A wealthy congregation. A flourishing winery.

Joe Stepanek knew his secret and had the power to take it all away.

I tried to get my head around it. Joe had been on the run for four years. Could he have blackmailed Hunt without putting himself in jeopardy? I could only assume he tried and paid with his life.

The last two weeks in May must have been excruciating for Sara. Caught in a power struggle she knew nothing about, she tried to make sense of a senseless situation. She wanted to be with her dad but not at the expense of losing her soul. In her altered state of mind, she believed bringing another child into the world was her road to salvation. Plans were made. It would happen this summer.

When her dad pressed for an answer, she stalled for time. Joe must have been going crazy. His was a desperate gamble. Until Hunt paid him off, Joe didn't have the resources to take Sara and leave, and he surely knew of Hunt-slash-Harris' obsession with his daughter.

Sara, ever more confused, had become an unwitting pawn in a dangerous game. At the end of May, she wrote:

Told Rob Dad wants me to go away with him. Rob begged me to wait a little longer. Dad told me to stay away from Rob. Don't know what's right anymore.

Assuming Sara didn't know about Joe's effort to extort money from Hunt—and nothing in her diary indicated she did—her words must have created even more anxiety for Hunt. Did he want Sara so badly he'd fork over the money? Was it then he decided Joe had to die? Or had he moved up the timeline, fearful that Sara would take off with Joe before he could do the dirty deed?

The last entry was a Thursday the day before Sara disappeared.

June 1. Dad said it had to be next week. But I can't. He gave me a key to the shed, said hide it. Tried to call Rob. Not home. Don't know what to do.

I shuffle papers and sigh. That's all she wrote. From her diary, I know Sara is screwed up, maybe even brainwashed, thanks to her trusted minister, Robinson Hunt. Hard to believe a so-called man of God could be so evil.

But then I think about pedophile priests. Teachers screwing sixth-grade boys. Doctors, lawyers, rabbis and even policeman cruising online for prepubescent girls and boys to meet and abuse. Maybe it isn't such a reach after all.

I also know the man responsible for her misguided beliefs has a stolen identity, is a convicted sex offender, and was desperate to get his hands on Sara. The presence of Joe Stepanek is not as easily explained. His appearance in Vista Valley, reconnection with his daughter, and apparent blackmail scheme will remain as mysterious as his death, unless Sara can be found.

Another thought has been circling in my brain. Sara may have gone with Hunt willingly and could be, at this very moment, screwing his brains out. But why, then, the letter to Nick and the phone call to me? She wanted us to find her Bible, the key to the storage locker, the doll, and the diary. If she'd gone willingly, she would have done everything possible to conceal her whereabouts rather than leaving a trail of clues.

Thanks to Marta, I know Gordon Venable has been a big player in Vista Valley's thriving drug industry, maybe still is. He and Hunt seem joined at the hip. Who holds the upper hand?

And what about Michael? I sweep up the papers and go downstairs to burn them. Then, by God, I'll make some phone calls. I might even call Sloan.

Nick is first on my list. We compare notes and make a date to drive to the WWJD Winery tomorrow afternoon.

Michael is next. From the sound of masculine voices and the clinking of glasses, I assume he's at the club. I waste no time on pleasantries.

"What makes you think I'll hear something bad about you, Michael?"

"I can't talk now. I'm with a bunch of guys."

"Why don't you step outside?"

"It's not a good time, Allegra."

His tone is angry, designed to make me scurry back into my corner like a good little girl.

"Play golf with Robinson Hunt today?" I ask. "You guys talk about Sara? About how you told your ex-girlfriend to back off? Why, Michael? What's in it for you? If you know where Sara is, you'd better tell me. Because I'm not backing off. No way!"

I hear Michael breathing into the phone then the scrape of a chair, the sound of footsteps, a door opening and closing. "It's complicated," he says. "There's stuff I can't tell you, but I don't know where Sara is. I swear it."

"If the stuff you can't tell me has to do with Hunt, you'd better be careful."

Michael's breathing accelerates. "Exactly what I was trying to tell earlier."

"Maybe we should get together and share information."

"I can't do that. Sorry."

He really does sound sorry. But then, Michael is skilled at sounding sincere. As we click off, I wonder what Hunt is holding over him. Sex? Drugs? I try to remember the seven deadly sins but give up after gluttony.

I dig out Sloan's cell number. Because he's out of town, I can pick his brain from afar without the risk of being banished to the sidelines. I'll dangle the name Gordon Venable-slash-B.G. in front of his nose and hope he'll snap at the bait. I'm on the verge of hanging up when, after eight rings, he answers.

"It's Allegra. Can you hear me?" I shout into the phone.

"Al? Can't hear you . . ." comes the reply.

"Where are you?" I scream.

"Colom—"

"You're in Colombia? The country of Colombia or the District of Columbia?" After I utter them, I realized how idiotic my words are.

"Country," he says.

I throw out Gordon Venable's name and my suspicions about Robinson Hunt. When I finish, I hear nothing but dead air. He's cut out completely and probably not heard a word I said.

"Sloan? Are you there?"

After an ear-splitting crackle, I hear. "Call you later."

Another dead end. I pace the floor, but it doesn't help. I need to talk to a real live person, and who is more alive than Grandma Sybil as evidenced by her unwavering devotion to the betterment of mankind? I've just started down the stairs when the phone rings.

"Ms. Thorne?" a booming, baritone voice asks. "It's Jack Cheeseman."

My heart stops beating, my mouth falls open, and the phone drops to the floor. Jack Cheeseman, assistant superintendent of the Vista Valley school district, is known by district employees as Monterey Jack. Hiring and firing are his forte. Especially firing. A call from Monterey Jack on a Saturday is not good.

I scramble for the phone. As I hold it to my ear, I see myself in the mirror. My face is ashen, my eyes wide and staring. "Sorry, Mr. Cheeseman. I dropped the phone."

"No problem. Call me Monty."

Why is he being nice to me? Is this his perverted way of putting me at ease before he gives me the ax? Should I stall for time and call Dorothy? Questions nibble at the edges of my mind like moths in a sweater drawer. I try to pull myself together. "What can I do for you, Mr. Cheeseman?"

"Monty," he corrects gently.

"Monty," I repeat like a dutiful child.

"Ms. Thorne," he says. I brace myself. "Relax, this isn't about you."

Giddy with relief, my knees give way, and I sink to the floor.

"It's about Coach Thorndyke. We need to talk."

Chapter 26

*a*fter a brief pause, I squeak, "Donny?"

"Mmm hmm," my new friend, Monty says. "It's come to my attention that, at some point in the past few weeks you made an effort to speak to Principal Langley regarding, shall we say, certain suspicions you harbor regarding Coach Thorndyke. Is that correct?"

(Yes, he really talks like that.)

My mind is swimming with confusion. How had Jack Cheeseman found out about my conversation with R.D. about Donny?

I swallow hard. "May I ask why you want to know?"

"No, you may not. But rest assured any forthcoming information will be held in the strictest of confidence. Furthermore, if Coach Thorndyke has acted inappropriately toward young female students, I think you'll agree he should not be in the teaching ranks."

Part of me feels vindicated. Monterey Jack is calling *me* to get the lowdown on Donny when my own principal blew me off like a pesky mosquito. All I have to do is say the word and Donny is history.

I can't do it.

"Mr. Cheeseman, uh, I mean Monty," I begin. "It's true I talked to R.D., but I need to speak to Donny before this goes any further. Can I call you back?"

Monty mulls over my request, his thought process punctuated by a series of exasperated *hmm*s and *harrumph*s. When he finally speaks, his tone has no trace of congeniality. "Fine. Call me ASAP."

As soon as he clicks off, I paw through the desk drawer for the school directory and dial Dorothy Simonson. I fill her in and ask that age-old question: "Am I in trouble?"

"You? Oh, my dear, it's not you who's in trouble," she replies.

"Donny?"

"I can't say too much, Allegra, but you know I hear things," Dorothy says. "If Donny's in trouble, it's only because of his association with R.D."

"R.D.'s in trouble?"

"You didn't hear it from me, but it's possible our nattily attired leader may have a lot more time to shop." She punctuates her comment with a single, "Oh, HO!"

"So where does that leave me? What about my evaluation?"

"At this point, probably not worth the paper it's written on. Don't worry. I'm on it."

Much comforted by Dorothy's words, I begin the tedious task of tracking down Donny Thorndyke. It's Saturday night. Donny could be at any number of watering holes. I call his home and get his answering machine. I even call

Brewski's. No Donny. I'm pondering my next move when I hear Grandma Sybil calling from the bottom of the stairs, "Allegra! It's spaghetti night. Come and get it!"

My meeting with Donny will have to wait until morning. Concluding that a hung-over Donny will be easier to deal with than a drunken Donny, I join Grandma for dinner.

Sunday

Sunday morning I stand on the front stoop of Donny's duplex, one hand lifted to knock, the other clutching a 20-ounce cup of black coffee purchased at Sid's Gas 'n' Grub. As I approach Donny's front door, my quivering nostrils detect the malodorous scent of stale beer and cigarettes. Donny's red Firebird sits in the driveway. I fervently hope his buddy Kelvin hasn't spent the night. "One sociopath at a time" is my motto.

My timorous knock gets no response, so I double up my fist and pound. No way I'm leaving until I talk to Donny. I've just kicked the door in disgust when I see the drapes twitch and a bloodshot eye checking me out through the narrow crack.

"Come on, Donny," I yell. "Open up!"

The door flies open, and I recoil as the fetid air pours out. Donny stands in boxer shorts and nothing else. I can't see his back but suspect his hackles are raised.

"What the hell are you doing here?" he snarls.

"Are you alone?" I ask, feeling like an operative in a spy movie.

"Yeah, why?"

Though every fiber of my being resists, I push past him into the depressing living room littered with empty beer bottles and old newspapers. I brush the crumbs off a saggy sofa and sit down. "I got a call from Monterey Jack."

Donny slams the door, kicks an empty beer bottle across the room, and explodes into a spate of curse words, the prominent theme being "that God damn Langley!" Had I not known Donny's secret, I would have cowered in fear. Instead, I wait calmly for the storm to subside.

Fury spent, he collapses into a chair opposite me. I hand him the coffee. He takes it in both hands and lifts it shakily to his mouth. "So what did you tell him? That I had the hots for little girls?"

I shake my head. "What's going on with R.D.? I thought the two of you were buddies."

He slurps noisily and scratches his chest. "R.D.'s about to get canned. Did you know that?"

Remembering Dorothy's caution, I gasp and say, "No way."

Donny nods. "All those conferences he goes to? He's been padding his expense account. You can fuck up a lot in administration, but you'd better not fuck with the money."

I can't argue with his logic. "So what's the deal with you?"

"When the shit hit the fan for R.D., he came to me. Threatened me. Said if I didn't help him, I'd be sorry."

"But what could you do?"

"He said people would listen to me. That I should draft a letter in his support and have everybody sign it."

"And you refused?"

"Are you nuts? Of course I refused. I don't want to get

tarred and feathered along with R.D."

"Oh," I say in a small voice. "So he's using what I said to get you fired, too."

He sets the coffee down on the floor and drops his head in his hands, his thumbs massaging his temples.

I clear my throat. Swallow hard. When the words come out, they sound forced through cotton batting. "Donny. I know about the brain tumor."

He lowers his hands and stares at me.

Like most people, I assumed Donny's bizarre behavior and partying were the result of his wife kicking him to the curb. But with a peanut-sized tumor growing in his frontal lobe . . .

My words come out in a rush. "It's a long story, but let's just say I had the opportunity to check my medical chart and accidentally grabbed yours along with mine. I saw the results of the CT scan."

He gives a shuddering sigh. "Who else knows?"

"Nobody. I swear."

"It's been a rough year," he says, staring at his feet.

"Do they know downtown?"

"Nobody knows."

"Are you getting treatment?"

He grimaces. "Surgery. Next week. Then radiation."

Sensing that pity will make things worse, I let my outrage show. "So what do you plan to do, tough guy? Soldier through on your own?"

He gives me a weak smile and shrugs.

"You have to tell them. If you don't, I will. You're sick, Donny. Partying and hanging out with thugs like Kelvin Koenig doesn't help. You're not just fighting for your job; you're fighting for your life. You need support from people who care about you."

I snap my mouth shut and wait. He runs a hand down his bristly cheek and finally meets my gaze. "I never touched any of those girls. I want you to know that. Yeah, I enjoy looking. Who doesn't? I haven't been feeling so good about myself lately."

"I have to call Cheeseman back," I say. "Here's what I'm going to tell him: 'Disregard any comments by R.D. Langley. Coach Thorndyke has a medical problem you need to be aware of. He'll be calling you later today to talk to you about it.' End of story. Got it?"

His face goes through a series of painful tics, and I realize he's trying to hold back tears. Finally, he nods.

I rise from the disgusting sofa and shake a finger at him. "Make sure you do. I'll be checking. And while you're at it, talk to your family."

He follows me to the door. "I need to tell you something, kid."

He swipes at his eyes and says, "I didn't tell him to, but it was Kelvin who spray painted your car. Sorry about that."

"Yeah, well Kelvin's a creep. But at least I got a new paint job out of it."

Before we part, Donny doubles up a fist and offers it to me. "Friends?"

After a brief moment of confusion, I bump his fist with mine. "Yeah, friends."

At noon on Sunday, we embark en masse on our short journey to the WWJD Winery. Grandma Sybil, Dodie, Susan,

Nick, and I.

Things quickly got out of hand last night when I unburdened myself to Grandma. No way would she miss out on a chance to check out the bizarrely named winery she believed was funded by her departed friend, Ruth Willard. Dodie, always up for wine tasting, decided to join us, and Susan is along to keep an eye on Nick.

To accommodate the size of our group, Grandma took the Olds out of mothballs.

Dodie rides shotgun. Susan, Nick, and I share the roomy back seat. Our pleasant Sunday drive ends abruptly when Grandma hits the on-ramp to the freeway. She stomps on the accelerator to beat an oncoming eighteen-wheeler, causing our heads to whip back and forth as if we're a bunch of crazed bobble head dolls.

I rub the back of my neck and try to stay calm. "Grandma, you might want to slow down a little."

She turns to give me an admonishing look as she whips around a lowrider, a Ford Explorer, and what looks like an unmarked state patrol car.

I scream, "Keep your eyes on the road. You just passed a cop."

She pulls into the right lane and eases up on the gas until the needle holds steady at seventy-five. I hear the bones in my neck crack as I turn to look out the back window, fully expecting to see flashing lights.

"Before you so rudely interrupted me," Grandma begins, "I was about to tell you most accidents happen because people merge onto the freeway too slowly. Did you know that, Allegra? Surely you remember it from drivers education."

"Which obviously you never had," I grouse. "And it doesn't mean you stomp on the gas so hard you give your passengers whiplash. I'm driving home."

"Only if you pry the keys from my cold, dead hand."

"That could be arranged."

"Hey, you two. Knock it off!" Dodie says.

She has one hand braced against the dashboard and, with the other, fans herself with Grandma's AARP magazine. Her face is scarlet with heat.

"Ha! Listen to you, Ms. White Knuckles," I say. "Would you please sit back? Your body's blocking the cold air. It's stifling back here."

A bizarre heat wave held Vista Valley in its grip, resulting in frayed nerves and short tempers. Like a wad of cotton stuck in the neck of an aspirin bottle, a high, thin layer of clouds sealed the overheated air in our inverted bowl of a valley. And it isn't our beloved dry desert heat, but a muggy, suffocating, hair-matting, sweat-dripping-off-the-forehead heat.

Grandma reaches over and cranks up the air conditioner. The cold blast of refrigerated air jolts Dodie back into her seat.

"We need a good windstorm to blow this out of here," Grandma says.

"No," Dodie says. "We need rain."

"Don't wish for rain." Grandma's tone is uncharacteristically sharp. "It splits the cherries."

"Rain doesn't split the cherries," Dodie snaps. "The sun makes them swell up and split *after* the rain."

"For the love of God!" I yell. "Who friggin' cares?"

Dodie looks at me and smirks. "Looks like Aunt Flo's

due for a visit. Panty shields up, Captain."

We lapse into sullen silence until Nick spots a colorful billboard emblazoned with the words *What Would Jesus Drink?* A larger than life, smiling Jesus cuddles a lamb in the crook of his arm. The other hand holds a cluster of purple grapes.

"There it is. Take the next exit."

Grandma steers the Olds through open wrought iron gates, punches the accelerator, and we zoom up a long, steep driveway flanked on both sides by rose hedges.

Dodie cackles and points at the small wooden signs spaced alongside the driveway. "Looks like Jesus drinks Holy Light whites, Blood of the Lamb reds, and communion wines."

From our vista high on the hill, the land stretches out to the west and south, a checkerboard in shades of green and brown. Bright green trellised grapevines bristling with new growth run up against darker hued orchards. The lush foliage of the orchards ends with startling abruptness as irrigated land gives way to patchy sagebrush and tumbleweeds. The soft purple foothills of the Cascades rise in graceful folds to the west.

As we pull into the parking lot, we have our first close-up view of the WWJD visitors' center. Built of cedar and designed to resemble a mountain lodge, it features stone pillars and overhanging eaves that surround the structure on all four sides. Carefully placed shrubs and trees combine with the overhang to bathe its façade in dark shadows. Even though I know the purpose of such a design—to provide shade on a blistering hot summer day—it gives me a feeling of unease.

We spill out of the car and fall in behind a family of four, the last of a group who arrived via chartered bus. Two women in brown cords, Birkenstocks, and matching backpacks march toward the tasting room. A pair of thin, non-gender-specific twins and a medium-sized boy with a round, merry face and bright blue eyes trail behind the two women.

"Seattle people," Grandma announces behind an up-lifted hand.

I nudge Susan. "Check out the boy," I whisper. "He looks like David Crosby. I hear you can buy his sperm on the internet."

Susan snickers but pokes me hard with her elbow. "Don't start."

Before the children are allowed to enter the building, one of the women says, "Okay. Whitman, Sinclair, Dawson. You may sample the snacks, but do not consume anything with meat. If you're not sure, check with one of us first."

The twins nod solemnly. The little round kid ignores her and darts through the door. Grandma looks at me and rolls her eyes. "Those twins could use a ham sandwich," she mutters.

We step into an elegant tasting room with oak floors, mammoth exposed beams, open stone fireplace and skylit ceiling. A loft overlooks the main room. The bar is busy as an elegantly garbed hostess whose name tag says, "Hi, my name is Tiffany," pours a tiny splash of red wine for eager visitors. Behind the bar, a glassed-in area allows visitors a peek into the barrel room. As predicted, two platters of hors d'oeuvres have been set for visitors, one marked *vegan*, the other unlabeled.

Dodie and Grandma get in line. Susan, Nick, and I sit down on the hearth next to a magnum of Blood of the Lamb red strategically placed at one end. A huge, polished slab of wood that serves as a mantle holds an array of wines featuring the WWJD label.

"Nice setup," Susan says.

Nick squirms restlessly. "We're wasting our time in here. Let's go for a walk."

"Yeah, okay." I say, standing up. "Want to go, Susan?"

She looks at Nick, who's gazing sullenly out the window. "I'll stick around and keep an eye on those two." She points at Grandma and Dodie, both sipping wine. Grandma's free hand inscribes graceful arcs in the air as she gestures and chats up a guy with a long, silver ponytail poking through the back of a Seattle Mariners' ball cap. I hope she's not recruiting.

As I turn to follow Nick, my eyes catch a flicker of movement from above. I glance up at the loft and see Gordon Venable, arms braced on the wooden railing, hooded eyes gazing at me. I acknowledge him with a nod and saunter casually over to join Grandma and Dodie. Now is not the time to go snooping around the grounds.

Nick grasps the situation quickly and heads for the snacks. I link arms with Dodie and pull her away from the group. "That's the guy I was telling you about," I say, surreptitiously watching Venable's ungainly passage across the loft and down the stairs.

"Piece of cake," Dodie says. "Just introduce me."

I take Dodie's wineglass and down the contents, seeking to counteract the dank, crawly feeling Venable's reptilian presence evokes. Though I chatter aimlessly to Dodie, I'm aware of his unwavering stare as he makes his way toward us.

"Ms. Thome," he says in his strange, rusty voice. "We meet again. Interested in wine, are you?"

"Oh, hi, Gordy," I say. "Not me. My aunt's the wine connoisseur." I make the introductions, take a step back, and let Dodie do her thing.

She places a hand on his arm and gazes at him in wide-eyed wonder. "I'm so delighted to meet you, Mr. Venable," she gushes. "Can you spare a few minutes of your time? I'd like to pick up a few cases of wine to take home."

A mottled flush creeps up Venable's sunken cheeks. He blinks rapidly three times and covers Dodie's hand with his own. His tongue flicks out to moisten his dry lips. "I'd be delighted," he says, looking deep into her eyes.

Before you could say "red or white, my dear?" the two are *behind* the bar with the hostess, who raises an eyebrow but keeps on pouring.

As Nick and I head for the door, I hear a strident voice call, "Dawson! No! We do *not* eat flesh."

I turn to see the jolly kid with the vegan parents poised over a snack platter, one chubby hand reaching for the cock-tail sausages. He looks at the sausages then at the women, as if gauging time and distance. Mind made up, he grabs a handful of sausages and shoves them in his mouth. Nick and I slip through the side door as all eyes turn to his horri-fied family moving toward him en masse.

Chapter 27

$\mathscr{W}$e step out onto a brick patio crowded with people sipping wine and sweating in the oppressive heat. The back of my neck prickles. I don't think Venable noticed our departure, but I take a quick peek over my shoulder anyway.

Picking our way through the crowd, we move into a grassy picnic area landscaped with blue spruce, arborvitae, and burgeoning annual beds. Overturned wine barrels are placed in conversational groupings under a gigantic weeping willow, a living reminder of another time, when it graced the front yard of a farmhouse long since demolished and sold for scrap. We stroll past a koi pond ringed by a low stone wall upon which a black and white cat lies dozing in the heat.

A shale footpath winds between the trees and leads to a miniature whitewashed chapel in the distance. On our left stands an eight-foot wooden fence bearing a sign that announces, "Danger. Keep Out."

"Chapel later," Nick says. "I'd really like to see what's behind the fence."

"Any idea how to get in?"

He gives me a look that says, "Don't ask," and takes off down the path, studying the fence as he walks. I jog a few steps to catch up. Though his face is ghastly pale, his expression is fierce and determined.

I put my hand on his arm. "I doubt he'd keep Sara here. Too many people around."

He jerks away, stiff with outrage. "You don't know that! If he's got her, he'd keep her close by."

"Don't get your hopes up."

"Hope is all I have left." His voice breaks, and he lifts his glasses to swipe at his eyes.

I want to eat my words. We step aside for a couple walking toward us on the narrow path. The woman glances at us curiously.

"You all right, son?" she asks Nick, glaring at me.

Nick nods and they walk on, the woman still casting suspicious glances my way.

The footpath ends at the chapel. Behind it, the fence veers away to the east.

"Gotta be a gate somewhere," Nick mutters.

"Probably back the other way."

"Can't risk it. Too close to the visitors' center," he says.

He squeezes through a thick curtain of shrubbery bordering the chapel and heads for the fence line. I follow reluctantly, my shoes sinking deep into the tilled earth as I step from the manicured lawn. "This is nuts!" I screech. "There's nothing out here but dirt. And look at us. We're like deer in an open field."

I can't shake the crawly feeling I've had since we arrived at the winery.

"Nobody here to see us. Go back if you want. I just want to see what's around the corner," Nick says.

"Shit," I mutter but keep on slogging. Puffs of powdery dust billow with every step, clinging to the white cropped pants I foolishly thought appropriate for a winery tour.

Nick rounds the curve, stops, and pumps a fist in the air."

"Gate up ahead. Told ya!"

I catch up with him and peer around the corner. A dirt road cuts through the vineyard and ends at a wide, double-hinged gate, its two sides fastened in the middle with a sturdy, brass padlock.

"Guess I'll have to toss you over the fence," I say.

Nick studies the padlock. "Combination lock."

He lifts the padlock so I can see the bottom. Four rows of numbers have to be lined up in sequence before it can be opened. He looks at me and shrugs, a thumb poised over the numbers.

"Wait," I say. "When you close it, you have to spin the numbers to lock it. If this gate's not used much, maybe somebody got lazy."

I take the padlock from Nick's hand and give it a yank. It falls open.

We open the gate a crack, slip through, and pull the two sides together so from a distance it will appear to be closed. Hopefully we'll be in and out before a winery employee chugs up in his tractor, notices the unlocked gate, and snaps the padlock shut. The same thought occurs to Nick.

"Hurry," he says, plucking at my sleeve. "We need to get back before Venable misses us."

A long, low-slung barn, probably a chicken house at one time, sits at the rear of the property, backed up against a tall chain-link fence topped with razor wire. The rest of the yard contains an assortment of outbuildings and a bewildering array of farm implements. The eerie silence makes the hair on my arms prickle. "Quick look around—then we're outta here," I say, trotting toward the barn.

Nick catches up with me. "Why the razor wire?"

I know where his mind is heading. "Expensive farm equipment. People steal it. That's all."

The barn door is ajar. I reach out to push it open when we hear the unmistakable sound of an approaching tractor. I freeze. *Run for the gate? Hide? What?*

Nick reaches around me, opens the door, and shoves me into the dark interior of the barn. Lurching crazily, I lose my balance and sprawl face down on the rough, wooden floor. Sucking in air, I scramble up while Nick slips inside and closes the door.

Dim light filters through a row of dirt-encrusted windows set high along the back wall. The sound of the tractor grows louder. The motor switches off. We dart behind a stack of cardboard boxes and wait. I'm shaking so hard I'm certain the mountain of boxes is vibrating like a mountain about to erupt. I grab Nick's hand. For once, he doesn't pull away.

The door bangs open, and a splash of daylight illuminates the interior of the barn.

"You sure you haven't seen a woman and a kid?" It's Venable's voice.

Another man answers. "No way they'd be back here. Both gates are locked."

"You look around in here. I'll go check the other end."

The man grunts an affirmative. I hear Venable walk away. Nick and I crouch behind our cardboard barricade trying not to breath.

The man mutters, "Enough work around this place without looking for some clueless twat who wandered off the path. God damn waste of time!"

His footsteps come closer. He kicks at a loose box. Nick jerks convulsively. I squelch a yip of surprise and wait for my heart to start beating again. A rivulet of sweat drips off the end of my nose. I crouch lower, and the back seam of my pants gives way, the ripping sound magnified tenfold in the silent barn. Nick inhales sharply and rolls his eyes.

Trapped in our cramped, airless space, we hear boots scraping across the wooden floor. Closer or moving away? Then nothing but complete and utter silence, punctuated only by the sound of our raspy breathing and pounding hearts. We wait, frozen in time, as seconds morph into an eternity.

Is he gone? I fight the urge to peek. Finally, after another round of cursing, we hear footsteps moving away and the door scraping across the floor. Thank God for slackers! I know who left the gate unlocked.

Shaking and weak with relief, we continue to crouch behind the boxes until the tractor starts up. Nick pops up, ready to make a run for it. I stagger out from behind the boxes, gasping in the overheated air.

"Not yet," I whisper. "He's waiting for Venable." We wait a full minute after Venable climbs aboard and the sound of the tractor fades into the distance.

Nick tiptoes to the door, pulls it open a few inches. "All

clear," he says and motions for me to join him.

I creep toward the open door and daylight. Nick holds up a hand, and I stop.

"Listen!" he says. His eyes are huge behind fogged-up glasses. "Somebody's playing a radio."

Snippets of thoughts boil through my brain. Radio playing. Not good. Somebody close by. Nick points at the far end of the barn. "It's coming from down there. Must be another room behind that wall."

"Venable said he'd check the other end."

We stare at each other. "Somebody's in there," I say.

"We gotta go see." Nick sounds frantic. "It could be her."

"Or a caretaker who lives on site." I pull him toward the gate. "No time, bud."

He digs in his heels, resisting me with every ounce of strength in his wiry frame.

"Nicky, don't do this! We have to leave now. Sloan will be back this afternoon. I'll call him. If Sara's here, he'll get her out."

I feel his muscles soften as my outrageous lie works its magic. We dash to the gate and push. It doesn't budge.

"No!" I wail. "We're trapped! I knew this would happen!"

"Latch must be hung up," Nick says, shoving me aside.

He lashes out with a foot, the gate pops open, and we barrel through. Nick padlocks the gate. Without speaking, we head for the chapel grounds and sprawl in the grass, waiting for the shakes to subside.

I take off my shoes, dump out the dirt, and take stock of my personal appearance. The dirt between my toes has turned to mud. White pants stained with dirt and filth. Ass hanging out. Hair frizzy and wild from heat, fear, and sweat.

Other than his dusty shoes, Nick looks none the worse for our ordeal. "So you'll call Sloan?" he asks.

"Absolutely," I avoid his eyes and stare at the tree overhead. "As soon as I get home. I don't have his number with me."

"Let me know what he says."

I nod and stand up. "Chapel next?"

The interior of the chapel is dark, cool, and deserted. The few brave souls venturing out in the heat have hastily returned to the visitors' center. A center aisle separates six rows of wooden pews on each side and leads to a broad, carpeted step up to the altar and raised pulpit. Soft light pours through a stained glass window set high in the back wall.

"Weird," I say, looking around. "Too small for a wedding."

Nick shrugs, clearly disinterested. "Let's head back."

I hear the door creak open behind us. I glance over my shoulder to see Gordon Venable framed in the doorway.

I'm not in the mood for Gordon Venable.

"Let's pray," I hiss at Nick.

I grab him and we kneel at the wooden railing, heads bowed, hands folded. Surely Venable won't disturb us at our prayers and, truth be told, it isn't all pretend. Since I'm already on my knees, I offer up a little prayer of thanks for our narrow escape.

My knees begin to ache after what seems like an hour but is probably only five minutes. "Is he still there?" I whisper.

"Yep," Nick says. "Looks like he's not leaving anytime soon."

"Oh, shit, let's get it over with."

Nick snickers. "Bad girl. Swearing in church."

When I stand, my left calf seizes up in a violent cramp. Muttering blasphemous phrases under my breath, I back away and place my hands on the step, dropping into a runners' stretch to release the painful knot. I see a flash of silver in the seam of the carpeted step. I scoop up the small object and stick it in my pocket.

Followed by Nick, I limp down the aisle toward the odious Mr. Venable, who perches in the last pew like a bony bird of prey. He stands as we approach, taking stock of my grubby pants, flushed face, and kinky hair. "Are you all right, Ms. Thome? You look a little, uh, disheveled."

I point at my leg. "Cramped up on me." I give him a cheery smile. "Nick wanted to walk out into the vineyards. Not a good day for that, with the heat and all."

Venable stares at me, without blinking, for a long moment. "I thought perhaps your nephew might be ill. A guest told me she met you on the path and the boy seemed upset."

I try to think of an appropriate response other than *nosy old biddy*.

Nick says, "It's the CF. I have a hard time breathing. That's probably what she saw." He launches into a violent coughing spell that I hope is faked.

"I was here earlier looking for you," Venable says and waits for me to respond.

Despite my feeling of unease, I force myself to look in his eyes, and I'm struck again by their opaqueness. No reflection of light. Devoid of life. Creepy.

"Like I said, we walked out to the vineyards," I repeat, holding his gaze. It's like I'm looking into the eyes of a cobra, fascinated yet terrified.

"Strange. I didn't see you out there," he says.

"As you can see, we're fine." I refuse to break eye contact.

Nick breaks off the staring contest by tugging at my sleeve. "We need to get going."

"I'll give you a ride to the visitors' center," Venable says.

We follow him through the door. A two-seater golf cart is parked on the path. When Nick starts to climb in the back, I pull him back. "I really need to walk off this cramp. Thanks anyway."

After another long, measuring look, Venable nods.

Though I want to see the last of him, I ask, "What's the chapel used for? Seems too small for services."

His eyes flick away then back to mine. "We wanted to provide a sanctuary, a place for people to meditate. Like you were doing. Do you have a church home, Ms. Thome?"

"Oh, many," I assure him. He frowns and drives away.

Halfway up the path I stop and dig around in my pocket for the item I found in the chapel. A tiny silver charm.

"I found this in the chapel. Looks like some kind of bird."

I set it on Nick's outstretched palm. He lifts his glasses and studies it carefully. "It's hers," he says in a choked voice. "It's Sara's."

He thrusts the charm under my nose. "It's a seagull. Her dad bought it for her when he got out of prison. It's hers. I know it's hers."

I look at the charm, a seagull soaring with outstretched wings, and remember the tattoo on Joe Stepanek's body. A setting sun bisected by three flying gulls. "Freedom," Sloan said. "The tattoo symbolizes freedom."

"Okay," I say slowly. "If it's hers . . ."

"It is hers!" Nick says, outraged by my lack of faith. "We can't leave her here! You gotta call the cops. We gotta do something!"

For the first time today, he sounds panicky. I try to get him to move. "We will. I promise. But not right now. Come on, Nick, we've got to be smart about this."

Finally, with one last look over his shoulder, he follows me up the path. His silence gives me time to sift through the jumbled events of the past hour. As the terror recedes, a flood of images rushes in. I stop suddenly.

Lost in thought, Nick steps on my heels.

"You know those boxes we hid behind?" I ask.

"What about them?"

"Juice concentrate," I say. "From Mexico."

"So what?"

"So why do they need juice concentrate when they grow their own grapes?"

He shrugs.

"I need to talk to your mom." I take off toward the tasting room.

We meet the bus people heading down the path toward the parking lot. I wave at my chubby little friend who appears to have cocktail sauce smeared on his face. Flanked on each side by a grim-faced mother, he grins and waves back.

Susan meets us at the door. She scans Nick for dings and

scratches and then gives me the once over. "Good God! What happened to you?"

I wave the question off. "Later."

"Dodie's tipsy, and your grandmother's helping the hostess clean up." Susan grins. "Apparently another bus is on its way."

Nick wanders off in search of water. I pull Susan over to the wine display. "Remember what you told me about imported grape juice? That you'd heard this vineyard is just for show?"

Susan nods. "Yeah, but this looks like the real deal to me."

She picks up a bottle of Merlot. "The label says, 'Cellared and bottled from grapes grown at WWJD Winery, Vista Valley, WA.' Why? Something to do with Sara?"

I tell Susan about the boxes of juice concentrate we saw. That the boxes were the only thing between her beloved son and danger remains my little secret. "Nothing to do with Sara. I'm just curious about concentrate. What's the juice used for?"

"Maybe the hostess can tell us."

She heads for the bar, ignoring my protests. All I need is Venable walking in while we grill the hostess about boxes of concentrate hidden away from public view. I hasten to join her. At least we can conduct the conversation at lower decibels.

Before Susan can ask her questions, Grandma sees me and shrieks in alarm. "Oh, sweetie! Did you fall?"

"Yep," I say, turning slowly for the full effect. "Tripped over a rock and fell in a pile of dirt. Split my pants too."

Grandma clucks her tongue and shakes her head at my slovenly appearance.

Susan traps the hostess behind the bar. "Could you answer a couple of questions for us, Tiffany?"

"Sure. What do you want to know?"

"Are all your wines made from grapes you grow here?"

"Except for the whites," Tiffany says. "We have another vineyard for that."

"Around here?"

"Just a few miles away. Why?"

I look around the room. No Gordy. "So you don't use juice concentrate?"

Tiffany chews her gum and ponders, a look of confusion blooming on her smooth, pretty face. "Juice concentrate?" she asks.

Suddenly the light comes on, and she giggles. "Is that what you call it? Concentrate? I thought it was called grape juice."

Eager to use her brand new word Tiffany explains, "Yeah, we import juice *concentrate* for our non-alcoholic wines. From Mexico. They bring it up in trucks, and we send back cases of stuff."

"Lots of Concord grape vineyards here in the valley," I observe.

Tiffany says, "Uh huh."

"Why import juice from another country when you can get it just down the road?"

Tiffany's eyes dart from Susan's face and back to mine, searching for a clue. It's painful to watch. "Jeez, I don't know. Probably has something to do with money."

I sigh. "Right you are, Tiffany. It's always about money."

We collect our little family and the three cases of wine

Dodie feels compelled to buy. As we drive through the open gate at the bottom of the hill, I turn for one last look. Will the gates be locked after dark?

As if he's reading my mind, Nick whispers, "We gotta get her out."

I put a finger to my lips and whisper back, "I've got a plan."

On the drive home, we recount a highly edited version of our adventure. No mention of our journey to the dark side. We pass around the seagull charm. I reiterate my intention to contact Sloan. Grandma beams her approval. When we pull into Susan's driveway, Nick won't budge. "Maybe I should come home with you, see what Sloan has to say."

Susan intervenes quickly. "You need your breathing treatment. Allegra will call you."

Nick knows better than to argue with Susan about health issues. "Yeah, yeah," he says and shuffles into the house.

We arrive home and offload Dodie's wine.

Hot, dirty and tired, I head upstairs and then check the answering machine. Three messages await. Marcy, bored out of her skull, wanting to meet me at Brewski's for a quick bite "and whatever." My new best friend, Donny Thorndyke, saying, "Babe, I talked to Cheeseman. Thanks again for stopping by. Talk to you later." And finally Sloan growling, "Call me."

I call and get Sloan's voice mail. Since I promised Nick I'd talk to Sloan, I feel compelled to leave a message. I start with "Where are you, Sloan?" before launching into a long, rambling message.

Conscience eased, I plan my agenda for the rest of the day.

Shower.

Nap until dark.

Return to the WWJD Winery.

Chapter 28

$\mathcal{I}$n the upper, left-hand corner of the U.S., traces of daylight linger long after 9 p.m. in mid-June. My plan to nap until dark is clearly flawed. Interrupted every twenty minutes by a phone call from Nick, I give up and plan a wardrobe suitable for nighttime skulking. Black tee shirt, black high-top sneakers, black jeans, and a black long-sleeved windbreaker with a hood. If I don't die of heat exhaustion, I'll be a veritable phantom in the night.

Nick finally relents when I tell him Sloan has the details and will handle it. I hear skepticism in his voice, but at least he stops calling. In truth, Sloan does have the details, though a slightly jumbled version.

At 10 p.m. I slip down the stairs and tiptoe across the entryway. Grandma and Dodie sit side by side on the couch, watching a movie. When I open the front door, Grandma's head whips around. "Allegra! What on earth are you wearing?"

"Storm's coming in tonight. I'm meeting Marcy. See

you in the morning."

I step out onto the porch and discover my faux weather report has come true. A sudden gust of wind rattles the maple trees, whipping through the branches in a frenzied rush, subsiding just as quickly. The air is still heavy and hot. A half moon appears briefly from behind scudding clouds. Unlocking the Ranger, I hear a roll of thunder to the north.

Armed with my cell phone and tiny flashlight, I head south, pondering my half-assed plan and praying to the gods who look after fools like me. *If this were a movie,* I ask myself, *would the audience be screaming, "Don't do it, you dumb shit"? Probably.*

But my options are few. Sloan is unavailable, I refuse to endanger my family, the police think I'm a nut job, and Michael is clearly involved up to his patrician nose. In spite of sketchy evidence, I'm convinced Robinson Hunt has Sara. Whether or not she's at the winery, I'll soon find out.

I have to get behind the fence. It is, after all, a working farm, so surely I'll find some useful item to boost me up. *Over the fence. Look for Sara. Run like hell for the truck. Drive home.* That's the plan. Simple.

The gates at the bottom of the drive leading to the winery are closed and locked. No problem. I'll walk in. I back up and park the Ranger well away from the overhead lights illuminating the billboard of Jesus.

I step out of the truck and listen. Other than cars whizzing by on the freeway, the night is utterly silent. I look both ways on the frontage road. No approaching headlights. I trot to the gate, slip around it, and head up the hill, taking care to stay close to the rose hedge.

I've arrived ahead of the storm. This side of the gap, the oppressive heat still lingers, undeterred by the absence of sun. After fifty yards of jogging uphill in the muggy air, I slow to a steady trudge and briefly consider stripping down to my panties and bra. Ten minutes later I stand concealed in the trees next to the visitors' center sucking air and mopping up sweat with my shirttail.

Dim light filters through the windows of the tasting room. I creep closer and check out the loft, half expecting to see Gordon Venable leaning against the railing. No signs of life. However, the shadowy, recessed areas behind the railing could conceal a half dozen Gordys. *Don't go there, Allegra.*

I'm not keen on wandering down the path to the gate Nick and I accessed earlier. With the moon obscured behind the clouds, the pathway is black as pitch. I could use the flashlight, but that would be like screaming, "Here I am. Come get me!" Instead, I'll use ambient light to see if I can find a way in behind the building.

I turn away from the visitors' area and follow a line of shrubbery leading to the south side of the building, where three giant stainless steel tanks sit on a cement pad next to a long, rectangular wing. The back of the building disappears into the night.

I feel like screaming, "What's the matter with you people? Where the hell are your yard lights?"

The shrubbery ends abruptly. Feeling exposed and vulnerable, I step out onto hard, packed dirt and creep along the side of the building. After a dozen steps, I pause to listen. A faint rustling sound: something stirs close by. I inhale sharply and hold my breath. Probably a rabbit.

Maybe a coyote hunting a rabbit.

Maybe something hunting Allegra.

In spite of the heat, I shiver.

I wait a full minute then move resolutely toward the rear of the building and a faint halo of light. I peer around the corner and see the loading dock and the wide concrete driveway leading to it, enclosed by a chain-link fence and padlocked gate. Staying in the shadows, I turn right, my back to the light and feel my way through the dark with outstretched arms. The fence has to be close by. With any luck, I'll run into it.

As I pick my way along, my eyes adjust. Squinting through the murky darkness, I head for what I hope is the shadowy outline of a tall fence. Picking up speed, I lengthen my stride, step in a hole, and sprawl face forward on the ground with a muffled grunt of surprise. I roll to a sitting position and wiggle various limbs. No harm, no foul.

Sweaty body now coated in dirt, I start to get up and then freeze in a half crouch. The rustling noise again. Closer this time. Behind me. Heart pounding, I turn slowly toward the sound, straining to see. Something brushes against my arm. With an aborted screech, I leap up and sideways, my legs churning in the air like the Roadrunner pursued by Wily Coyote.

Upon landing, I hear a familiar *Rowr?*

My legs collapse, and I sit down hard. The winery cat, delighted by my unexpected visit, rubs against me in the dark.

"Nice kitty," I whisper between gasps. I reach out with a trembling hand and stroke his silky fur. A sudden swirl of wind rustles through the grapevines, bringing with it the smell of rain and a distant rumble of thunder. The storm is catching up.

On the move again, this time using more caution, I reach the fence. Keeping my hands in contact with the wood, I slide to the left, groping for a gate. After a dozen steps, I feel the fence make a 90-degree turn. I ease around the corner and take a couple more steps. I reach with the hands. Slide with the feet. Pat. Slide. Pat. Slide. One final step, and my left hand shoots off into open space. I've found the gate, and it stands ajar.

I creep through the opening and stop to reconnoiter. I can barely make out the humped forms of the outbuildings. The barn is at the far end. Keeping in mind the farm implements scattered around the yard and my inherent clumsiness, I'll have to take it slow. To complicate matters, my kitty friend has followed me through the gate, bumping me with his head and pouncing at my ankles. Probably Vlad's evil twin.

After two tentative steps, something makes me stop. The air is heavier and charged with energy. An elusive scent fills my nostrils. I stop, my heart thudding painfully against my ribs. I'm not alone. I clearly hear the sound of breathing, and it isn't mine. My brain screams, *Run!*

Before my legs get the message, I hear the flick of a switch, and then a floodlight positioned atop the fence switches on.

"Welcome, Ms. Thome," says a rusty voice. "Took you long enough to find the gate."

No hesitation this time. As I whirl to make a run for it, I'm brought up short by a hand gripping my right arm. I flail violently until Venable jerks me back and something hard presses against my ribs. My heart sinks. He has a gun.

"I knew you'd be back tonight," Venable says with a chuckle. "All I had to do was stand here and wait. I heard you coming a mile away."

A dozen smart-ass comments come to mind, but I bite my tongue. For a bully like Gordon Venable, fear will be an aphrodisiac. If he wants me to be scared, I'll be a sniveling basket case and wait for an opportunity to show my stuff. Providing I have stuff to show.

I fake a sob. "Just let me go. I'll forget about Sara. I promise."

"If you weren't such a nosy bitch, we wouldn't be having this conversation."

"I'm sorry. Please just let me go."

I drop to my knees and wail.

"Get up!" He jerks me up and then sighs in mock distress. "*You* caused this to happen. When I couldn't locate you earlier today, I knew you'd been snooping around back here. Just be glad the kid's not with you tonight."

"Why?" I say. "What are you going to do?"

"You're about to have an accident. Your truck will be found in the river tomorrow. You'll be inside. Dead."

"Nooo!" I scream, dropping to my knees again. "You can't shoot me! Pleeease!"

"You're a goddamn nut job."

Breathing hard, he tries to jerk me up. I pretend my knees are noodles.

"I'm not going to shoot you, you idiot. It has to look like an accident," Venable says. He pokes me hard in the side and barks again, "Get up."

Without imminent danger from the gun, I stall for time. "Ow!" I whine, crouching and cringing. "Quit poking me, and I'll get up."

"Jesus," he mutters under his breath. His grip on my arm eases up a little.

I take my time getting up. "Tell me how Hunt did it. How he got Sara. She's here, isn't she?"

"Pastor Rob has, shall we say, a special interest in Sara," Venable says. "Against my advice, he moved up the timeline for her counseling."

"Counseling?"

He doesn't answer.

"Joe Stepanek was blackmailing Hunt, wasn't he? Which one of you killed him?"

"You *have* been a busy little girl . . . Joe got greedy."

He steps forward and gives my arm a yank. "Enough questions!"

The cat darts between us. Venable swears and lashes out with a vicious kick. Yowling pitifully, the cat goes flying.

While he's off balance, I slam into Venable with every ounce of strength in my body. My shoulder hits his midsection, and we fall to the ground. At the edge of my vision I see something dark fly from his hand, landing in the shadows a few yards away.

The gun! I claw at his face, trying to break his iron grip on my arm. Sweating, panting, and cursing, we roll in the dirt, all traces of humanity lost in our desperate struggle. He reaches for the gun with his free hand. If I can get to it first . . .

I double up a fist and swing hard at his Adam's apple. He gags and grabs his throat with both hands. I crawl toward the gun. He catches the hood of my jacket and yanks me back. As he scrambles after the gun, I dive on his foot and sink my teeth into his bony ankle, nearly gagging from the rancid taste of his skin. He gives a yelp of pain. I bite down harder.

"Crazy bitch!" he snarls, flailing away at me.

I try to deflect his wild swings, but he lands a fierce blow on the side of my head. Stunned and deaf in one ear, I feel my jaw go slack. He jerks away and goes for the gun. I scramble up. Gun or no gun, I'll make a run for it and pray he's a poor shot.

I take off like a scalded rabbit, Venable on my tail.

As I head for the wide gate, a car pulls in and parks in the opening.

Robinson Hunt steps out.

"Stop her!" Venable yells.

Hunt blocks the narrow passage between his car and the gate. I try to dart around the front of the car to the other side. He kicks out at my legs, and I go down, sprawling face first in the dirt. A sharp knee in the middle of my back pins me to the ground. I feel the gun press against me.

Venable is breathing hard and cussing. "Nighty night, sweetheart," he says.

I don't have to pretend this time. "No, please. Don't do it. I'll . . ."

My plea is interrupted by a jolt of excruciating pain. The breath leaves my body. All rational thought gone, except for *Please, God, make it stop. If I'm dying, let it be quick.*

Locked in a spasm of agony, unable to move or speak, I'm borne aloft for a dozen steps. A metal door opens with a *screech*, and I'm tossed unceremoniously onto a dirt floor. Rough hands dig through my pockets, removing flashlight, car keys, and cell phone.

I hear the door slam, the *snick* of a padlock, and Gordon Venable's parting comment: "Have fun with Betsy, our black widow spider. She's looking forward to company."

Chapter 29

Twitching muscles. Waves of nausea. Someone moaning. Me?

My power of reasoning returns slowly, bits and pieces of information sifting through my brain . . . not a real gun . . . a taser . . . I'm not dead . . . I'm locked in a metal storage shed with . . . *a black widow spider*!

Mobilized by panic, I roll to my stomach and squat in the stifling shed. In my dazed, crazed state, I think I see Betsy's shiny, black body as she marches toward me on eight hideously long legs, spidey senses atingle. This scares me more than a dozen Gordon Venables.

Filthy, sweating and cringing in the dark, I take deep breaths and talk to myself in my head: *Get a grip, Allegra. That spider's not interested in you. She's busy eating her mate.* But, oh, shit! What if she's still hungry? Maybe he was just an appetizer, and here you are all warm, sweaty, and tasty. *Don't go there! Even if she bites you, you won't die. On the other hand, if you don't get out of this shed, you will die!*

I visualize in sickening detail how Venable will do it. He'll hit me with the taser again, and I'll be in the river before the clock strikes midnight.

I stand on quivering legs and do an abbreviated version of my spider dance, flicking a hand through my hair and stomping my feet. Carefully pulling the hood over my hair, I vow to forget about Betsy. I stumble around the shed, groping in the dark for something to use as a weapon when Venable comes for me. A hoe or shovel would be nice; a hammer, even better.

A gust of wind tosses dirt and gravel against the side of the metal shed and brings in a welcome draught of fresh air. Suddenly, briefly, the interior of the shed is illuminated with a flash of lightning. Automatically, I pause and count, *one thousand one, one thousand two, one thousand three,* as Grandpa Mort taught me years ago. *One thousand six.* Thunder booms. Six miles away. The storm is coming closer.

I have to find a weapon.

Taking baby steps, I shuffle through the shed waving my arms in front of me. Thanks to the lightning, I've had a quick look around. The shed, made of corrugated metal, is long and narrow with a high ceiling. A few more steps, and I bump into a dozen heavy bags stacked up against the wall. Manure, I deduce from the smell. No hammer. No hoe.

Two long steps to the left, and my toe strikes something hard. Groping blindly, I trace the outline of what feels like a broken wine barrel probably tossed into the shed by a day worker. With only my hands for eyes, I locate a stave that's come partially loose. I grab it with both hands and yank, bracing my foot against the body of the barrel. It resists for a moment and then pops free with a squeak and groan. I feel the heft of the board and smile.

I have a weapon.

The wind picks up. Rain pounds against the metal roof. Another flash of lightning and a few heartbeats later, a deafening crack of thunder makes me shriek and clap my hands over my ears. The storm is directly overhead. Gripping the board in my left hand, I explore the rest of the shed and hear a pitiful *meow.*

"Kitty, kitty," I call. Though I doubt he has Vlad's killer instinct, I'll settle for companionship. I track the sound to the corner where I found the barrel. I tap on the wall and talk to the cat. "Hey, buddy. What's up? You staying dry?"

I hear him answer, and it's coming from above. Must be a tree next to the shed. The cat, bruised, battered, and frightened by the storm, probably took shelter there.

Another flash of lightning. I count and wait for the sound of thunder. Ten seconds this time. The rainstorm is over, blown further south by the brisk wind. Through a good-sized crack in my corner of the shed, I can see the moon starting to appear behind fast-moving clouds.

I reach up to investigate the crack and get a handful of sticky spider web. I scream, flicking and rubbing my hand against my jeans, the hair on the back of my neck prickling with horror. I dance around my cramped quarters like a woman possessed, hoping in the process I'll stomp a spider or two.

Shaky and sweaty, I return to the corner and use the board to scrape away the rest of the web. I poke my finger through the crack and trace the opening. Part of the metal roof has pulled away from the wall. Rivets are missing. Probably damage from last winter's heavy snowfall.

Maybe, just maybe . . .

Using the barrel stave, I whack at the opening, cringing at the hideous clanging noise. I fervently hope Venable and Hunt are at the other end of the compound. Weak moonlight filters through the crack in the shed. I can see tree branches whipping in the wind and hear the plaintive cries of the cat.

I look around for something to boost me up. From my present position on the floor, I can't apply the leverage I need. My only option is the bags of manure. I drag five heavy bags, one by one, to the corner and stack them up.

Sweaty and out of breath, I crouch atop my makeshift platform, my head bowed and pressed against the ceiling, and pry at the opening with my multipurpose weapon-slash-tool. When prying proves fruitless, I use the board as a battering ram, gratified when a rivet gives way and the crack widens. At this speed, I'll be out of here, say, by the time school starts in the fall.

I fall into a pattern of banging and prying, prying and banging, pausing occasionally to listen for the approach of my execution squad. When it's big enough to poke my head through, I check out the surroundings. Venable killed the floodlight, but after stumbling around in the inky darkness, I discover the moonlit farmyard appears as bright as a city street.

A tree branch, tantalizingly close, waves in the wind. Close enough to grab if I can squeeze through the crack. I see a flicker of movement in the shadows.

Hurry, Allegra. Hurry. You're on borrowed time.

No time for prying and banging. Sucking in deep, anxious breaths, I flop on my back and kick at the roof with both feet, noise be damned. After two hard kicks, I've made the gap wide enough to accommodate my shoulders.

Sadly, my hips are a different story. Spurred on by the ridiculous image of myself stuck in the crack, waiting for Venable to finish laughing before he finishes me off, I lash out with another kick. The gap widens. I rotate on my back 45 degrees and kick the other end of the crack. With a noisy squawk, rivets pop and metal shrieks. I'm free!

I hoist my body halfway through the gap and look down. I need to go through feet first, grab the edge, and drop down. Take off my jacket. Lay in over the jagged edge, or . . . maybe I can reach the tree!

I wriggle my hips so that my upper torso is hanging out further, no mean feat with sharp pieces of metal snagging my clothes. A little farther and I can grab the branch, climb down the tree, and beat feet to the highway, where I'll hitch a ride to the police station. This time I won't take no for an answer.

The sweep of headlights and sound of a car motor put a swift end to my plan. I freeze, praying the lights won't hit me. The car stops outside the gate, and the lights flick off. I hear the murmur of voices then silence. Friend or foe, it doesn't matter; I'm busting out of this damn metal box.

No time to take off my jacket. I put my hands on the bottom of the opening and push until I can throw one leg over the edge. I bite my lip to keep from crying out as the jagged metal lacerates my palms. Face down and straddling the narrow opening, I teeter crazily in the gusting wind. Panting and swearing under my breath, I try to pull my other leg up and over, but my jeans catch on a bit of metal. I jerk free, lose my balance, and make a desperate grab for the waving tree branch.

I miss by inches and plummet to the ground, landing with a *thud* on my outstretched right arm. I feel something tear in my shoulder.

Moaning softly, I take stock of my body. I roll to a sitting position and watch the arm flop uselessly to my side. I try to lift it, but a burst of agony stops me.

I grit my teeth, stand up, and slip into the shadow of the shed. I can't exit the way I entered, not without knowing who lurks outside the gate. Soon, Venable will know I've escaped. What he'll do then is anybody's guess. Panic? Track me down? Leave the country? And what about the people outside the gate? Have they been summoned by Venable to do the dirty deed?

Hunt is a cipher. His car is gone. If Sara has indeed been on the premises, perhaps they've decided to move her.

Okay, think, Allegra. Physically, I'm in no condition for another confrontation with Venable. Though I long to run like the wind, I'll do the opposite. Look for a place to hole up, keep my eyes open, and wait for an escape route.

I listen for voices, look for signs of movement, then wait until the moon ducks under a cloud before I scurry to the far side of the next outbuilding. Moving in this fashion, I work my way down to the barn, the side Nick and I weren't able to check out earlier. This end of the barn is dark, but I can see a halo of light leaking through the tall pine next to the back corner.

Despite the danger, I'm drawn to the light and the possibility that Sara might be close by. Cradling my useless right arm with my left, I sidle along the end of the barn toward the light. I hear a door open and close, a man's sharp cough and footsteps coming my way. Stepping with care, I slide behind the tree. A flashlight clicks on, and Gordon Venable rounds the corner. I stop breathing. He passes within three yards of my hiding place but strides off toward the upper end of the farmyard and my former prison.

If I'm going to check out this end of the barn, it has to be now. I peek around the corner and see a small porch and a windowed front door. A light is on behind the tightly closed mini blinds. Nick is right. This end of the barn contains living quarters.

I step up to the door and put my hand on the knob. Though the blinds are closed, they're too narrow for the window, leaving a half-inch gap along each side. I press my face against the glass and see a small slice of living room. Battered couch. Old recliner. A coffee table strewn with paperback books and fast-food cartons. No signs of life.

I've just moved to the other side when I hear a door shut and footsteps. Heart pounding, I scoot back into the shadows, pressing up against the side of the building. I wait a few beats and creep back onto the porch. Peering through the crack, I see a hand come into view and hover over the stack of books. It's followed by a sweep of dark hair and a familiar profile. *Sara!*

I don't realize I've said her name aloud until she turns her head slowly toward the door, eyes wide with shock. I grab the doorknob and twist. Locked.

"Sara, open the door," I urge in a low voice while I rattle the knob. "It's me, Miss Thome. Nick and I have been looking for you."

Her eyes are wide and staring. She doesn't move. *What the hell's the matter with her? It's like she doesn't know me at all.*

I glance over my shoulder, positive that Venable will be back any minute. Decision time. My arm is useless, and my shoulder throbs painfully. Sara appears to be in some sort of trance. Can I get both of us out safely? Doubtful.

I feel like I'm failing the people who trust me the most when I step off the porch. I'll go to ground until the first workers arrive. Venable won't dare harm me in broad daylight in the presence of others . . . I hope.

Two steps into the shadows, I hear the click of a deadbolt lock and the door flies open. Sara peers into the night. "Ms. Thome?" Her voice is weak and shaky. "What are you doing here?"

When I step onto the porch, she recoils and backs into the small living room. In better light, I see that her face is pale and drawn, her body painfully thin in oversized denim shorts and a tank top.

With a quick glance behind me, I enter the room. "I've come to take you home," I say as gently as possible.

She reacts in horror, throwing up her hands, her dark eyes wide with fear. "No. You can't . . ." she begins. "I have to, uh, I have to . . ."

She glances toward a hall leading from the living room, takes a tentative step toward it.

Shocked, confused, and in pain, I'm temporarily without words. What has Sara endured to cause such panic at my sudden appearance? I turn back toward the door. "Sara," I say softly. "Don't tell anyone I've been here.

I hear a door open, footsteps in the hall. Sara's eyes

come alive. Robinson Hunt steps into the room. She runs to him and throws herself into his arms.

"Rob. It's my teacher, Ms. Thome. She's come to take me home, but I want to stay with you." She clings to him and stares into his face, a face that turns pasty white when he sees who stands in the living room of his little love nest.

I bolt for the door and slam into Gordon Venable and a very large, black gun. A real gun.

I back slowly into the living room, hoping I'll regain my power of speech and my wits. What else do I have?

Chapter 30

$\mathcal{V}$enable steps through the door. "I should just shoot you now, you fuckin' pain in the ass." Two spots of red burn high on his cheekbones. His left eye twitches, and a knotted muscle works in his jaw.

"But that would spoil your little plan," I hear myself say. I have nothing to gain by showing fear.

"Plans can be changed."

He glances at Hunt still frozen in place with Sara clinging to him. "Jesus Christ! Don't just stand there," Venable snarls. "Get something to tie her up. I'll deal with her after we get the girl out of here."

Hunt gently disengages Sara's hands and tells her where to find the rope. She shambles slowly toward the back of the apartment. When Hunt looks at me, his expression changes. No longer the compassionate saver of souls, he looks like what he is: An ex-con. A pedophile.

"Sara!" I yell. "His real name is Roy Harris. Your dad knew him at Chino. Do you know your dad is dead? One of these men murdered him. I went to the funeral. I talked to your mom. I saw your little brother."

My words come out in a rush. Sara stops and turns to stare at me, her eyes huge and frightened.

"No!" she whispers. "He can't be dead." She takes a step toward Hunt.

"It's all right, baby." Hunt gathers her into his embrace. "Don't listen to her. She doesn't understand."

I press harder. "You were great, Sara. You left clues. You wanted us to find you. Remember your letter? The key? Your diary?"

Her head swivels, and she stares at me. I see the dawning of recognition in her eyes, like a person awakening from a deep sleep.

"These are bad men, Sara. They killed your father. Don't listen to them!"

"Shut the fuck up!" Venable screams.

His eyes flick over to Sara. "Get the God damn rope!"

She looks up at Hunt. He nods. She leaves the room. My heart sinks.

Venable yanks a straight-backed chair away from a small wooden table and shoves me into it. I grit my teeth when the back of my shoulder hits the chair. I hear Sara rummaging through drawers.

Hunt moves close to Venable. "Where are we taking Sara?"

"Let me worry about that," Venable says.

"You're going to kill her, aren't you?" I say. "Just like you killed Joe Stepanek. Just like you killed poor Peggy Mooney. It's the only way you can clean up this mess."

Hunt looks shocked.

"*Your* mess," Venable tells Hunt, the corners of his

mouth drawn down in disgust. "'Sara's the last,' you said. 'She's special,' you said. How many times do I have to save your sorry ass?'"

Good, the hyenas are turning on each other.

Though the gun is still aimed at my heart, Venable and Hunt lock gazes in some sort of manly, visual smackdown. I see a shadowy movement at the front door window and turn my head slowly. There! A brief blackout of light on the left edge of the window, like a head bobbing up for a quick peek. Somebody is outside the door.

Hunt finally breaks the silence. "I'm going to pretend you didn't say that, Gordy."

The menace in his voice is unmistakable. "You don't touch that girl. Understand?"

"I guess you're the only one who gets to do that," I chime in, hoping to keep their eyes away from the front door.

Hunt flushes. "Sara was in pain. I helped her. I don't expect you to understand."

"What about your wife? Does she understand?"

Hunt clamps his mouth shut.

Venable jerks his head toward the kitchen. "Go see what's taking her so long. Rope, duct tape, whatever. Just hurry it up."

Torn between defying Venable and protecting Sara, Hunt says, "This conversation isn't over," and leaves the room.

"Massive cover-up, huh, Gordy? Since you're planning on *killing* me, you might as well tell me how you did all of it."

I speak loudly, hoping whoever is on the porch does not condone murder.

Venable smirks down at me. "It's not rocket science, Ms. Thome. My friend in the kitchen . . ."

"Roy Harris," I say loudly.

Venable shrugs. "Names aren't important. It's all a matter of perception. He's a charming guy. People are drawn to him, important people who don't like snippy little bitches causing him trouble."

"Important people like high-ranking police officials and city council members?"

"Exactly." He looks pleased at my astuteness.

"But Joe Stepanek showed up and wanted a piece of the action."

Venable grimaces. "When Stepanek found out Roy was interested in his daughter, he went crazy. Barged into the church. The two of them had a hell of a brawl."

I remember the broken lamp in Hunt's office. "Who shot him up with heroin?"

When he doesn't answer, I say, "What about Michael? The night we met him at the club for dinner, he got us all out of the house so somebody could break in."

Venable gives me a grim smile. "Your notes were extremely helpful."

He continues, "Some people just won't cooperate, like your ex-boyfriend. It's just a matter of finding out the right buttons to push. Michael has a certain standing in the community so . . ." He fumbles around in the breast pocket of his shirt and removes two photographs, placing them, face up, on the table beside me.

I recoil in shock and close my eyes, but the images are burned into my retina. Michael. Naked and sprawled on a king-sized bed, his right arm around a young boy, his left around a barely pubescent girl. I open my eyes and look up at Venable. "Michael wouldn't do this."

He shrugs. "The camera doesn't lie."

Hunt and Sara come into the room. Hunt carries a length of clothesline rope. Sara is my only hope. Anguished in body and spirit and running out of time, I give it one last shot.

"Sara, Robinson Hunt beats his wife. He hides behind religion to prey on young girls like you. You're not the first. They killed your dad. They killed Peggy Mooney. They'll probably kill you and, for sure, they're going to kill me!"

Sara screams and claps her hands over her ears.

The front door flies open, and Heather Hunt bursts through, followed by Nick. In Heather's hand is a small, silver revolver.

Holy shit! The chicken house at the WWJD winery is turning into the O.K. Corral.

"Nick!" I shout. "Get down." If Venable doesn't kill me, Nick's mom will.

The events that follow are like snippets of a movie. Heather kicking the door shut. Nick ducking behind the sofa. Hunt shouting his wife's name. Venable's gun drifting toward Heather, his face a ghastly shade of gray. Me, frozen in a half crouch.

Heather strides toward her husband, her eyes wild and crazy. Hunt pushes Sara away and holds out a hand to Heather. "Heather, sweetheart, give me the gun."

She takes a step back. "I'll just hang onto it for a while," she says. "Until I hear what you have to say."

She glances over at Venable. "You want to shoot me,

Gordy? Go ahead. My life's not worth shit anyway. But I promise you I'll get a shot in before I go down. It might be you instead of Rob."

I hear the raspy sound of Venable breathing. The heavy gun wavers in his hand.

"Sit down, Allegra," Heather orders. "You'll want to hear this."

I plop down on the chair.

"Remember your little speech about spousal abuse?"

"Uh huh."

"It wasn't Rob using me for a punching bag; it was good old Gordy. I asked too many questions. About missing girls. About Peggy Mooney. About a lot of things that didn't add up."

She pauses, her chest heaving with emotion. "Rob didn't hit me. He was too busy doing the Lord's work. How many girls have you saved, Rob?"

Sara begins to keen, the mournful sound too full of pain for one small room.

Hunt's eyes dart between his wife and Sara. "It's not like that, Heather. Sara had an abortion. She wanted to be cleansed."

"Bullshit." Heather pulls the trigger.

Hunt crumples to the floor. I brace myself. Now Venable will surely kill us all.

"Hey, Gordy! Over here!" Nick pops up from behind the sofa. He grabs a sofa pillow and starts racing around the small room like two-year-old on a sugar high.

I scream, "Get out! Go get help!"

Distracted by Nick's actions, Venable looks wildly around the room. Heather, steely-eyed with determination, swings her gun around and takes careful aim at his chest. It occurs to me, and apparently to Venable, that Heather truly doesn't care if she lives or dies.

Like a manic moth to the flame, Nick darts between them, directly in the line of fire. Heather's gun wavers. Venable makes a grab for him but misses. Nick throws the sofa pillow in Venable's face and runs for the door. Off balance, Venable fires and hits the doorjamb, splintering the wood. Nick opens the door and vanishes into the night.

Deafened by the gun blast, I'm vaguely aware of Sara screaming and Heather trying to get a bead on Venable, who lurches toward the door after Nick. Suddenly the doorway is filled by the massive body of Arnie Vasquez, Nick's buddy and my classroom peacekeeper. Lifting a hand the size of a Virginia ham, Arnie swats Venable to the floor and kicks the gun away with a size 15 sneaker. Venable scrambles through the open doorway on all fours. Arnie smiles pleasantly and makes no move to stop him. I hear a thud and a groan.

Arnie steps into the room. "Hi, Ms. Thome. How are you?"

Shaky with relief and muddled of mind, I stand up and try to lift my arm in greeting. My bad arm. Sickening pain shoots through my shoulder and, for the first time in my life, I faint.

I awake to a cacophony of sounds and blurred images. Sara softly sobbing. Hunt moaning. Venable, hog tied on the floor, cursing nonstop. Heather, rocking silently on the sofa.

Approaching sirens. My throbbing head cradled on a pair of bony legs—Nick's legs. Arnie peering down at me, his moon face crinkled with concern.

Too tired to take in any more, I close my eyes.

When next I open them, the room is crowded with people, some in uniforms and sporting badges, others wearing gray polo shirts embroidered with the words *Vista Valley Emergency Services.*

I see Hunt being wheeled out on a gurney, which evokes memories of my passion-filled ride across the basement of Mystic Meadows. I begin to laugh hysterically.

I hear Nick tell an EMT, "She hit her head on the table when she fainted. I think something's wrong with her right arm, too."

I try to stop laughing long enough to tell my gurney story but can't seem to get the words out. Gentle hands examine my shoulder, probe the lump on my head, and lift me onto yet another gurney. I giggle all the way out to the ambulance.

Exhausted from all that laughing, I fall into a fitful sleep and dream of running on leaden feet through a darkened vineyard toward Red Ranger. The headlights are on, the motor's running, and the doors are open. Before I can reach it, I'm brought up short by a grapevine, whose tendrils reach out and snake around my left arm, squeezing and hissing.

I awaken, hooked to a blood pressure cuff. Dr. Myers, the elder, is frowning down at me. Various and sundry medical personnel hover nearby. Dr. Myers thrusts a hand in front of my face.

"How many fingers do you see?"

"Why?" I say. "Are you missing some?"

I snicker. Dr. Myers, however, is not amused. "Always with the smart mouth. Just answer the damn question, Allegra."

When I identify the correct number of digits, he bobs out of sight to consult with his colleagues.

"Her pupils aren't dilated. Vision's okay. Her nephew said it was a glancing blow. But she seems disoriented."

Another voice responds. "No evidence of a concussion. She's been through a hell of an ordeal. People react in different ways to trauma. Some laugh; some cry. She's a laugher."

Doc Myers pops back into view. He pats my cheek. "You're finer than frog's hair, kid. See you in the morning."

I feel the prick of a needle. Before I succumb to the waves of bliss crashing over me, I giggle and say, "You're funny, Dr. Myers."

Chapter 31

I awaken to the smell of lavender and a soft hand stroking my cheek. Cotton-mouthed and hurting, I struggle to open my eyes. The room is dark and quiet. Grandma Sybil's face is barely visible in the dim light spilling in through the open doorway. I try to smile but can only croak, "Water."

Grandma starts pushing buttons on the hospital bed's remote control device. Down goes my head. Up go my feet. Then back down. I moan as the middle of the bed humps up under my butt.

"Sorry, sweetie," Grandma whispers.

She turns on a light and studies the remote. After a couple of false starts, I'm in a semi-sitting position with a flexible drinking straw between my parched lips. Water never tasted so good; the act of drinking it, so exhausting.

I manage to stay awake long enough to take inventory of my injuries. Both hands are bandaged. My right arm is bent at a 45-degree angle and held in place by a shoulder strap hooked to a contraption that loops around my chest. It's a strange disconnect, like I'm outside my body looking down at a stranger.

Grandma Sybil explains, "Dr. Myers said you had a partial dislocation of the shoulder. You have to wear a shoulder immobilizer for three weeks. Then therapy."

"Three weeks," I repeat and close my eyes. In my present state, three weeks sounds like a lifetime. The very thought makes me tired, and I drift away.

The smell of food and daylight streaming through the windows tugs me back into the world. Grandma is gone, having relinquished Allegra watch to Dodie, who is examining a tray of food, the corners of her mouth turned down in distaste.

An adolescent voice says, "I think she's awake."

Arnie Vasquez stands at the end of the bed, flanked by Nick and Jimmy Felthouse. Nick looks pale but happy. Arnie and Jimmy stare at me with the shell-shocked look kids get when they realize teachers don't live in their classrooms.

"You look like shi— Uh, I mean, you don't look so hot." Jimmy ducks his head in embarrassment.

The memory of the previous night's events returns slowly, my brain arranging and rearranging pieces of the puzzle. Venable. Heather Hunt shooting her husband. Nick's heroic actions. Arnie's surprise appearance.

Some pieces don't fit. Like why is Jimmy here? I struggle to clear away the cobwebs.

Dodie raises the bed and fluffs my pillow. I stare wordlessly at the trio, trying to get my mind around the notion of Nick and Arnie with Heather Hunt.

Arnie looks at Nick. "Tell her how we did it."

"Please," I croak. "Enlighten me."

Jimmy puffs out his chest. "We had a three-part plan."

"We? You were there, Jimmy?"

"Well, duh," he says. "Who do you think clobbered the geek who was trying to run away?"

Taking turns and frequently interrupting each other, the three boys fill in the blanks.

Nick stopped by the house shortly after I left. When Dodie told him I was out with Marcy, he didn't buy it. He went up to my apartment to find her cell number. When Marcy confirmed his suspicions, Nick was sure I'd gone back to the winery. He was mulling over options when my phone rang. Thinking it might be Sloan, Nick answered it. It was Heather Hunt, sounding distraught, insisting she needed to talk to me.

Nick told her he believed Sara was at the winery. Heather went ballistic. She said Hunt was gone almost every night, not returning until late and lying about where he'd been. She offered to drive Nick to the winery to catch that "son of a bitch."

Not knowing what he'd encounter at the winery, Nick called Arnie and Jimmy.

I remember the car driving up, the hushed voices and the silence that followed. "So that was you guys outside the gate. You didn't see me fall out of the shed?"

Nick shakes his head. "We were having a little disagreement."

"Yeah," Jimmy adds. "Arnie and me wanted to go in

294

first, you know, so I could use my ball bat and Arnie could beat the shit—oops—I mean persuade them to let Sara go. But Nick said, 'No way.'"

Arnie says, "That's when we decided I'd guard the door and Jimmy would be backup. We didn't know Ms. Hunt had a gun."

Nick picks up the story. "When we got to the door and saw Venable pointing the gun at you, we weren't sure what to do. That's when Heather took over."

"We did good, huh, Ms. Thome?" Jimmy's freckled face glows with pride.

I want to correct him but stop myself. "No question. You guys saved my life." Without warning, tears well up and trickle down my cheeks.

All three boys avert their gaze at this unseemly display. *Damn! I'm either laughing or crying. This has to stop.*

Dodie hands me a tissue, and I mop my face clumsily with my bandaged left hand. After blowing my nose, I ask Nick, "Is Sara okay?"

He bites his lip. "Psych unit. They won't let me see her. Sloan said she needs an exit counselor. He knows a guy."

"Sloan's back?" I ask.

Nick purses his lips in disapproval. "Yeah, he is *now.*"

"Okay, he wasn't exactly in town, but I said I'd talk to him and I did. At least, I talked to his voice mail."

Dodie says, "He dropped by, but you were asleep. Said he'll be back later to debrief you."

The word *debrief* evokes a flood of memories involving a panoramic view, a pizza, the business end of a hearse, and a mind-blowing orgasm. I gaze out the window and smile, happy to be alive.

"Aunt Allegra?" Nick says. "Want to hear the rest?"

I refocus. "What about Hunt? Is he dead?"

"Naw, his wife just winged him," Arnie says. "They patched him up, and the cops hauled him away."

"Is Heather in trouble for shooting him?"

The boys exchange a look.

"Well," Nick says, "I didn't see anything because I was behind the couch."

"We didn't see nothing," Jimmy adds.

I can't stand it. "Didn't see *anything*."

Jimmy grins. "You neither? Guess she got away with it then."

The guys take off. A local television station is waiting to interview them.

Sloan shows up in my hospital room late in the day.

Dodie is gone, driven away, she claims, by my incessant whining. I want to go home, and one of her Doctors Myers can make it happen. Much to my dismay, she's refused to interfere.

Sloan leans against the wall. His eyes are red-rimmed with weariness, his demeanor all business. Stone-cold Sloan. "Shoulda locked you in your room when I left town."

"Had to do something. Nobody else would."

I stare out the window and bite my lower lip to stop it from trembling. Sloan stands silently for a moment then mutters, "Ah, shit."

He crosses to the end of the bed and pulls the covers loose. Big, warm hands close around my left foot, massaging it gently before moving to the right. It feels so good I can't stay mad.

After an involuntary groan of pleasure, I ask, "When did you get back?"

"About the time all hell was breaking loose down at the winery. I was up all night interviewing Hunt and Venable."

"And?"

"They couldn't wait to rat each other out, hoping for a plea bargain."

I narrow my eyes at him. "Did they get one?"

"Hunt, probably. Venable, highly unlikely."

I feel a rush of anger. "But Hunt's a damn pedophile, a sexual predator. Maybe even a murderer. You know he used to be Roy Harris?"

Sloan grunts an affirmative and tucks the covers around my feet. He collapses in the chair next to the bed. "Yeah, your nephew gave me the floppy disk and the newspaper article. Smart kid. Wanna hear how it all went down?"

I nod. "But first, let me tell you how I think it happened."

"Deal." He scrubs a hand over his bristly jaw.

"When Roy Harris gets out of Chino, he becomes Robinson Hunt, an itinerant man of the cloth with the canny ability to separate folks from their hard-earned cash. Am I right so far?"

Sloan gives me a grudging smile. "You're not just a pretty face, Al."

I continue. "He comes to Vista Valley and somehow gets noticed by Gordon Venable. Maybe Joe Stepanek mentions him to Venable."

I pause and look at Sloan. He nods.

"I'm not sure of the timeline, but Venable must have

needed a way to launder drug money. What better place to park a lot of cash than a church collection plate and a winery tasting room?"

"Yeah," Sloan says. "Venable had a sweet deal going with a bank official. After the Stepanek bust, his guy got antsy, took his hush money, and moved to the Bahamas. Venable definitely saw Harris's potential."

"So Harris gets a makeover and a shiny, new church," I add. "Was Ruth Willard a client of Venable's?"

"You got it."

"Here's the part I can't figure out. Some high-level cop stonewalled the investigation. Why? And what about Peggy Mooney?"

Sloan says, "Venable micromanaged Hunt's every move. They built the church with Willard's money. It attracted the right kind of people, rich and powerful. Hunt learned to play golf and joined the country club, which gave him even more access. A captain in the police department is his buddy. Hunt convinced him you're a hysterical broad trying to make trouble and that Sara ran away with her boyfriend."

"Kinda like what you thought."

Sloan reaches over and tousles my hair. "Ah, come on, Al. I already feel like an asshole for not being here when you needed help."

Wow! Was this Sloan making a semi-apology?

He continues, "One thing Venable didn't count on: Hunt reverting to form. When he got the hots for Sara, things went bad and Venable had to clean it up."

"What about the Hewitts and Peggy Mooney?"

Sloan says, "Venable and Hunt intervened when a foster kid died in the Hewitts' care."

"So the Hewitts helped with the cover-up and got a new car and TV to boot."

Sloan nods. "Peggy Mooney was a different story. She had a crush on Hunt and would do anything he asked. Hunt was afraid Sara was going to take off with her dad and spoil his little plan, so he told Peggy to pick Sara up that Friday and tell her Joe had been arrested."

"Did Peggy know Hunt was a pedophile?"

"Her co-workers say she believed in Hunt's ministry and thought he was trying to help Sara. We've applied to have her body exhumed. It's likely she was murdered to keep her from talking."

"Who killed her?"

He averts his eyes. "She started to get suspicious and told Hunt she wanted to talk to Sara. When he refused, she threatened to go to the police."

I fight back tears. "If I hadn't gone to see her, she'd still be alive."

Sloan leans close and strokes my cheek. "Don't beat yourself up, Al. She probably had her doubts long before your visit."

I want to believe him, but I know my capacity for taking on guilt far exceeds his ability to grant me absolution.

"What about Joe Stepanek? Venable told me Joe and Hunt fought at the church."

"Hunt thought Joe and Sara would take off after the last day of school. Sara disappeared before that. Right?"

I nod.

"When Sara didn't respond to his messages, Joe figured Hunt had her. They fought. Hunt knocked Stepanek out and panicked. Venable arranged the overdose and put the fake letter from Sara in his pocket."

I wait.

"Yeah," he mumbles. "You were right."

I cup my hand over my ear. "I didn't quite hear you."

Sloan is saved from further torment by the delivery of long-stemmed red roses. The aide sets them on my bedside table and hands me the card.

"Somebody loves you." She winks and bustles out. The card says, "From Michael."

The words bring back, in sickening detail, the photos Venable was so eager to share. I crumple the card in my hand.

Michael is exonerated by an unlikely source: Sloan. He pries the crumpled card from my hand and tells me detectives cracked Venable's safe. Along with illicit drugs, they found a treasure trove of incriminating photographs, many of them featuring prominent citizens. Sloan interviewed Michael as well as others.

"Venable had access to GHB," Sloan says. "Liquid ecstasy. Slip some in a drink, and you've got the perfect date rape drug. Venable hasn't copped to it yet, but I'm sure he drugged these guys and posed them, probably at one of Hunt's little fellowship gatherings. Everybody I spoke to complained of nausea and headaches the next day."

"Venable made Michael get us out of the house so somebody could break in and see if I'd found . . . what?"

"Fishing trip. Joe was trying to blackmail Hunt. Venable knew he had concrete evidence and wanted to see if you'd found it."

I can't let go of the anger I feel at Michael's betrayal. "Michael was joined at the hip with Hunt and Venable."

"You need to cut LeClaire some slack. Venable threatened to show the pictures to his parents."

I need time and solitude to sort out my feelings about Michael, neither of which I'll get in the hospital. Besides, I have more to tell Sloan. "You need to check out the chapel at the winery. Something's not right."

Sloan's mouth twitches. "Woman's intuition?"

I feel a surge of fury at his smug remark. "Fine! Don't believe me."

Sloan heaves a weary sigh. "Aw, come on, Al."

"Hunt's a pedophile, and Venable's a stone killer!" My voice rises in outrage. "He shot me with a stun gun. He locked me in a shed with a black widow spider. He pointed his big, black gun at me and he . . . he . . ."

Sloan stands and gathers me into his arms. He strokes my hair and pats my back.

"Screw you, Sloan." With my face buried against his neck, the words come out muffled and without heat. *Damn!* I'm going to cry again.

While I blubber like an oversized toddler who missed her afternoon nap, Sloan speaks soothingly of many things. Even though Sara insists she went with Hunt willingly, a multitude of other charges are piling up against him, including accessory to the murder of Joe Stepanek. Add to that his knowledge of money laundering and extortion, not to mention his stolen identity, and Hunt, Sloan tells me, will be a guest at the gray bar hotel for a long time.

Sloan holds me until the hiccoughing stops and then drops a chaste kiss on my forehead before heading for the door.

I call after him. "Check out the juice concentrate from Mexico. The hostess at the winery told me the truck that brings it drops off the concentrate and loads up stuff for the return trip. I bet it's another way Venable is laundering money."

"FBI's on it," he says with a wave of his hand. He pauses at the door. "By the way, when Joe confronted Hunt, he told him to forget about the money. He just wanted his daughter back."

After he leaves, I think about the sad life of Joe Stepanek, ex-con, drug dealer, lowlife, and how, in the end, it all came down to family. Someday, Sara will need to know that.

Chapter 32

The next morning I awake feeling semi-normal, i.e. crabby and in need of something better than hospital coffee. Before I start my campaign of harassment to go home, I have one last thing to do.

The Venable-Hunt-Harris story is front-page news, and the flowers pour in. A mixed bouquet from the Vista Valley teaching staff, balloons from Marcy with a card that says, "My hero!" and a plant from Donny Thorndyke.

I reach for the phone and call Donny. "I need a favor," I say. "Isn't your ex's dad a big wig here at the hospital? And, if so, are you still speaking?"

Turns out Gwen's father is indeed important. Chief of staff important and, yes, strangely enough, he still likes Donny.

An hour later, I'm escorted to the psych unit for a short visit with Sara. Before I'm allowed through the locked doors, Sara's therapist preps me.

"Remember, her perception of reality is pretty screwed up right now. It's not your job to point that out. Okay?"

I tell him what I plan to do. He frowns and mulls it over. Finally, he says, "Yeah, I guess that's all right. If she starts to get upset, drop it. And don't say anything about her dad dying."

"But I already did," I said. "Sunday night at the winery."

"Her mind isn't ready to accept it, so, unless she asks, don't bring it up."

He takes me to a large, cheerful room filled with comfortable furniture. One shelf-lined wall holds books, magazines, and board games. A television set, its volume turned low, sits against another wall. Sara is at the end of an overstuffed sofa absorbed in a book and twisting a lock of hair around her fingers, a gesture so familiar I catch my breath.

She looks up and smiles. "Hi, Ms. Thome. Where's Nick?"

Her color is better. Her eyes look slightly vacant, probably due to mind-altering drugs. I wonder how much she remembers about Sunday night.

I sit down next to her. "He was just here. He brought me the letter you wrote the day you went away."

I hold out the letter. She studies it curiously, her brows knit in concentration.

"Oh, yeah," she says. "That letter."

She traces the words with her finger. "That was a pretty weird day. Know what I mean?"

"Absolutely."

"My dad flipped out. Did Nick tell you I was seeing my dad?" She pauses and searches my eyes.

"I made him tell me. We were trying to find you."

"Anyhow," she continues. "Dad told me to stay away from Pastor Rob. He wanted me to leave with him after school was out. I didn't know what to do."

"But Peggy came to get you on Friday," I say.

"Yeah. Peggy said the cops arrested my dad and that Pastor Rob wanted to counsel me. She said it might take a few days."

She tugs on a lock of hair. "I knew it was a lie. My dad's too smart to get picked up by the cops."

I wonder if she remembers he's dead.

"It didn't sound right," she continues. "Why would Peggy lie to me? I told her I was supposed to meet Nick that night, that I wouldn't leave without writing him a note. She watched me write it, so I had to leave hidden clues."

"You had us going for a while. Especially the bit about Clementine."

I hope I'm not breaking the rule when I ask, "Why did your dad tell you to stay away from Pastor Rob?"

Her face closes up, and she stares at her hands. "He said Pastor Rob was bad."

She begins picking at a hangnail. "That was the hard part. I knew Pastor Rob was trying to help me. I *wanted* to see him. I *needed* to see him. He was the only one who could help me."

She bites her lip. I wait. When she speaks again, her voice sounds thin and strained. "Did Nick tell you I killed my baby?"

"Sara," I say gently. "You were thirteen. You were a child."

"No!" she says. "I knew I had to get right with God. I had to! Don't you see?"

I want to dismember Robinson Hunt with my bare hands.

Sara takes a deep, shuddering breath. "It wasn't so bad, really. Rob loves me. He said he loves me."

Not your job to change her mind, Allegra. I have to bite the inside of my cheek to keep from trying. "You called me. You asked me to help you."

She flushes. "Yeah, I was scared. I found a cell phone underneath the sofa cushion. Rob caught me and grabbed the phone. He said people wouldn't understand."

An attendant appears and tells me my time is up. I give Sara a hug with my good arm and promise her we'll talk soon. When I leave, she picks up the book. When I see the title, I curse under my breath.

Great Expectations: A Pregnancy Primer.

I go home the next day. In the week that follows, I receive a visit from Chief of Police Randall O'Dell and Captain Peter Lembeck. Chief O'Dell alternately smiles reassuringly at me, and glares at Lembeck, who, judging from his demeanor, would rather eat carpet tacks than be in my presence.

I smile sweetly and wait while he sputters and chokes. He finally manages a weak apology. "I hope you understand that Robinson Hunt is, uh, was a close friend. I'm an elder in his church, for Christ's sake."

Frowny face from Chief O'Dell.

"It wasn't that we were stonewalling," Lembeck says.

"Of course not," I say.

"Hunt said not to worry about the kid, Sara. He told me she'd run off with her boyfriend. It's not like we don't have *real* crime to worry about in Vista Valley."

"Let's not lose our focus here, Pete," the chief warns.

Lembeck digs a deeper hole. "Hunt said you were *way* overboard and acting like it was a major crime or something."

I look at the chief and wink. "Don't you just hate it when that turns out to be true?"

Lembeck flushes. "Yeah. Well, anyhow, consider this my official apology."

"Thank you," I say. "Your sincerity is heartwarming."

By the weekend I'm sick of lying around and nag Dodie until all three Dr. Myers grant me their collective blessings and say I'm fit to teach summer school. But I still have the heavy hitter to convince.

Grandma Sybil insists we go for a test drive in Red Ranger to make sure I can drive one-armed. I pass with flying colors, leaving Grandma free to concentrate on her new project.

Upon Sara's release from the hospital, Grandma put her therapeutic career on hold and welcomed her into the Thome family circle. She'll stay with us until Marta comes home. Grandma's good with screwed up teenagers. Look how I turned out!

Back in my normal routine, the week whizzes by. After school on Friday afternoon I'm tidying my desk when an unlikely couple enters my room. Heather Hunt and Michael.

Heather smiles and walks to my desk. Michael stands in the doorway looking miserable. He removes his cap and twists it in his hands, looking everywhere but at my face.

"Come in, Michael," I urge. "Close the door if you want."

I plop down in my chair and wait until they slip into student desks.

Heather says, "Since you've been in this thing from the beginning, you have a right to know."

She pauses and looks at Michael. A jillion things flash through my mind. Are they secret lovers? Old prison mates? What?

Michael finally speaks. "My golf game's been in the crapper. I need a new challenge."

"This is about golf?" I ask.

Michael flushes. "No, it's about me buying the winery."

"What Would Jesus Drink Winery? That winery?"

Michael grins. "Yeah, that one. But I'm changing the name to Valley Vintage."

I stare at the two of them, mouth agape.

Heather fills in the blanks. "The church board of directors met. Since the church owned the winery free and clear, they've allowed me to sell it and keep the proceeds."

They wait for my reaction. For the past month, I've been sucked into a world spinning crazily out of its prescribed orbit. After it hurled me out, bruised and bleeding, I've been unable to find the normalcy I crave. But hearing their words, I feel the universe shift with an inaudible cosmic *click*. My life is back in sync, bright with promise, right and wonderful. I want to clap my hands for joy. Instead, I pound the desk with my left hand and laugh out loud.

"What a great solution! I'm happy for both of you."

Michael looks relieved. Heather digs around in her purse and pulls out a checkbook.

"Michael paid more for the winery than we were asking," she says. "We talked it over. We want to help Sara.

Would you see that she gets this?" She hands me a check for $50,000.

I've never seen that many zeros on a check. "But it's made out to me."

"We want you to be the trustee on her account," Michael says. "I talked to Sloan. He's working on getting Sara's mother out of prison early. They'll need a place to stay. And Sara will need counseling."

"And if Sara is pregnant . . ." Heather begins. Her voice breaks, and she swallows hard.

"I heard she isn't," I say, thinking, *even though she wants to be.*

Heather breathes out. "Thank God."

Entirely of its own accord, my lower lip starts to tremble. I thank them and blot my eyes with a tissue. Michael stays behind after Heather leaves. He has a few tears of his own.

"Baby, I can't tell you how sorry I am about the break-in. Venable drugged me. I would never . . ."

"It's okay, Michael. Sloan explained it to me. Let's just forget about it." As I say the words, it really *is* okay.

Before he leaves, I warn him about Betsy the black widow and tell him to be sure to feed the winery cat. He promises to show me around after he's made his changes. I tell him we might have to wait a while for that.

Sloan is waiting for me when I get home, drinking coffee and eating leftover bread pudding from the second shelf. Grandma sits next to him on the couch. Then I show them the check. Sloan whistles. Grandma claps her hands in delight then leaves to get ready for Melba and KFC night.

Sloan pulls me into his arms and nuzzles my ear. "About time for date number four."

"Four!" I say. "We haven't had a real date yet."

"Keeps things interesting."

"I've had enough excitement in my life for a while."

He gives me a warm, wet, lingering kiss. "See ya tomorrow."

"No way! I'm going out with Marcy."

He narrows his eyes. "Bet I can find you."

He starts for the door then pauses. "Looks like you were right about the chapel. There's a trapdoor under the lectern."

Feeling vindicated, I ask "What's down there? Not a body, I hope."

"Cash. Lots of cash. The juice concentrate gets trucked up from Mexico. Nice and clean coming into the U.S. On the return trip, the truck's carrying cases of wine and bundles of cash stashed in a special compartment. No problem going back into Mexico. The juice people in Mexico take their cut and write a check to the WWJD Winery. Everybody's happy."

"The FBI will probably offer me a job," I say. "Since I was all over this."

"Yeah, yeah. See you tomorrow."

After Sloan leaves, I wander upstairs and take a twenty-minute power nap. I awake refreshed and go to my closet to get my running shoes. I'm not up to a jog, but Vlad and I will take a nice, long walk. Before I close the closet door, I notice a single strappy sandal with a dangerously high heel and pick it up, idly wondering why I don't wear the shoes more often. Then I remember. When I can find both of them—one would invariably go AWOL—they look great, feel great for a while. But then, when I least expect it, they start to rub and I have to take them off and walk around in my stocking feet, shoeless. Sexy as hell and unpredictable. Exactly like Sloan.

I rummage through the jumble of shoes and pull out a black leather pump with two-inch heels. Suitable for attending funerals, winter weddings, or a business appointment. Good leather. Expensive. Capable of a high, glossy shine. Sensible but slightly boring. Michael.

I set the shoes side by side on the floor and curl up on the window seat. Noe is edging the lawn with a weed whacker. I bang on the window and wave. He looks up then points at the tree across the sidewalk from our house.

There, perched on a lower branch of a stately old maple sits Lefty, our droopy-winged friend, a bit of string dangling from his beak. With a flutter of wings, another robin swoops in for a companionable chat before they both dart into the lush foliage. Our misfit robin has found a mate.

I laugh out loud and give Noe a thumb's up. He grins and returns to his edging. I gaze out the window thinking about Sara, my wacky family, and the unbridled joy I feel each day for having cheated death. I think about Lefty, the one-eyed robin and his unrelenting search for love. As Grandma Sybil is fond of saying, "To everything, there is a season."

Which leads me back to Michael and Sloan. I wiggle my toes in the carpet. It's summer. Who needs shoes? I'll go barefoot for a while.

But then the phone rings.

"Al," Sloan says. "I forgot to tell you something."

"Oh?" I glance at my watch, curious to see how many seconds will tick by before he speaks again. But, without warning, the silence is shattered by a staccato burst of gunfire. An icy hand of fear closes around my heart, and I yell, "Sloan! Ohmigod! Sloan! Say something."

"I'm at the firing range." His voice holds a hint of laughter.

"You might have warned me," I huff.

"Yeah, well, the reason I'm calling . . . I should have told you earlier . . ." His voice fades away.

Hmmm. What's Sloan's big secret, and, more importantly, will he ever manage to get it out? I murmur, "That's okay. You can tell me now."

"Well, uh," he stammers. "What I meant to say is, I lo– lo– . . . I really like you, Al."

I bite back a yip of surprise. Sloan uttering the first syllable of the *l* word. Unbelievable! But, I'm not *that* easy.

"What color are my eyes?"

Without hesitation, Sloan says, "Green with flecks of hazel."

"And your first name is?"

"Marlon," he mumbles.

"Nothing wrong with that name," I say. "Marlon Brando. Marlin Perkins. All manly men. What's your problem?"

"My mother spelled it M-A-R-Y-L-N."

Ouch! "So everybody called you . . ."

"Marilyn."

"Bummer." I pinch myself hard to keep from laughing

312

and try to think of something to cheer him up. "How would you like a big slice of warm apple pie?"

"À la mode?"

"À la Legra."

"I'm on my way."

Be in the know on the latest Medallion Press news by becoming a Medallion Press Insider!

<u>As an Insider you'll receive:</u>

• Our FREE expanded monthly newsletter, giving you more insight into Medallion Press

• Advanced press releases and breaking news

• Greater access to all of your favorite Medallion authors

Joining is easy, just visit our Web site at <u>www.medallionpress.com</u> and click on the Medallion Press Insider tab.

twitter

Sign up now at <u>www.twitter.com/MedallionPress</u> to stay on top of all the happenings in and around Medallion Press.

For more information about other great titles from Medallion Press, visit

medallionpress.com